THE MAGICAL ADVENTURES OF EVIE JONES

AMIE GIBBONS

Printed in the United States of America

First Printing, 2020
Gremlin Publishing
Nashville, TN.

https://authoramiegibbons.wordpress.com/

ISBN: 9798562056856

For my Grem Monster.
Here or in Heaven, I love you, baby.
Always.

ACKNOWLEDGMENTS

It's never easy to thank everyone who helped with a book, and I'm sure I'll inevitably leave people out; it's not on purpose, I swear.

First up, of course, thank you to my parents. Mom, you taught me to love reading. Dad, you were right, never should've taught me how to read, look what happens. And to the Sully monster, the next generation of stubborn apes.

To my first reader, my twin six years removed, and my inspiration every day. Probably shouldn't have subjected you to some of those terrible first tries, but look how well it turned out, baby brother.

And then to all the people who cheered me on during writing, then beta read and edited this book: Sam, my best beta reader. Tiffany, one fantastic editor. And my many wonderful beta readers who helped smooth out the rough spots.

PART I. EVIE JONES
AND THE CRAZY EXES

"**I** COULD CURSE THE PUTZ," I said, giving up on the dishwasher for now and propping my arms on the counter, phone pressed to my ear.

The townhouse smelled like cat, apple juice and the dirty dishes that were scattered across the counters like soldiers fighting the good fight for the king of germs.

"*Evie!*" Faye said. "For the love of the Goddess, do *not* do anything crazy."

The small voices from the TV erupted into a laugh track. The background noise kept me from jumping every time the wind rustled a tree branch or the neighborhood kids outside ran by. How they could run in the July heat was beyond me.

I put my hand on the gun at my hip and took a deep breath. *Nothing's going to happen. Your imagination's just freaking out because...*

I looked out the window above the sink. The mountains loomed, huge and obvious even in the dark.

A protective wall against the world.

Salt Lake wasn't the most happening city, but it was mine. And even staying in Faye's house, I was still home, still safe. I'd keep telling myself nothing was out there, I was fine.

Until I believed it.

"Oh what?" I rolled my eyes. "Anyone hearing that would think it was a joke."

"We're not supposed to talk about *that* over the phone."

"Yeah," I snorted, "because the NSA is listening in along with the Council. Hey, Council, if you're listening, you're a bunch of dictators. Magic. Magic. Magic! I cast spells, make potions and light things on fire, and right now I want to. And if anybody wants to tell me I can't talk about magic over the phone because somebody *might* hear and know witches are real, then bring it on! I could use a good fight."

"See, this is why I worry about you. You need to talk about this. We all have exes, Evie. We all have someone who's made us crazy, and we've all been the person someone went crazy on. You don't want to be the crazy, jealous ex. *Trust me*, the person you'll hurt most is yourself. What does your dad always say?"

"Grrrrr." If she pressed this, I was going to be hitting something alcoholic or something wall-like, but I was going to be hitting something.

"Your dad says before you seek revenge, dig two graves," Faye said. "There's a reason. You curse your ex, not only would *you* be the putz, the Council will catch you and throw you in jail."

I turned. "Gah!"

"What!"

Missy sat not three inches from my feet, staring up at me with big green eyes.

"Your cat's invisible and *evil*, but hey," I said. Missy rubbed against my jeans, purring like a lawnmower. "Okay, she's actually very sweet."

Missy meowed and shot off towards the living room. Probably so she could sneak up on me again, the stinker.

"So-" Faye started.

"Nope."

"Evie, if you don't talk about it, especially when you're extra stressed, you're going to repress until you explode and actually do something crazy. And I am *not* visiting you in prison. Witch *or* human."

Thud came from the living room. I jumped, grabbing my necklace and running to the archway just in time to see Missy scramble up from the pile of books she'd knocked down and run out the cat flap in the front door.

I took a deep breath. Then another.

"What are you guys doing tonight?" I asked.

"Evie-"

"Nope. Because people out there have real problems. Real things going down. There are crimes and car accidents and people being diagnosed with cancer as we speak. Real problems they deal with every day."

"A broken heart is…"

I tuned her out.

Scritch scritch scratch, came from the living room. I looked up and didn't see the cat anywhere.

Maybe she's scratching outside the door?

"Meow."

I jumped, whirling and biting down on the surprise as I clutched my hand to my chest. Missy sat right behind me.

I covered the receiver, looking from the front door to her and whispered, "How did you do that, cat? Do you have a friend out there or something?"

Faye was still talking.

"*Faye*," I interrupted sharply, "if I start, I won't stop, and then your one-year-old will be subjected to my bitter vibes, and that can't be healthy. *So*, what are you doing on a Friday night in New York City?"

Faye sighed. "We're going to a play. Ki… someone recommended it. We're just getting cleaned up in the hotel."

"You can say his name."

"You mean your ex who's getting married tomorrow? I don't think I can, because you're trying not to talk about it."

Scratching came from the front door again and Missy ran in a second later.

Oy vey! When did she leave the kitchen? You'd think Faye fed her espresso instead of kitty kibble. She ran past me and halfway up the kitchen's sliding glass door before slipping down.

I opened the door and she walked out, every step pure cat dignity, and sat on the deck, licking her front paw. I rolled my eyes, closed the door, and turned away.

"I'm repressing so I won't be pissed that you guys are going to the wedding of the biggest sociopath the legal profession has ever seen." I snorted. "Which is sure as hell saying something."

"Good, get it out. Deal with your emotions."

"I'm going to be a lawyer; I don't have emotions." I gulped. "Don't shrink me, please."

Thump!

I jumped, grabbing my necklace again, knees shaking. Goddess, I was a wreck! There were kids and wind outside, and no reason to think the thump was bad. And even if it was, with magic and a gun, what couldn't I take down?

"Merow." Missy ran straight at me and I stumbled back into the wall. She hit the blue and gold throw rug in front of me, sending it sliding two feet, used it to get traction, and turned to shoot back into the living room.

I sagged against the wall, heart pounding. "Your cat is a menace." I sighed. "If he's ready to settle down and get married and all that, why not me?"

I was pathetic!

"And you *get* to think that. You *get* to be upset." Faye paused. "We've got to go. Watch TV, study, have a glass of wine. Relax. Okay?"

Scratch, scratch, scratchscratchscratch, came from the front door, making me cringe. Bad kitty!

"Okay." We said bye and I upped the TV volume, sat on the couch and grabbed the book on top of the pile of blue Bar Exam study books I'd brought.

"I *could* curse him." I glanced down at my book, tapping my finger on the pages. "Impotence? That's a classic. A curse would constitute crazy though. Then again, you're supposed to get crazy on an ex, like scratch his car and shit like that. I never scratched his car like a normal girl. Because I figured that constituted crazy."

Scratch, scratch, scratchscratchscratchscratch.

I jumped off the couch. "So does *that*, Missy." I stomped to the door. "You have a cat door! You can get in." I threw the deadbolt and yanked the door open. "Crazy fluff-"

"Argggg." The man outside lunged at me, swinging a meaty fist in haymaker that'd leave me a pumpkin if it landed.

I JUMPED BACK ON PURE INSTINCT, bumping into the couch's arm before I even registered there was a person there. I scrambled to the side and back.

Wet dirt and something like meat spoiling in the fridge wafted off him like cologne. Cold, rotting, but not growing *friends* quite yet. I recognized the smell before my eyes caught up and transferred what I was looking at.

He was sallow under the heavy makeup, and his black wool suit hung loose on him. Like he'd lost weight before he died. And he was most certainly dead.

Zombie, flashed through my mind, and I shook my head like that'd kick the thought out.

Now *that* was crazy. There weren't vampires, werewolves, or freaking *zombies*! Except… zombies weren't originally stories made up to scare children. They were based in real voodoo. Not my religion, but, but… possible. There were golems, demons and ghosts, so why not zombies?

We'd know if there were ways to make zombies, right? The Council would've told us.

The man lunged at me again, teeth bared and fists raised, and I screamed, pulling my tiny gun from my hip and pointing it at him.

"Arggggggggg." Fetid breath washed over me as he swung at my arm.

I ducked and shot, the *ping* of a magically suppressed bullet surprising him into stillness for a second, and not doing much else as the bullet buried itself in the doorjamb.

Fire. Right. Duh.

I focused my mental energy on him, willing the life force in his body to turn against itself, to make the molecules speed and burst.

Fire kills zombies, right?

Magic rushed out of me in a huff of energy, leaving me sagging and exhausted, but at least he was…

Standing there.

He was still fucking standing there!

The zombie looked at me, confusion painting his face.

My magic doesn't work on him!

"Argggggggggggg!" He leapt at me, suit clad arms swinging.

I screamed, backpedaling into the kitchen with another wild shot. The man dove to the side, hitting the fireplace under the TV with his shoulder.

"Ehhhh, ehhhh, ehhhh," came in stereo, light scratch tinted mechanical cries from the baby monitor next to the couch and muffled wailing from upstairs.

My head snapped to the spiral staircase between the living room archway and kitchen. I lunged a second before the zombie. Up the stairs, round the tight corner and into the nursery, clattering telling me he wasn't far behind.

I slammed the door behind me, sealing it with a sloppy push of magic. Daphnie stood on her knees, holding onto the bars of her crib. She stopped crying and stared at me with big blue eyes. They matched her footie pajamas. I scooped her up, climbed onto the chest under the window, opened it and held up a hand, blowing the screen out with nothing coming close to finesse.

The large window was built for teenage girls to sneak out. Something I'd pointed out to Faye with glee last week. It was a few feet tall and opened right onto the sloping roof. I bent and crawled out, holding onto the window's edge with one hand and the baby on my hip with the other, not looking back as the door crashed open behind me.

I focused on the air below, making it bubble up soft and accommodating, and jumped, hugging the baby so hard to my chest I was surprised she could breathe. I hit the bubble with my back. It sagged, taking most of my weight and I had a second to tuck my chin before it popped.

Dropping me the last two feet to the ground.

"Oy!" My back slammed into the hard-packed dirt. I gave it a beat to catch my breath, then pushed to my feet. I held Daphnie up with both hands. She stared at me, blue eyes wide, her mouth in a little O. She seemed fine, shocked maybe, but fine.

"I swear if I live through this, I'm going to practice my magic more," I said, looking up at the broken window. "Where the *hell* did I put my gun?" I searched my brain. When I ran for the baby, I'd had my gun. I probably dropped it without thinking when I grabbed Daphnie since I needed both hands to pull her out of her crib.

The man appeared at the window. He pointed at me and climbed out.

"Sh…" I looked at Daphnie and bit down the curse.

Who was he? Who made him? Didn't matter.

I turned tail and ran.

A suburban maze just north of Salt Lake City wasn't exactly where you'd think zombies would pop up. It wasn't like Voodoo mixed well with Mormonism.

Or salt!

Salt breaks the hold on zombies, right? Where do I get salt?

Hysterical giggles bubbled up and I quashed them. Needed the air to run. And if I started, I wouldn't stop. But there was a zombie literally in the salt city. That was freaking hilarious.

I risked a glance behind me just before turning the corner onto the next street. The zombie was out of the house and pounding the pavement behind me, his longer legs gaining on me.

Oy gevalt! I couldn't run any faster. I'd never exactly been a track star and the extra weight of a baby wasn't helping. I couldn't keep this up.

I scanned the street. One house a few down didn't have lights on. I ran up the steps, flipping the deadbolt lock and opening the door with a tug of magic and barreled in through a bubble of resistance.

Walls, fences, barriers, they were all words for the same thing.

Protection.

They kept stuff out… or in. Faye's home didn't even faze the zombie, meaning he wasn't magic. He was animated by it, but that was it.

But, he couldn't open the door and hadn't busted through the walls or windows, meaning the psychosomatic barrier a home made *did* work on him.

I slammed the door behind us, breathing so hard I wondered if I was going to pass out. *Maybe he was scratching at the door to mimic a cat, hoping I'd open it?*

Magic rules were weird. You couldn't go into someone's home and kill them in their sleep with magic without an invite, but you could magically float a bomb through a window or just walk in with a gun after the locks were flipped. And apparently zombies could walk in once the door was open.

Coming in here, uninvited, I checked most of my magic at the door like a coat.

Then again, it hadn't worked against this guy anyway, so what did it matter?

I peeked through the front window's blinds, hands shaking on the baby. She stared up at me, quiet, like she knew one sound could give us away. Better than me. My heart pounded so hard someone walking by outside could've heard it.

"The fire spell didn't work," I whispered.

It used living animals' natural energy against them. The zombie didn't have the same energy, he was animated by something else. The spell didn't work because he didn't have the right fuel. I could've just set him on fire with a push of magic instead of trying the spell.

"Goddess, I'm an idiot."

I stared out the gap in the blinds. *What are the odds he'll let me see him coming?*

Bupkis.

Where did he go?

Fear crept up my neck like spiders and I grabbed my necklace with my free hand, pulling away from the window. What if he got distracted and went after someone else? Salt. I could hunt for him with salt... if the lore about zombies and salt was true.

I could hide, call the cops, call Dad!

Cops couldn't deal with a zombie, and anyway, bringing humans into magic *wasn't* an option. If I lived through the zombie by calling the cops, the Council would kill me.

"Get salt, go back to Faye's, get my phone, call Dad."

Okay. Plan. Good.

I held my necklace tighter, walking into the kitchen with my hackles as high as a cat facing down a pack of wolves.

Daphnie tightened her arms around my neck like she could feel it. But she stayed silent.

"You got chutzpah in the best way, baby girl," I said, kissing her hair. "You're going to be one hell of a witch; just like your mama. She's really good with the dead, too. Too bad she's not here when an actual undead attacks me."

I gulped and walked towards the kitchen, my flats too loud on the hardwood floors. The kitchen was behind the living room, through an archway in a wall with holes strategically carved out to play shelves. These guys had books and magazines piled up in them. My kind of people.

"What are the odds they have a landline?" I looked around, straining my eyes. Nothing remotely phone-like on the walls or counters. Yeah, welcome to the twenty-first century.

Salt then. I opened the cupboard next to the stove. I could barely see lumpy shapes in the dim glow from streetlights shining through the windows so I reached up and ran my fingers over things.

The bottom shelf held a wall of boxes, some stacks neat and even, others with boxes jutting out, like they were shoved in quickly. Tea?

I felt above the tea shelf and… *there*! Bottles lined up like cooking soldiers. My fingers ran over the ones at the front and pushed them to the side, searching for the bigger container most salt came in.

Scritch, scritch, scratch. My heart seized and I gave up pretenses and swept the smaller bottles out, letting them shower to the counter and floor. Daphnie made a small noise but that was it. Chutzpah indeed.

And I was a wreck! The scratching was probably just a tree branch in the wind. Or another damn cat.

"Do you think Missy knew there was someone outside and was trying to warn me?" I whispered. Daphnie cooed and grabbed my hair. "Ow. And yeah, I think so too."

I switched my hand around, fingers brushing a larger container near the back. I stretched on my toes to get another inch or two of arm through, got my hand around it and pulled it down. The glint of the spout said I had the right one.

I sighed. "Okay, phone, but…"

But I still didn't know where the zombie was. Something told me he didn't wander off. He was way too focused. Definitely more sentient than the media said. Stupid zombie movies.

"Begging the question, why me? And who sent him?"

It wasn't like *I* had anyone who'd want to sick a zombie on me. Hell, I didn't even have any exes who'd possibly want to do something crazy to me, no matter what Faye said about everyone having someone like that in their past. All my exes were nice guys, except the one.

I scanned the backyard through the sliding glass door. The door and deck were like Faye's, and the backyards were a uniform line of wooden fences. We could camp out back so I'd have my powers if the zombie popped up, but then we'd be waiting for him to jump us again. I wanted to end this mishegoss on my own terms, preferably with my dad to back me up. So I needed a phone.

What about Daphnie?

I couldn't go to possible battle with her riding shotgun on my hip. For one, my left arm was numbing out pretty quick, and for two, I didn't want her caught in the crossfire.

I walked back to the front, scanning the street through the living room window's blinds. Nothing.

Well, nothing obvious.

My stomach burned and my heart did backflips that'd make my younger gymnast self proud as I put Daphnie down.

I poured salt in a solid line around the room, making a circle along the walls. I glanced around; these guys definitely had kids. There was a stuffed turtle on the couch and giant blocks piled in the corner, with nothing harmful to children obvious. I picked Daphnie up and put her next to the blocks then grabbed the turtle and put him beside her.

"Back in a bit, baby girl," I said, whispering a blessing to the Goddess. You *don't* leave one-year-olds alone, but I had to handle this. And I couldn't do it with a baby as my sassy sidekick.

I walked out the front door without letting myself think about it anymore, careful to step over the salt, and closed the door behind me before the wind could blow away any of the line.

My powers rushed back, like armor I'd donned at the door, and I flicked the deadbolt closed with a push of magic. The night *felt* more alive. I hadn't noticed the bugs in the background, crickets cricketing, and other things making their squeaks and squishes before. The smells of fresh grass and heated asphalt met my nose without so much as a sprinkle of death.

But there was… *something*. That sense of wrongness, of something being where it shouldn't be. The laws of nature being spit upon.

I walked down the steps, raising a hand to sense the world. The zombie wasn't supposed to be here. All I had to do was feel out the wrongness, like playing hot and cold… only with magic, and of course, with a fight if I found the thing, but hey.

I *did* say I could use a good fight.

Damn, careful what you wish for had never been so literal before.

My heart pounded as I focused on what the zombie *was*. What he represented. A tear in reality. I just had to let the world tell me what wasn't supposed to be here.

Nothing came to me. I closed my eyes, breathing in the heat.

Bupkis.

"Okay." I poured salt into my hand and walked to the sidewalk, looking every which way as I quick walked up the street. Why did I think he was even chasing me? Maybe he was just lurching around? No. He'd pointed and ran after me. Where was Faye when I needed her? She had the strongest necromancy magic of any of us in the Coven.

I shivered and walked faster, looking over my shoulder again, expecting him to just suddenly appear.

Honestly, I kind of wished he would, if only to stop the wondering. That's what scared me, always had. Uncertainty. Loose ends…

The lack of closure.

I paused, brain chewing on… something.

When my ex had broken up with me, he'd said it was because he didn't want anything serious, what he'd meant was he didn't want anything serious with *me*. Took a long time for me to accept I was just a girl he was keeping himself busy with; I wasn't who he wanted.

Faye said that crazy ex thing like she's been there. When the zombie lunged in, he hadn't done anything to me besides lunge in and start swinging. I'd just been there and was something to swing at, but he'd ran for the stairs when Daphnie cried and then he came after us.

"Not us," I said, horror sinking my heart. "*Her.*"

It. Wasn't. Me. He was after *her*!

"Oh fuck!"

I turned and bolted back down the street, praying between the door and the salt circle she'd be safe.

I FLIPPED THE LOCK AND OPENED the door magically as I mounted the steps, then hopped over the salt circle. I barely even noticed the power check at the door this time.

Daphnie looked up at me from the corner and clapped two bright green blocks together.

"Ugh," I breathed, clutching my hand to my chest and turning to close the door.

So of course, the zombie decided now was a great time to make his special guest appearance.

He bust through the half open door so fast it bounced off its hinges, the air swirling the salt and breaking the circle.

Where had he been hiding!

He ran straight for Daphnie. I threw myself at him, hitting his knees and tackling him before he made it past the couch. He thumped to the ground on his belly.

I scrambled to my feet and dumped salt out of the container on his back.

Nothing happened.

"Oy vey," I huffed and dropped the container and the salt I'd palmed as he shook his head and pushed to his knees. I put my fists up and kicked him in the back of the head like I'd practiced a thousand times in self-defense class. The shock traveled up my leg and I gritted my teeth.

Real life fighting wasn't anything like practicing in class.

The zombie ignored me and crawled for the baby.

I screamed at the top of my lungs, jumping on his back. I put my hands on the top of his head and under his chin, yanking to break his neck.

"Arghhhhhhhhh!" He flailed his arms and I hopped off just in time to avoid getting hit in the head. He turned, jumping to his feet, way too agile for a corpse. Weren't they supposed to lurch? He came at me and I back-peddled. He lunged and I skittered backwards faster, bumping the wall. I threw myself to the side and the zombie hit the wall.

He pushed off it and marched towards me.

Oh goody, I'd made him mad.

But he stopped and turned back towards Daphnie.

"Oh, hell no!" I ran and jumped on his back again, looping my legs around his waist, holding on with an arm around his neck, hitting him with my free fist.

He whipped us around and I lost my grip.

"Omph." I hit the floor so hard I swear I bounced. My bruised butt screamed in protest as I pushed myself back up.

He stared at me, his chin… drooping, like melting wax.

"What the?" I looked down at my hand. The one that had held the salt. There were a few granules attached to the skin. I'd grabbed him under the chin with salt still clinging to my skin. It didn't work when I'd dumped it on his back because it'd just hit his suit.

"I'm not too bright tonight." I dove for the container and scooped it up, pouring salt on my hand and blowing it in his face as he rushed me again.

He froze, mouth working, eyes wide. Strangely like the expression Daphnie wore when I'd jumped out the window with her.

Child-like shock, innocence wondering why it was hit.

He fell to his knees, and I walked up to him. He looked up at me, mouth still fighting to talk.

"Can you tell me who did this to you?" I asked.

"H… H…" he said. I poured salt in his mouth and he made a face… kind of like I would if I were eating pure salt. "Her ex." He met my eyes. "Hurts."

"It hurts?"

He nodded, bottom lip following his chin down so I could see the inside of his mouth was melting too. His gums merged down, clogging his useless airway and his tongue stuck to the fleeing bottom of his mouth.

I covered my mouth, holding down a gag as I switched to breathing through it. "How do I… put you back?"

He held up his left arm and pointed to his wrist. I pushed the suit and shirt sleeves back, careful not to graze the lifeless skin, just enough to see the string tied around his wrist.

"Will you be okay if I leave your body here for the cops to find? They'll be able to put you… *it* back, I'm sure."

He nodded, meeting my eyes with pain, mouth still trying to form words.

"It's okay. I'll find who did this to you and put him down like the dog he is. It's okay. You don't need to tell me. Rest." I slid my hand under the string and snapped it with a tug.

He slumped to his side, the life blinking out of him so fast it was like flicking the death switch.

The air lightened, wrongness clearing from it like blood washing out of white cotton, and I took a deep breath, wiggling my shoulders.

"At least there was a reason I felt so off tonight," I said to Daphnie as I picked her up. Oy vey, she was going to be so screwed up after this. Even a therapist mom wouldn't be able to treat this trauma. I walked out, leaving the door open.

Hopefully someone would notice something amiss and call the cops before the family with kids returned.

"YOU MISSED ONE HELL OF a show," I said, leaning against Daphnie's crib as I cradled the phone to my ear. I'd moved the crib to the bedroom so I could keep an eye on her. "Know anyone into voodoo?" I asked before Faye could say anything.

She drew a sharp breath. "What happened?"

I gave her the quick version, ending with. "Someone must've called the cops because I saw sirens going down that way a minute ago. Hopefully they'll get the poor guy back to his grave."

"He said an ex? Are you sure?" She whispered something under her breath

"Faye! What is it? Who did this? And why?"

"I… I think it's my first husband," she said.

My jaw dropped. *First husband?*

"He… He said he'd get me back. I just didn't think… It was seven years ago! I haven't even spoken to him since I got engaged to George."

"If it's him, why now?"

"He… I think he got out of prison last month."

"Prison?" My voice jumped two octaves. "For what?"

"Just theft… a few times. And attempted murder."

Oh *just.*

"I figured by the time he got out, he would be over it, move on with his life. He wasn't supposed to be out this soon!"

"You're telling me this is a crazy, jealous ex trying to get back at you for dumping his sorry butt seven years ago by kidnapping your kid?" I pinched my nose. "That's it? *Seriously?* Suddenly I'm glad I never did anything crazy to Kieren."

We talked a bit more about what to do and how to find her ex. Her and George were hopping on the first flight home tomorrow morning and just missing the wedding.

Until then, I'd ward the house and stay up with my trusty revolver.

I hung up and looked down at the sleeping baby. The poor thing would probably be scarred for life after the violence tonight.

She giggled in her sleep.

Then again, maybe not.

I shook my head and stroked her hair before going downstairs. "And I thought I had ex issues."

I warded the house, poured a glass of pinot, grabbed my book, went back upstairs with Missy on my heels, and flopped on the bed. I wouldn't be sleeping tonight, but I could enjoy myself.

I pulled up *The Big Bang Theory* on my laptop and took a sip of my wine. When I got home tomorrow, I was treating myself to a bubble bath... hell, maybe a spa day. And I'd talk to my therapist about Kieren getting married at our next session.

Because Faye was right, I needed to deal with my issues and de-stress.

And I'd be damned if I'd let myself become that ex.

"You'll be okay," I said to Daphnie. "Everybody has issues. Most of us deal with them just fine, without conjuring zombies... or, you know, cursing our exes."

PART II. EVIE JONES AND THE GOOD LUCK FUNDRAISER

"I'M GOING TO FAIL the bar again," Ashley said, eyes wide. She took a gulp of her beer, staring past me into the restaurant like she was watching her legal career wash away. "I'm going to fail and get fired and that'll be it. In this economy, when employers find out I took three tries to pass the bar and lost my firm job because of it, I won't even get hired at the Public Defender's office."

The bar last July had killed all of us, and I'd seriously thought I'd failed until the results came out in October.

Everyone thinks they'll fail the bar. It's just that kind of test.

But one of my best friends actually had failed, and it'd hung over her and her future for the last four months.

"Oy vey. *No*," I said, shaking my finger at her. "Hey, look here."

She sighed, looking me in the eye.

"You are *not* going to fail again. You had some bad luck last time. You were sick and got blindsided with harder questions than expected. That's *all.*" I held up two fingers about a centimeter apart. "You failed by this much. Which sucks! Because you were right there. But that means this time." I tapped the wood table. "*This time*, you got this."

She looked at me like she wanted to throw her drink in my face. "Evie, I say this with all the love in the world, but shut up and stop being the perky pixy. I want to wallow. I want to cry, and say why me, and bitch about the fact that I failed by half a percent. Because being *right there*, knowing if I'd checked A instead of B on one or two multiple choices, or put one more paragraph in an essay, and I wouldn't be going through this hell again, is *devastating*. Okay?"

"Nope, because if you believe you're going to pass, you'll do better. It's all about positive thinking."

She rolled her eyes. "You know I don't go in for all that New Agey stuff."

I bit my tongue. No, literally, because I wanted to say, "I come from a long line of witches. I practice techniques to track and move energies, and I do spells and potions dating back to the Druids. My ancestors helped build Stonehenge. I'm *old* age, baby."

You can't say that to normal people in modern day Utah.

Or, you know, to Mormons.

Hey, if they get to call me weird for my charms and crystals, I get to call them weird for their magic underwear. Fair's fair.

I stuck my tongue out at her.

Ashley smiled and took another swig of her beer.

"No really," I said. "Studies have shown if you believe something, like you'll do well on a test or in an interview, it affects your body and brain. It's why placebos work. It's the mind telling the body it *should* be getting better, so it does. You wear a good luck charm to a test, you think it'll work, just *slightly*, so you're more confident on the test. And that's usually what gets people. They get scared, lose confidence, second guess themselves, and eat up time."

"So you're saying it's like Friday the Thirteenth? You think there's bad luck, so there's more accidents and stuff? People are all… what's that word you use? Shlimzl? Or…?"

"Shlimazel," I said, grinning because she wasn't too far off. "You know, since people in western cultures believe it's a bad luck day, their good luck floats off them and then black cats scoop it up."

She stared at me for a moment then burst out laughing. "Where do you come up with this stuff?"

Ha! She thought I was kidding.

It's not luck per se. It's good energy. The stuff people make every day with their thoughts and deeds. It's been called luck, karma, chi, the Tau, and of course, the Force. It's all the same idea. Energy.

And when millions of people have the idea a day is bad luck, even if they don't *really* believe it, they shed a little of their good energy just by the collective thought that it's possibly a bad luck day.

I grinned, shrugging. "Oh, you know, it's in my New Agey books." I took a sip of my wine. "Though, it's not only black cats that can scoop luck up, they just have better marketing people, built their trademark as the bad luck kitties. All cats can do it."

She snorted. "Too bad we can't get those cats to pass some luck to me."

I froze with my glass halfway up to my lips.

Now *there* was an idea!

"I HAVE A GREAT IDEA," I said to Faye on the phone. "Actually, it was Ashley's, and she was joking. You know the Cat Luck Scramble on the Thirteenth? What if we do that this year, only instead of keeping the energy, we donate it to Ashley and your husband, so they have more luck on the bar this time?"

Faye didn't say anything for a moment. Then, "Are you high?"

"Haha, you're hilarious. No. I'm serious. You already know how to do the spell. You have Missy do it every Friday the Thirteenth. What if we ask the others to have their cats do their normal gathering, but instead of using it themselves, they donate to a good cause? We'll store it in the necklaces, or something more manly for George, and give them to George and Ashley the day before the bar."

Another pause. "You're serious?"

"Yeah! Why not?"

"Welllllll, I mean, it's possible. The cats never gather a lot. It's more a silly novelty than anything anyone's ever put to good use. But if we got our friends with cats to do it and put it in just two places, it might be concentrated enough to give them a boost."

"And they've both been studying so hard," I said. "*While* they've been working. They need the extra good vibes. Ashley is strung out and barely functioning. I had to drag her to dinner tonight to get her to take a break, and I'm sure George is right there too. The mindset Ashley's in? She's going to psych herself out of passing. *And* there's a Friday the Thirteenth right before the bar. It's bashert! What do you think?"

She paused. "I know why I'd want to give it to George, he's my husband. Why are you so hell bent on helping Ashley? This isn't going to be easy, and it won't make a big difference, especially if she doesn't believe in it."

"She's my friend. This is what friends do. Even when one of them is cranky-pants."

"Yeah, Ashley can be a bit of a downer."

"So can *I*. And when I was a downer mess One-L Spring finals, she was one of the people kicking my sorry butt to study so I didn't flunk out. You were another one of those people, which is why I babysit your kid. It's more of a trade. See, I'm not a good friend, I'm a good vibes capitalist."

She laughed, making me grin.

"Okay," Faye said, "I'm in."

"Yay! I'll call the Coven."

THE COVEN RENTS A HOTEL lobby for our monthly meetings to accommodate the two hundred or so of us who usually show up. But since this was an informal meeting called with two days' notice, Dad suggested we rent out the party room loft at Squatters Pub instead.

We reserve places as a book club. In some states you can say coven and people go with it. Usually with a thumbs up and a blurry-eyed, "New Age? Duuuude." In Utah, New Aged, Pagan, Wicca, even Goths equals devil worship. Salt Lake's better than the rest of the state, but still, not worth the attention.

"Faye!" I bounced off my barstool and rushed Faye soon as her dark blonde hair caught my eye across the bar. "Gahhhh, haven't seen you in like a month."

We hugged and she laughed as we broke apart. People always think we're sisters because we're both slim with similar cheekbones and noses. But she's blond, blue eyed and pale to my blonde highlighted brunette, brown and naturally tan.

"So, how does this work?" I asked.

"Usually we let the cats out on Friday the Thirteenth and they wander their neighborhoods, bringing whatever they scoop up back where we use the energy gathering spell to take it in. We capture the luck in crystals, and whoever gets the most wins the prize."

"There's prizes?" I asked. "Good ones?"

"Last time's was a seven day cruise in the Bahamas."

"Nice!"

"Yeah. Wish you'd gotten a cat earlier, huh?"

I nodded. "Little bit. Almost worth dealing with the furry sociopaths. Almost."

Faye went to the front of the room after it looked like we weren't going to get any more than the thirty or so people. Since she did this every year, she could explain and ask everyone for their help. I'd jump in if needed, but cats weren't my area.

She ran through the idea, stressing they wouldn't miss out too much since Friday the Thirteenth was in February and March this year, so they'd get a chance to gather luck next month.

"But how will we know who wins this time?" one of the guys asked after Faye finished.

"Same as before," Faye said. "Use the crystals. But this time, after we measure it, we pool it and give it to my husband and Evie's friend. It's more of a cute idea than anything we think will make a difference on the bar. It'll just help with their confidence."

"How will this help them though?" Maggie, the old crone that painted all witches with that stereotype asked. From her cheap, tacky jewelry to her Walmart shoes, she screamed welfare mom, even though she was middle class with no kids.

"They'll get the luck and take it into the test," Faye said.

"Yes, but how will it help if they don't know about it?"

My eyes flew wide and I waved at Faye from the back of the room, swinging my arms wide and shaking my head.

She must've not seen me because she said, "We'll tell them the necklaces have luck in them."

Oy vey! And there it was. I slammed my palm to my forehead. I loved Faye, but there were times I wanted to give her the stupidest smart person award.

"No," Maggie said, smugness obvious in her voice even though I couldn't see her face. "You know we can't tell humans about us."

"No, no, no," Faye said with an easy smile, like she anticipated this.

I shook my head. She didn't know Maggie like I did.

"We're going to tell them as kind of a joke," Faye said. They'll have it in their heads that it's good luck without really believing it. It should still work, though."

At least she wasn't clueless enough to say her husband already knew. If you're married, everyone knows the spouse will know, but they don't *know*.

"No," Maggie said. Gee, wonder what her favorite word was. "It either won't work because they won't believe, in which case, you're taking from everyone for no gain, or they'll believe it." She paused for dramatic effect and I resisted the urge to make gagging sounds. "And then we'll be facing the next witch trials."

Oy vey.

"Come on!" I shouted from the back, making the crowd whirl. Haha, it was like a witches' line dance. "This is ridiculous. Humans buy charms all the time." I pointed to Hallie. "Hallie's shop wouldn't stay open if it was just witches buying stuff. Humans go in there for all kinds of New Age crap. Have you seen any witch hunters going after her? No. Would humans spend the money if they didn't believe at least a little? No! And this is Utah! If there's any place in America people would go after witches, it'd be here."

I crossed my arms as Maggie stared me down over the crowd. She wasn't that old, maybe fifty. But she may as well have been a hundred for how she acted.

"Anyone who wants to help out, please raise your hand," I said. "If you don't want to, no hard feelings. This is us asking for donations, not demanding them at gunpoint. It's a fundraiser, not taxes."

People laughed and hands started going up.

"You're all-" Maggie said.

"Anyone who thinks Maggie is a bitter, old yenta who needs to get a fucking life, and butt out of other peoples', raise your hands," I said over her.

More laughter ran through the crowd as hands shot up and I grinned at her. Okay, it was bitchy, and normally I'm not that mean. But she'd been knocking me down since I was old enough to spell because she hated Dad.

"You try this, I'll report you to the Council," Maggie said, face twisted in a smirk.

The laughter shut off like she hit a switch.

My mouth dropped and I closed it, shaking my head.

"No way. She's bluffing," I said loud enough for everyone to hear before meeting her eyes. "You wouldn't call attention to us like that. You *know* the Council would be up *all* our asses at even the hint of letting humans know something. Forget about me, what about people like Hallie? The second they knew she sold anything that could be used to make real magic? They wouldn't just shut her down, they'd toss her in Oz."

Maggie's smirk widened.

"You are not that petty," I said, my tone a challenge. If she went ahead with this, everyone would be on my side. They'd think she was a treacherous, fear monger.

Hopefully.

"Following the rules isn't petty. It's being a good citizen."

"Not when the rules are totalitarian bullshit meant to exert power over people!"

She grinned. She would've been pretty if she wasn't so full of spite. "So typical of the Joneses. The rules don't apply to you. Everyone else should be good, follow the rules and make sure society keeps on going. But if a few break the rules, everything will be fine. Just as long as you Joneses are the ones who get to benefit by being the rule breakers, right?"

I opened my mouth but she kept talking.

"And anyone trying this or even helping those stupid enough to try this, I will report you to the Council, making sure they know the rest of us tried to stop you. I think letting them know there are some of us here policing their rules will keep them from checking in on us too much."

"NO," FAYE SAID. "YOU HEARD that… that…"

"Bitch?" I said. "Harpy? A few other words I couldn't kiss my mom after saying?"

"Yes." Faye pushed her blond hair back, holding her head for a moment. "We can't do this."

"I could beat her up. I've been practicing since the zombie attack. My magic's never been stronger."

"I still can't believe you left my kid alone."

"I can't believe you're still harping on that. It was months ago. It was either leave baby, or wait for the zombie to attack."

"Wait for the zombie to attack! It's *always* wait for the zombie to attack." She reached up like she was going to wring my neck but grinned. "You could've holed up inside and waited."

"He could've gone after someone else. We've been over this. Heat of the moment, I was going off adrenaline, and… yeah, that's pretty much it. We're getting off topic."

"I meant to." Faye sighed. "She'll tell the Council."

"You know, I'm getting really sick of the Council hovering over us."

"And that's *why* I was trying to get us off topic."

I ignored her. "Can't do this. Can't do that. What if the humans find out? It's for the good of us all. It's the twenty-first century! Humans *should* know. And you know what, the Council can *bite me*."

Faye paled, looking around her living room like she was afraid they were listening in. Hell, for all I knew they were. It wasn't like they had any respect for privacy. It was for the good of us all for them to keep an eye on witches, to keep us in line so we didn't hurt ourselves or expose our secret.

Antiquated bullshit used by dictators that got off on power.

"Evie," Faye said, "I know you don't like the Council and they can be… heavy handed." She looked around again and I rolled my eyes. "But they're our governing entity, and they have thrown witches in Oz for less. Be. Careful."

"Grrrrrr," I said, picking up my glass of wine. "Okay, fine. I'll be a good little girl and not say anything that could get me a treason charge, well… anything *else* that could get me a treason charge. But we should still do the Luck Scramble."

"And we can. I'll do it with my cat and you can get a cat and do it with her." She looked around and twisted her fingers, making the air pop.

A sound shield, just in case anyone was listening. I grinned.

"This whole thing started as a joke anyway," Faye said, "not as a legitimate way to give them enough luck to make a difference. I mean, the questions are already made, how much good could luck really do?"

"It's a boost. It makes people think clearer, have more energy… more *confidence*. Hell, it's a triple espresso wrapped up with some good ol' liquid courage." I toasted her with my glass. "They know the material. That's not the problem. Their mental states are, or at least Ashley's is. You haven't told me how George is doing."

"He's freaking out." She took a gulp of wine and I nodded at her to continue. "He keeps looking at stats, saying not even twenty percent fail the Utah bar and how could he be so stupid. He's drinking more and he has a hard time sleeping… yeah, he could use the confidence boost."

She stared into her wine like it held answers to marriage she could dig down to find.

"How bad?" I asked.

She looked up, meeting my eyes. "Bad. He's… broken. And I can't help."

I nodded. "That settles it. I'll get a cat. At the very least we'll give them what we catch on Friday, every little bit helps."

"AND ALL OF OUR ANIMALS are fully up to date on their shots, free from parasites, spayed or neutered, and looking for a good home," Ariel, the woman who bounced up to us when we entered the shelter said, clapping her hands together before folding them in front of her.

Good, I was another minute of her chatter away from letting loose a verbal attack of Little Mermaid jokes, including a few bars of "Part Of Your World." She'd been talking since we entered. It'd been at least ten minutes and I was worried she was going to suffocate. Okay, I got less worried and more hopeful as the spiel went on.

"Okay," Faye said with a head shake, like she needed it to recover from the onslaught. "We're going to look around."

The shelter was nice at least. And it wasn't a puppies and kittens only place, where the shelter found homes for unexpected litters while they were still tiny and cute. Those guys would do fine.

If I was going to subject myself to a self-centered monster whose poop I had to clean up, it was going to be one who really needed a home.

"Okay," Ariel said. "Oh yeah, we have an adoption day this Friday where you can get your animal half off if you want to pick someone and come back then."

"It costs money to adopt?" I asked.

"Yes," Faye said. "They have to make money to run this place somehow."

"Actually," Ariel said. "It's a hundred dollars and that's just to help pay for the animal's basic health care, like the shots. Most of the time we run on donations, but the shelter's getting pretty low on funds. We've been in the red, or whatever it's called, for the last few years."

"What about a fundraiser?" I asked, staring down the line of cages. There had to be at least fifty dogs and cats here. How long did they keep them before the poor things got put down?

"We do one every fall, but last year we didn't pull in enough to keep the place running. I don't even know how to set up a fundraiser. I mean…" Her voice picked up speed and she was off and jabbering.

I shook my head. *Not another ten minute monologue, please. And it's not like it's hard to run a fundraiser. It's hard to get money. That's why…*

I whipped my head around. Lightbulb!

"What about doing one during the adoption day?" I asked, interrupting whatever she was babbling. "Cute animals to play with will be the gimmick, the event to bring people in. Add some food, music-"

"We couldn't put one together that quickly, I mean-"

"I could," I said before she could get going again. "Go get me the info of the person in charge. I've ran the fundraiser for the hospital I work at every year since high school."

"Are you a nurse?"

I took a deep breath. "*Lawyer.* I work for the hospital's General Counsel now, but I've been there forever. Putting a fundraiser together in a week won't be hard since you've already got an event set up. Getting the word out to the right people is the problem. I can do that."

Ariel's mouth worked and she made some noise I'm sure got the dogs' ears perked up before running back towards the front desk.

"Whatever you're thinking, no," Faye said.

I grinned, holding up two fingers. "Ohhhhhh yes. Two birds." I dropped a finger. "One stone. We're going to do our fundraiser, and help out some of these little guys in the process. It's, wait for it." I held up my hands. "Purrrrfect."

Faye groaned. "Oh, that's bad. That's so bad."

Ariel came back with the info and I shook my head at Faye, mouthing we'd talk later.

I'd get people to the fundraiser, handling the animals and playing with them, holding different ones to decide who to take home. I'd put the Luck Scramble spell on the cats, and when I took the cats back from the people handling them, I'd store whatever the furballs gathered.

But I still had my own fuzzy friend to find.

"HE'S ABOUT FIVE," I SAID on Friday, taking the tiny tabby back from the woman. "They said he had a family that dropped him off last month because they were moving."

The fundraiser took a hell of a lot more work to set up than I'd thought it would. On top of my job, it'd been a long ass week, but it was worth it.

The section of the park roped off for this was filled with dogs, cats, even some rabbits, from shelters all over the city. We'd talked them into joining and helping us promote. I got restaurants to donate food, a giant tent, heaters to keep everyone toasty against the February chill, and managed to wrangle us a band to play some rock/alternative music. If it wasn't Utah, I'd probably been able to get us some booze.

Alcohol licenses in Utah are a nightmare and sure as hell not happening in one week.

People crowded our tent and bunched around the warmers. They were wrapped in coats and stomping snow off their boots, but they were pouring in.

Animals were everywhere. Some in their cages and resting, a few dogs running around in their little playpen. The cats couldn't really be let out like that. Furry little escape artist Houdinies. But they were being held and passed around.

Volunteers helped handle the animals and keep everything clean. I ran the table at the back of the tent, bringing the cats out for people to check out and putting them back in their cages, helping people choose their new babies.

Mine licked his paws next to me on the table. He was a two-year-old black Maine Coon named Gremlin who'd grabbed my heart in five seconds. I brushed him with the luck collecting spell, but so far, he hadn't gathered anything, purrrrr-fectly content to stay by me and eye the other cats like he knew he could beat them up.

"They said he's very good with other cats, dogs, kids," I said to the woman, scratching the tabby's head.

"Oh, I don't know," the woman said, looking around. "I think I'm just going to keep looking."

"Okay." I swiped the energies off the tabby's fur with one last pet before putting him back in his cage and grabbed the necklace in my pocket to deposit the energy there.

"Hey." Faye inched out of the crowd moments later and dropped into the seat next to me. Gremlin gave her a fish eye, meowed, and went back to cleaning himself.

"Great turnout," Faye said, scritching Gremlin's head and making him purr. "And the shelter has already raised nearly five thousand dollars. How did you pull this off?"

"Years of building connections doing the fundraisers for the hospital with my mom. The key to something like this isn't a cool theme or even a worthy cause. It's knowing the right people to invite and convincing them all the other right people will be there. Mom tells her society friends to show because it's this fresh, new thing and that everyone will be there, they all show. This isn't the hospital's Fall Society Ball or anything, but it's not a bad turnout."

"The-" Faye's phone buzzed and she pulled it out, frowning as she read the text.

"What?"

Faye pursed her lips, staring at the screen. "She… that *bitch* Maggie is asking where I am. They've gathered for the Luck Scramble and she thinks it's suspicious I'm not there."

My heartrate spiked. "Oy vey! What do we do? What if she comes here?"

"At least she's not tech savvy. Probably didn't see all the Facebook posts and Tweets and whatever else you do for this stuff."

"Is she going to do something? Like try to figure out where we are or what we're doing?"

Faye's phone buzzed again and her eyebrows flew up.

"I'm afraid to ask," I said.

"She said she heard about a pet adoption day, and thinks it'd be a good place to hit for the Good Luck Scramble. She's going to mix her cat in with the ones here, pretend the cat is here to sniff other ones and see who would get along well with her cat or something like that."

"She wants to bring her cat here?"

"Yes."

"She's onto us."

"I don't think so."

"How do we keep it that way?"

FAYE INTERCEPTED MAGGIE AND HER group at the entrance to the tent nearly an hour later. I found someone to cover for me, and watched from behind one of the band's speakers.

Oy vey. This was going to go bad so freaking fast.

Faye and Maggie started walking around together as the other witches scattered. I shook my head. This wasn't going to work. There was no way Maggie being here was a coincidence. She knew. She *knew*…

And that meant the Council did.

I took a deep breath. *Stay calm. Just stay calm.*

The necklace in my pocket was heavy with the energy I'd pulled so far. The near identical one on Faye was probably the same way. If Maggie so much as thought we were still trying to pull this off and tested Faye's necklace, she'd see there was a ton of extra energy and realize Faye didn't just get here to meet the group, she'd been here since this thing started at five.

And that'd only lead to more questions.

"Hey pretty lady," someone said behind me.

"Ah!" I jumped and whirled.

One of the guys from the band smiled down at me from the stage, winked, and lifted his guitar in a greeting before launching into the next song.

I grinned, rolled my eyes, and turned back around.

The smile disappeared. Maggie had worked her way down the first line of cages and was headed right for me, Faye behind her with wide eyes.

I met Maggie halfway, crossing my arms and staring her down.

She mimicked my pose and stared back. I shrugged. No way in hell would I speak first.

"Fancy seeing you here," she finally said.

Point for me. I fought down a grin.

"It's for a good cause. These little guys need homes, the shelter needed help, and I'm good at fundraisers. What are you doing here? Never pegged you for the civil minded type."

"Cat Luck Scramble. Seemed like a good place to gather energy. Of course, *you* thought of that first, didn't you?"

She smiled, wicked and tight.

It sliced through my belly, making my knees shake.

"I'd say see you around, but I have a feeling the Council's going to have you… tied up for a while."

Fear dropped into my stomach like ice and I grabbed her arm as she turned to leave. "You're not telling them anything."

"Get your hands off me."

"Nope." I looked around. We weren't attracting much attention yet, but we would if this went down in here.

Faye shook her head at me, making a throwing motion.

Throw the necklace away because of some bully? Oh, hell no!

"Come on," I growled, yanking her arm.

I pulled Maggie through the tent's back flap, night draping us as the flap fell back over the lighted inside. Cold bit my nose and ears, making me shiver.

Wish I'd had time to grab my coat.

I dragged her behind the line of trees half a football field away from our tent before I stopped and looked around, eyes straining in the dim streetlights lining the park.

Thank the Goddess for the cold keeping the park mostly empty.

"What do you want?" I asked, trying to keep my voice even. "Nobody does something like this without an agenda. What's yours?"

"Keeping witches protected," Maggie said like it was the simplest thing in the world.

"Bullshit. You're not telling the Council on me."

"Are you going to kill me to keep me from talking?"

"That would be overkill, don't ya think?" But I narrowed my eyes, drawing up my power.

I didn't have to kill her, just make her see things my way.

"You can't take me," she said, but her eyes widened. "I have twenty-five years of spelling on you."

I shrugged, using the motion to cover up pulling my phone out of my pocket. I fumbled for its power button behind my back, turning it on. How could I get through it without her seeing me and wondering what I was doing?

"And?" I asked. "My family's always been more powerful than yours. One of the reasons you hate us so much. I can take you, Maggie. Only question is, are you going to make me?"

She didn't move so much as twitch, but it was enough warning.

I dodged to the side, grabbing the necklace around my neck. It's my wand, for lack of a better term. It focuses my magic.

Maggie's spell flew by me, something icy that'd probably leave me hollow as a cold shower. Our powers reflect our temperaments, and she was a water witch who was a cold bitch down to her core.

I shot flames at her, not bothering to keep the spell invisible like she had.

I was done pussyfooting around.

Maggie jumped to the side, almost too slow. Her age gave her more experience and power than me, but left her seriously outmatched in anything physical.

Goddess, why didn't I bring my gun! It'd be easier and take a hell of a lot less of my energy to shoot at her.

I spit another whip of flame at her, keeping it powered so it didn't flicker out. I raised a wall of fire on the right as I flicked more at her on the left and curved them behind her, boxing her in.

The flames hardened into ice and fell to the cold, hard ground, shattering into chunks.

I ducked behind a tree and shot a fireball at her. She dodged, raising her hand. Water hit the tree, visible and obvious under the streetlights.

I pulled fire from my belly, growing a wall in front of her face. I swished the flames around her, making them flick and twitch at her, and fumbled with my phone to hit the right buttons.

I tossed my phone, holding it in the air and veiling it with a puff of magic as the flames fell from her face with another splash. I hurled a fireball straight at her, and she dodged. I pulled up another and another, lobbing them like baseballs as my power waned.

I grabbed my necklace and yanked power from its core, breathing in a rush of smoky goodness, and shot a wall of flames at her, moving fast as a cheetah.

She paled and threw up her arms, making a visible wave of ice crash over my flames. The ice charged forward and I flung myself to the side, grabbing my phone and making it visible.

I grinned, holding it up. "Smile, Maggie. You're on Candid Camera."

Her arms fell, sending the ice smashing to the ground, and she covered her mouth, eyes wide as she looked around the park. Nobody was out and about, but they could've been. She pulled her hands from her face and stared at them like they were possessed and pulling her intestines out an inch at a time.

"No," she said almost too quiet for me to hear, and shook her head. "I didn't mean… I was scared…" Her face hardened but she didn't look up. "You tricked me!"

"And yet," I said with a smirk, stopping the recording and emailing it to Faye and my dad just in case Maggie tried anything. "The Council won't care. All they're going to care about is we did this in public. Just like they wouldn't care all I wanted to do was give my friend a confidence boost with no real risk of exposure. Just like *you* didn't care."

"But… but…" She dropped her hands and looked at me. "I had a reason. You were attacking me!"

I shook my head, tucking my phone back in my slacks. "I show this to them and you know as well as I, they won't care about either of our *reasons*. Those rules you love so much? They don't leave room for any kind of reason or exception."

"They'll… to both of us, they will *punish* us."

"And *I* could've killed you when I put that fire in front of your face. At the very least severely burned you. I *didn't*. This video goes nowhere besides the people I just emailed it to unless you tell the Council on me." I paused, taking a deep breath. "I don't expect us to be friends, Maggie. But I do hope you'll take this and consider maybe, just maybe I'm right on this one now that you're in my shoes."

I turned and walked back to the tent and the cute fuzzies.

Maggie didn't try to stop me.

"ALRIGHT," I SAID, HOLDING THE necklace up by its chain. "Open your eyes."

Ashley's eyes popped open and she looked from the necklace to me and back. I'd gotten my hands on dozens of kitties, and at least twice that many people's loose energy, and stored it all in the necklace. Faye made out even better. It wasn't enough good vibes to magically change the test for Ashley or George, but it sure as hell was enough to give them the boost they needed.

"It's a good luck charm for the bar tomorrow," I said with a laugh. "Here." I put the crystal pendant on her hand and poured the chain around it with a silent blessing. "Wear it both days of the bar. It'll give you luck."

"Evie, you know-"

"You don't go in for all that New Age stuff, yeah, yeah, yeah." I curled her fingers around the spelled talisman. "But this is old age, baby. I spent Friday the Thirteenth collecting this good luck for you at that pet fundraiser I did."

She threw her head back laughing. "Oh man, you are hilarious." She squeezed the necklace, forehead wrinkling up. "You know what? I actually feel better."

I smiled.

We had our people equipped for the battle ahead, dozens of animals found homes while the shelter got a nice boost to its coffers, and I hadn't heard boo from Maggie in ten days. That was pretty damn successful in my book.

I stood, looking around Ashley's apartment. "Wear that tomorrow. It'll help. I'm not kidding."

"It's not going to *really* work," she said, snorting.

I raised my eyebrows. "You're holding it and you said you already feel better. Wear it, and then tell me it doesn't really work."

"You can't be serious. How could it…" She shook her head and stared at the necklace. "It feels warm. How…?"

The Council can suck it.

I smiled and winked. "Magic."

PART III. EVIE JONES
AND THE MAGIC MELTDOWN

"EVIE! GET YOUR SKINNY ASS out here," Chet yelled and pounded on the door, making the cheap wood dance like a stripper twerking.

I rolled my eyes at the bedroom door and put the last of my wrapped crystals in their bag. "Give me a minute. I'm packing up my girly stuff." I shook my head, muttering, "Oy vey."

"What, like your vibrators?"

I snorted and closed the bag, looking around to make sure there were no other magic items lying around before slinging it on my back. The carpet squelched under my feet as I crossed it, leaving footprints in my wake.

The damn flood took out the rental house's (I use this term loosely) carpets, the smattering of cheap tables, loveseat, and bed I'd brought to save me from renting the who-knew-who'd-done-what-on it furniture from this small town's Rent-A-Crap. The stuff was cheap, but it was mine. And now it was in the trash.

Chet and Zach came with their truck to help me toss the stuff growing mold, and pack up and schlep home the TV, kitchen stuff, and random knickknacks I'd brought to keep me company in this middle-of-nowhere, backwater town while I was stuck here for a month.

"Merow!" came from the living room. I got my tuchus out of the bedroom so fast you'd think I teleported. My giant Maine Coon, Gremlin, ran up, sitting next to my feet.

Zach was still mid-crouch and stared at me with big eyes. "How did you do that?"

I crossed my arms. "Don't pull my cat's tail."

"I wasn't! I was petting him and he just screamed and hissed at the door."

"Bull, ya putz. Don't mess with my cat."

"Dude," Chet cut in, "come on, don't mess with her cat. That's her baby; she'll kick your ass."

"I didn't do anything to the damn cat." Zach stood, towering over me. "And she's like four feet tall, what's she gonna do to me?"

I looked at Chet and he held his hands up in the universal apology siblings everywhere give for their big-mouthed brothers.

I glared at Zach. "I'm average height, not four feet, for one. For two, I'm trained in Aikido, carrying a knife and a *gun*, and I just moved so fast I made you freeze." I lowered my voice and raised my eyebrows. "I'm Kung Fu Jew, bitch."

Zach burst out laughing and I couldn't keep the serious anymore, laughing too.

"Okay," I said when I caught my breath. "This is the last bag." I scooped up Grem, cradling him in my arms like a baby. "We good?"

We piled into the truck, Zach driving so Chet could sit between us, my bag by my feet, and my Grem-baby on my lap.

"I can't believe this rain," I said, petting Gremlin's bush of soft black fur. "It's Utah, not London, for the sake of the Goddess. It's a freaking desert."

I glanced in the rearview mirror at the little house in the rain as we pulled out from under the covered driveway that passed for a garage.

A small figure with long, straight black hair stood in front of the house.

I twisted around so fast Gremlin jumped into Chet's lap.

No one there.

I looked back at the mirror and she was gone. My heart raced and fear shivered down my spine.

"You okay, Evie?" Chet asked, resting a hand on my cat and the other on my knee.

I ground my teeth together as another stab of adrenaline pierced my heart. My belly jerked and I shook my head. "Fine. Just… seeing things in the rain. I'm tired. It's been a long month."

He stroked Gremlin but left his other hand on my knee and my attention zeroed down to it like a teenager. *I'm a grown woman. I'm not getting gooey over a friend who sees me as one of the guys.*

We'd met when I hired his band for a fundraiser last February. When I ran into him again at the gun range, we'd hit it off and had been friends since. He'd had a girlfriend until a month ago, and I was his buddy who happened to have boobs.

"What were you doing out here anyway?" Zach asked.

"I'm one of the Assistant General Counsels at my hospital. We're expanding. We put a satellite hospital out here in two-hours-from-civilization-ville, and they needed someone to train the staff on patient privacy issues. Guess who pissed off the new boss?"

"Sucks."

"It's been hell. Small town, USA. Where the existence of a Walmart and a hospital makes it a city in the redneck populace's minds."

"Damn girl, tell us how you really feel," Chet said, rubbing my knee.

I looked down and the puddle of water at my feet reflected a flash of dark hair back at me.

Wait, water!

I jerked my legs up, Chet pulled his hand away like I'd slapped it, and Gremlin jumped into Zach's lap. Zach swerved with a curse and pulled the truck back into the lane. A blink later the water was gone. An empty chip bag, two water bottles and a smattering of papers decorated the truck floor, and that was it.

"What the fuck?" Zach said. "Did you see a spider or something?"

Chet shot me a worried look and Gremlin climbed over him back to me.

"I'm seeing things," I said. "Sorry guys."

"Seeing things, like you're off your meds?" Zach asked.

"Ha ha. I'm not on meds."

"At least you admit it."

"I'm not crazy! Just tired. It's fine."

What if it's not? What if something's after me?

I couldn't call my dad and ask if this could be anything magical with the guys in the car. I'd wait till we stopped for gas. If I could wait that long. I looked over at the dash; the gas gauge was down to about a fourth. We'd have to stop soon anyway.

"Hey Zach, pull off at the next gas station. I've got to pee."

"Already? Are you shitting me?" Zach rolled his eyes. "Girls."

"THANKS DAD, LOVE YOU TOO," I said, hanging up the phone in the disgusting excuse for a bathroom. Of course it *could* be something magical. It always could be, but it wasn't likely. Tired, stressed lawyer was a hell of a lot more likely than magical thingamabob after random witch.

Unless I'd pissed someone off.

The only magical people I've pissed off are Maggie, but she'd never break magic law, and Faye's ex, um… something Payton, when I stopped his zombie, but wouldn't he go after her first?

I'd been texting Faye so we could get drinks when I got back to Salt Lake. She was at her office and perfectly fine.

Leaving me with the far more likely explanation of exhausted lawyer who'd been so bored the past month her brain started making meshugaas up for entertainment.

I checked the bathroom door to make sure it was locked, and put my phone back in my purse. I looked drawn and grey in the mirror, my normally tan skin a nice pasty color just in time for summer. I snorted and pulled up the toilet seat.

A face decorated with stringy black hair stared up at me.

"Ah!" I jerked back and looked down at the toilet again, pinching myself when nothing was there.

While we were stopped, I had to pee, otherwise I'd hear it from the guys in an hour when I actually needed to pee. Still… water was a dangerous thing right now.

I pulled down my panties, hiked up my suit skirt, and straddled the seat, looking down as I squatted over it to make sure a hand didn't reach up from a watery grave to grab something I didn't want grabbed unless it bought me dinner first, and told me I was pretty.

I have never peed so fast in my life. I got out of there after a quick hand wash and half ran out to the counter. Why would I hallucinate things in water? Maybe it was because I was a fire witch and water was my biggest weakness. There's a reason the Joneses settled in the desert, and it wasn't for our Jewish heritage's sake. We didn't do well with our elemental opposite when magic came a-callin'.

"You okay, girl?" Chet asked, rubbing my arm as I waited near the doors for Zach to finish filling the truck and pull it around front. I'd paid then ran in. The guys were nice enough to spend their Friday moving me, the least I could do was pay travel costs and spring for dinner and drinks when we got home.

"Yeah." If he'd been anyone else, I would've shrugged him off. "Just one of those days… or months, you know?"

"Yeah, can't believe your place flooded. Do water lines normally break like that?"

I paused, shivering. They really didn't… not without help. I shook my head. *You're being crazy. It was a crappy house with crappier plumbing. What, you think it's some big plot of water witches to get you? Who and why? Be reasonable. Oy vey, I'm even a bitch to myself when I'm tired.*

"Not that I know of," I said.

I squinted out of the convenience store's double doors into the rain, tapping my foot. The truck sat across from the doors, the gas pump had to be done by now, unless the truck had the gas tank equivalent of Rosie O'Donnell's stomach.

"Where's Zach?" I asked, walking closer to the doors. They zipped open automatically and thunder cracked the sky open, making me jump. *I guess I missed the lightning flash?*

"He's getting gas." Chet walked up behind me and looked around. "He *was* getting gas. Punk's probably sneaking a smoke. He knows I'll get on him."

"He trying to quit?" I searched the parking lot, trying to focus through the rain. It bounced off the roof and asphalt with a deafening pattering usually reserved for stampedes of sugared up kids, falling so fast and thick, it'd be like walking into a hail storm.

"Yeah." Chet popped his jacket collar up and pulled a wool hat out of his pocket and shoved it on his head, covering the gelled brown spikes. "I'll find him."

The rain sang its rhythmic taunt as Chet stepped forward, and the doors swished open. Fear hit my chest like a shot of epi, nausea turned my stomach, and I grabbed his arm with both hands like a melodramatic silver screen queen.

"What?" he asked with a grin that made me almost want to smile back.

"I…" Why did I grab his arm? I had a bad feeling? Yep, pretty much it. My hackles were up, I was tired and I was seeing things. I couldn't look at him so I looked outside again. The water shimmered on the asphalt in the dreary cloud blocked sunlight like razorblades.

"Just got a little dizzy." I let him go. "It's passed."

"Hey, if you pass out, I'll carry you back to the truck all *Gone with the Wind*." He winked.

I pushed his arm. "Yeah, yeah, move it, Rhet."

He grinned and flicked his windbreaker's hood over his warm woolen hipster cap, and walked into the rain, broad shoulders hunching down like it was a physical hand pushing on him. He walked around the edge of the building and out of sight.

I shivered and rubbed my arms, the long-sleeved blouse not doing a lot to keep me warm.

My jacket was in the truck. I could grab it, but that'd mean going back out into the rain. My belly burned, rolling with sugared fear balls, and I wanted to sink to the floor and shake until it passed.

Damn, I hadn't felt this on edge since…

"Since last year with the zombie," I whispered.

I'd felt wrong the entire night. Just figured it was because my ex was getting married, and I'd been down. I had been, but that wasn't what made the hairs on the back of my neck rise like my cat's.

Gremlin!

He was in the truck. If something was out there and wanted me, it'd go after my cat. My knees shook and my stomach roiled up again. I tried to force my feet to move and they wouldn't.

Quit being a wussy! I mentally screamed like a war cry, grabbed my necklace, and ran into the rain, the force of the drops pounding me down two seconds out. Magic?

Not that it mattered. Something was out here either way. I ran faster, slamming into the truck's door hard enough to bruise me and make my Grem jump. I yanked the door open, scooped up an armful of cat, slung on my bag with my magic items, and turned.

The rain swirled, mini tornados forming around the parking lot. Gremlin snuggled to my chest, eyeing the lot and convenience store with the same jerky apprehension I was. "Merrrow."

"Yeah, I think we should get inside too." I ran, breaths coming out in short bursts, and bust through the doors.

The clerk looked up from her magazine and pulled out her earbuds as I set the bag on the floor. "No pets allowed, unless they're service animals," she said in the bored tone of someone spouting out a spiel memorized from a dry handbook.

"He's my familiar," I said. Her dyed black hair, black nail polish and Elvira dress said it was worth a shot.

She shrugged, going back to her magazine, and Gremlin jumped out of my arms, running to the first aisle and sniffing the jugs of motor oil.

I turned to watch the doors. It couldn't take Chet that long to check around the gas station. Sure enough, a Chet shaped water monster stomped back into sight a minute later, holding his hood closed under his chin with one hand and hunching down into his jacket, moving slow against the rain, almost like it was pushing him back.

I stepped closer to the doors and they whooshed open, letting in a blast of iced air. "Chet!"

He looked up and grinned. I waved at him to hurry up and he didn't move any faster.

Oy vey! Come on, come on.

The rain twirled up behind him in another weird whirlpool and I grabbed my necklace. No way… nuh uh. It was the wind, it happened, that wasn't a cyclone and there's no way in hell it was controlled by magic. Because what did that? A witch? Why?

"Chet, get your tuchas in here. It's cold!" I yelled.

The girl appeared in front of me, just outside the doors. Black hair hung over a pale, naked body shorter and slimmer than mine. She met my eyes.

And smiled.

WHAT TEETH WERE LEFT STUCK OUT, like a girl born in a time before dental care. Her flat, oval face and almond eyes said Asian.

She said something. Her breath smelled of fish so strong I had to breathe through my mouth even five feet away. She turned on Chet.

"Holy fuck!" he screamed, like he just saw her now and not a few seconds ago when she appeared.

"Chet, run!" I ran outside, holding my necklace. I threw my hand out, pulling magic from my core and letting it take its most natural physical form in my hand. I pointed and blasted the bitch with a whip of fire. My flames died on her chest with the sputters of drowned fireworks, and she appeared next to me in a blink.

I threw up a shield so fast I got whiplash, and she placed a hand on it.

Chet pulled his gun from his hip, focusing the laser pointer on her. "Freeze!"

She said something probably along the lines of, "You asked for it," and raised a hand. Hoarfrost grew from the nose of his gun and up like a flesh-eating disease of the metal kind, and he dropped it before the cold could catch his hands.

I pulled water out of the air, gathered it around me and turned up the heat, using my diamond necklace to focus the magic. Steam burst out like a cloud and I wrapped it around the water ghost thing, sealing it with a prayer. Chet ran towards us, grabbed my hand and yanked me inside.

The steam hit the ground and dispersed, leaving rain and nothing else on the blacktop as the doors swished shut in front of us.

I looked over and the girl wasn't at the counter anymore. *Is she in on this? Is she that thing? It'd explain why there's a goth girl in middle of nowhere Utah.*

I walked to the counter and peeked over it. The girl was curled up on the floor, little shushing noises saying she was merely asleep.

"A sleeping spell, or maybe a potion?" I said out loud. "Why? If the demon or ghost or whatever could do that, why not do that to us?"

"Potion? Demon?" Chet asked behind me.

I whirled, slamming my hand to my cheek. "Oy gevalt!"

"What!" He looked around, whirling and checking behind him too.

"No, nothing's there," I said as he turned back around. "You're not supposed to know about magic. Humans can't know! We get in serious trouble with our government if we let humans know."

Gremlin walked over and sat at my feet. "Meow?"

I picked him up and slung him over my shoulder like a big, furry baby. "Yeah, we're in trouble."

"He talks!"

I gave Chet a look. "Yeah, he says food, no, outside, mom, and now. Usually in the form of a meow, but you learn to differentiate."

Chet closed his eyes and took a deep breath before opening them. "Okay, so you're magic, the cat isn't, and the thing outside is…?"

"You're the anthropology doctoral candidate. You tell me. Any Asian magic water thingies you know about?"

"You don't know?"

"I'm not Asian! You want a golem, that's my people's magic. That thing out there is sooooo not."

He shrugged off his windbreaker and rubbed his head, crunching his short spikes. "I don't know. I can't think. This is crazy!"

"Well, you're handling your first magical attack better than I did."

"What did you do?"

"Dropped my gun."

He made a small noise, letting go of his hair and meeting my eyes, horror sliding over his. "Where's Zach?"

"Um. If he wasn't outside, then maybe in the storage room in the back?"

Chet ran to the back door and disappeared through it faster than Gremlin could vanish when I turned on the vacuum.

I tried to go after him. My feet wouldn't move. Fear boiled my belly. What if he didn't come back? What if that thing could get inside? What if it was behind me!

I whirled and Gremlin pushed off my shoulder and ran down the first aisle, scrambling on the slick floors. No one else there. The florescent lights made the white floors gleam. My heart rate ticked up and my chest constricted. I couldn't breathe!

I'm panicking. Why am I panicking? That thing out there hasn't even done anything yet besides…

Besides scare me.

I slapped my forehead. "Oy vey, it's a *fear demon*."

I'd been off and panicky all afternoon. No wonder. An Asian water fear demon. Did someone summon a creature out of a horror movie and plop it in my life? Last time someone did that, it was Faye's ex. Could be him again, but why an Asian demon?

I kneeled by my bag and opened it. Crystals, herbs, candles. I had the basics, but no research books, no talismans, no way of finding out what…

"Duh. Dad." I almost slapped myself on the forehead again, and pulled out my phone. I pressed the button to turn it on and typed in my code before realizing the screen didn't light up. "Oh *fuck*! You've got to be kidding me!"

"I don't think I've ever heard you use that word." Chet walked back in, shaking his head and holding his jacket. "He's not there and my phone's dead."

"Mine too."

"Can't be a coincidence."

"Nope." I stood up. "I've got ingredients here, but they're not a lot of good if I don't know what I'm fighting."

He walked towards the doors.

"Wait! What are you doing?"

"I'm gonna throw down with that bitch and get my brother back." He didn't have to roll up his sleeves, his dark shirt clung to his arms so tight they'd go nowhere. "What are you doing? You're the witch, figure you should be doing something about this shit."

"I need to know what it is before I can fight it. And I'm having a little problem."

He raised his eyebrows, jaw clenched so tight his dentist would need to surgically separate his teeth.

"I'm scared." I held up a hand before he could say anything. "I don't mean this situation's scaring me. I mean the whole thing. I'm *terrified*. Can't move, can't make a decision, can't even think about going outside. I'm not a puss." I turned to my Gremlin as he rocketed past me. "No offense, baby."

I took a deep breath. "I'm scared. I think it's some kind of fear demon. Is there anything from your studies that could be something like this? Add messes with electronics to the list. Unless it has a partner."

"Tons of things could be something like this. There are mythologies on water spirits and fear ones, and ones that overlap, from all over the world. And that's just mythology. *Stories*. It's not supposed to be real. What are the odds this thing is something ever studied by humans?"

"Okay, good point. I don't know how to fight it, though."

"You don't want me to die, you're going to figure it the fuck out, because I'm getting my brother back." He walked out of the store.

Go after him! my brain screamed.

I can't!

I pinched myself and focused on my foot. *Just step forward.* It didn't move. *One step. Come on!* Bupkis. "Grrrrr!"

I grabbed my necklace, using it to center myself. I was a witch with blood lines running back to the early Jews and the Druids. I took a deep breath, closed my eyes and ran for the door. The doors opened with that whoosh just fast enough to get out of the way before I probably would've smacked into them, and I opened my eyes as I hit the rain.

"Bring it, bitch!" I yelled.

Chet turned in a slow circle, arms up, second gun drawn.

"Where did your first gun go? The one she froze?" I asked, pulling my revolver from the holster on my belt.

"No clue." He kept turning, freaking doctoral candidate playing cop.

"Aren't you worried about the damn demon getting it?" My voice sounded high and squeaky, and I gulped. "I mean, it could use it against us." I searched the ground.

"Seriously, girl. That's all you got?" He got in my face, bending over and grabbing my chin. "You're whining like a little bitch baby. Dammit, girl. Get your head in the game. Get pissed off! Whatever you need to get over the fear. I need you!"

"I don't know how." Rain pounded my skull and Chet stared down at me.

"Whatever it is, I don't know how to fight it. And it's out here. It's going to pop up any second. Get over it, Evie! Where's the firecracker I know! Where's the bitch who took on that prick at the shooting range and put him in his place?"

I stared into his eyes.

He threw his hands up and walked a few feet away, pausing and screaming at the sky, "Give me back my brother, you bitch! You want me? You want Evie? We're right here. Come and get us!"

The rain pounded down and the clouds cast the parking lot in shadows, but nothing came for us. It was like she disappeared.

I shivered and rubbed my arms, forcing bile down as I holstered my gun. Had to. Had to pull this off. "I don't think she's here anymore," I said, making my voice shake. It wasn't hard.

"No." Chet looked around, eyes wild and wide. "No! Dammit! Zach!" He fell to his knees, pushing his hair back. "Zach! You fucking brat, get back here!"

I walked over to him and touched his shoulder, leaning down to his ear. "It's still here," I whispered so light I couldn't hear myself over the rain. "I can feel it. It's playing with us or trying to draw us somewhere. I'm terrified right now. So are you. That feeling of helplessness, that's the demon. It's. Still. Here."

He hung his head like he was defeated and I kneeled in front of him. Chet hugged me close, whispering, "What do we do?"

"What we would do if we believed Zach was gone. Go inside and call the cops with the landline. I'm betting it'll be down too, but we'll look like that's what we're doing."

"And then?"

"We see what the demon does. It's got a plan. This isn't random."

"Is he still alive, Evie?"

"Yeah."

"How do you know?"

"Because it's trying to scare us. If he were dead, it'd string him up for display to see us scream."

"That's… comforting."

We stood, and I slung an arm around his waist, fears buried under the blanket of someone else needing me. He held his gun slack by his side, like he almost forgot it was there. We walked towards the building with the slow shuffle of people who knew they were defeated and couldn't outrun anything, so why try.

The wind shifted, blowing in from the street and carrying the soft, sweet smell of gasoline, making me flashback to boating in the mountains.

And fish.

Not rotted. Good fish, like sashimi salmon, delicate and mouthwatering.

I let go of Chet, pulled my knife from my hip and whirled in one motion, catching the demon's arm with the four-inch blade.

"Eeeeeeeeee," she shrieked, jerking away with a flash of blurred limbs as I whipped my arm up and stabbed at her belly. Blood sliced through the air and decorated the asphalt.

"You can bleed, you can die," I said, grinning like I wanted to split my face.

She came at me. Too fast. Too many pale, slender limbs flying, and I backpedaled, swiping at the air in front of me with my knife.

"Merrowwwwww!"

Twenty pounds of black furred fury slammed into the demon's face. Gremlin moved so fast he scratched the crap out of her, jumped away, and disappeared into the night before I got my gun fully out.

"You get fish tonight, baby!" I screamed, pulling the trigger three times. The demon stumbled with each hunk of lead, blood leaking out of her chest.

She didn't fall, just looked at me.

One by one, hunks of metal inched out of her flesh and fell to the ground. Why did the knife do more damage? *It's silver! She's silver sensitive.*

Blood decorated her white flesh where the holes had been. She tossed her knee length black hair back and flashed those jacked up teeth at me.

They caught the gas station lights. So did something at her ear. A silver earring. A hunk of metal, but so much more. Nothing sensitive to silver would wear it willingly.

Silver's a binding agent, used across cultures in spells older than my peoples to bind and control others. The original handcuffs.

"Chet!" I yelled, bringing my knife up. "She's being controlled by someone. They've got to be close to keep the spell going. Find them and take them out! They'll be watching us and have some sort of talisman on them."

"What about her?" came from behind me.

"She's already got a dance partner. Go find your own."

She rushed me, moving with the smooth, slick motions of a cat. At least she wasn't doing the damn jerky thing from a horror movie. I dropped the gun and sliced with my knife. She danced back, moving with grace that'd put my Aikido instructor to shame.

I advanced, slicing down like I'd been taught, and turning slices to jabs randomly, trying to catch her off guard. Water whirled up around me, keeping me from her. The only witches who liked water were born water witches. To the rest of us? It was dampening magic of the oldest kind, literally.

I sliced at the wall of water as it closed in. My knees knocked together and nausea rolled my belly, but I took a deep breath, closed my eyes, and dove into the water wall.

It smacked against me like wet concrete and I pushed forward. *It's maybe six inches of water. She can't control much more than that.* If she could, she wouldn't have allowed some human to capture her and force her to fight.

I walked through molasses, lungs burning, heart pounding. *I'm going to drown.*

NO! I THRUST FIRE FROM my hands, sloppy and power draining, but effective. Water steamed around me, pressure lifting like a lover rolling off you.

And I *breathed.*

The air had the humidity of a Southern summer, but it was air. I opened my eyes. Mist and steam clouded my path, but it wasn't enough to hide that the demon was gone.

"Chet," I said, lifting my hands, focusing on the energy pulsating through the world.

Life flashed on my radar a few feet away and I turned. Gremlin sat by one of the pumps, licking something off his paw. I retrieved my gun and holstered it, then walked over and picked him up.

"Is that blood? Stop that. You don't know what's in a demon thing's blood."

Gremlin chirped at me and jumped out of my arms, licking the *treat* he'd won.

"That blood better not do anything to you," I said. "I am not dealing with demon kitty… which is redundant." I raised my hands again, the water smacking against them with less ferocity than only a minute ago.

I closed my eyes and focused on Chet. On his spiked rocker hair, thick arms with the Hindu tattoo, and full cupid's bow lips.

His focus was ancient cultures. He was writing his dissertation on ancient Indian religious rituals, had spent a semester in India learning from the locals. He wrote the music for his band, mixing eastern tunes in and updating them to give the rock-alternative music more flavor.

And he smelled like pomegranate shampoo and Zest soap.

I breathed in, drawing that smell through my brain like a shoestring flung down to tease a cat. I followed it upstream through the world... and opened my eyes.

The *trail* lit up the dark afternoon like red emergency lights leading to the exit. I focused to keep the line going and followed it. Gremlin trotted next to me, tail down and head high, pointy ears that gave him his name twitching and alert.

"You are so much better than a dog," I said to my baby. He meowed his agreement.

The trail twisted behind the store and across the street into the Dairy Queen's parking lot.

It's too bright and there's workers there. I shook my head. Then again, the gas station was lit up in the gloom and it had at least one worker, probably more in the back, and that didn't stop this thing.

I brought my gun out, holding it left-handed, and put my knife up, ready to twitch at the slightest movement. I crossed over the patch of grass dividing the parking lot from the street. The dining area visible through the restaurant's giant walls of windows showed the few patrons inside were awake and eating. The red line ran behind the Dairy Queen, and I followed it.

The rain had definitely lightened, not that it made a difference now. My button-down clung like I was in wet t-shirt contest, and the skirt stuck to my legs. My hair hugged my head and water squished under my feet in my sandals.

I circled the building, raw dumpster stinging my nose with that patented stench of thrown out food, wet cardboard, and feces all restaurant dumpsters seemed to have.

Chet sat on his knees next to the dumpster, staring down like he had been at the gas station. Only now he wasn't moving.

"Chet!" I ran up to him, gun and knife up and at the ready. I looked around for people, anyone I could accidently shoot if I was trying to aim with the gun in my weak hand. Only one car was parked out here, and it had tinted windows so I couldn't see if anyone was inside, but why would they be hanging out in the parking lot?

I reached Chet and fell to my knees next to him. "Chet?"

His eyes stayed fixed on the street like I wasn't there and he didn't respond. His mouth worked like he was talking, but I couldn't catch anything over the pitter-patter of the rain.

"Chet, get up! What happened?"

"He's dead," Chet said so quietly I barely made out the words. "My brother's dead."

"No." I shook my head. "The demon's messing with you. Zach's fine. I just saw him. This is the demon getting in your head."

"Are you sure?"

"Positive." I looked him in the eyes, forcing conviction into my voice and eyes.

"I… I thought-"

"It's a fear demon. It's making you think you saw things. Get up. Where's your gun?"

He pulled it out of the holster on his hip.

I nodded. "You got any knives on you? Anything silver? I mean, real silver?"

"My piercing is." He flicked the small hoop in his ear.

"Okay, that's not much help. And I've just got the knife on me."

"Bullets?'

"Not helpful."

"Then why-"

"Because the person controlling her is a person and can be shot."

"How do you know it's a person?"

"Demons don't bind other demons. It's a courtesy thing. It's a human, and it's one with a grudge against me. Unless you've pissed off anyone lately?"

He looked at me with big eyes. "I don't think so."

"It's magic, makes me think it's got to be aimed at me. And it has the same feel as the night my friend's ex sent a zombie after me. I think it's him."

"Zombie?" Chet pushed to his feet.

"Yeah."

The demon appeared in front of me and I stabbed her in the chest with reflexes born of training, so fast Gremlin would be proud. Gremlin shot out of the dark hedges surrounding the parking lot and landed on the demon's arm. He bit her hand, sinking his teeth and claws in and hanging on as she flailed her arm.

I jumped in and grabbed the ear holding the silver earring. Magic glowed around it, sickly and yellow, twisted. I sliced her ear off and it fell to the ground as a splash of water, leaving the silver earring lying in a puddle.

She flung Gremlin off and he twisted, landing on his feet. He ran under the hedges lining the lot and disappeared in their shadows. The demon looked down at the earring then met my eyes.

She said something and I didn't need to speak whatever ancient language it was to get the message.

I nodded. "You want to point me at the bastard who bound you?"

She disappeared, flicking back into existence next to the car with the tinted windows. She reached through the glass like it wasn't there and pulled the door off its hinges.

"What the fuck…" Chet breathed next to me.

The demon yanked a man easily twice her size out of the car by the scruff of his neck, and threw him at least ten feet through the air. He hit the ground in front of us in a heap. He was bulky with muscle, and I recognized his bulldog face from pics Faye had shown me.

Her ex. The guy who made a zombie last year and sicced it on her kid while I happened to be babysitting.

"Why didn't she throw us like that?" Chet asked, walking past me.

I grabbed his arm. "She was fighting the binding. She was trying not to hurt us while he was commanding her to. I'm guessing it's why she led us over here. He doesn't have Asian magic."

"How do you know?"

The demon appeared behind the man and grabbed his neck, twisting so hard the sound cracked through the dim afternoon like a gunshot.

"That's how," I squeaked.

She dropped his body and pointed a finger at me.

I held up my hands. "He enslaved you. Clean kill. I have no beef with you."

She must've understood the words or at least the hands up gesture. She disappeared.

My shoulders dropped and I lost ten pounds of stress in my chest. The rain smelled like rain again, and the parking lot shone a little brighter in the stormy afternoon.

"Wow," Chet said. "She's gone?"

"Yeah."

"How did you know he wasn't Asian blood?"

I turned and walked back towards the gas station. "You don't enslave things more powerful than you in your own religion," I said as Chet walked next to me. Gremlin ran ahead of us.

"It's a good way to get yourself dragged into whatever afterlife the tradition believes in," I continued, picking up the pace to keep my cat in sight. "He raised a zombie last year. That's something meant to be controlled, like a golem, but it wasn't powerful enough. He wanted something that could think for itself instead of just following orders, something with magic of its own.

"He didn't use a loa, meaning they probably didn't want to help him or he didn't want to pay their price. He enslaved something outside his religion, so once he let it go, he had a chance of living through it. Probably had some way to send it back to wherever it came from once he was done with it. If he had Asian blood from whatever religion that thing came from, he wouldn't have risked it."

We hit the station and walked in through the back.

"Where did you see Zach?" Chet asked.

"Oh, I didn't," I said. "I lied to get you up."

Chet stopped in the middle of the backroom, the stacks of boxes and random cleaning instruments flanking him like backup. "*What!*"

I looked around. The storage room had industrial shelves lining the walls, and boxes stacked nearly to the ceiling. I slid between two towers of boxes. Zach lay under a shelf behind the piles, head to toe with two gas station workers, even breathing making a soft, almost sweet noise.

I whirled my hands like a game show ditz from the nineties at the sleeping bodies as I stepped back through the gap in boxes to get out of the way. "He's so cute when he's sleeping."

Chet pushed the two towers of boxes, sending them scattering across the floor and making me jump. His jaw dropped. "Is… is he going to be okay?"

"Oh yeah, sleeping potions aren't like in the movies. They only last as long as they're in your system. He'll wake up in a few hours and be fine, probably thirsty."

Chet grabbed Zach's arms and pulled him out from under the metal shelving. He squatted and lifted his brother over his shoulder like a fireman, rising with a grunt. "Do we just sit him up in the truck?"

"Yeah, let's get home. Don't know about you, but I need a drink. Or three." I pulled out my phone. Still dead. "Of course, this wouldn't magically be fixed when the demon left."

"Why not?"

"Because magic doesn't work that way. If you short out someone's phone, it stays shorted. If you drain the battery, it's drained till it recharges."

"Here's hoping it's the second one."

"If it isn't, I'll buy you a new one. Least I can do after today."

Chet put Zach in the car and I put piles of napkins under the clerks' heads so they'd be more comfortable, put my stuff back in their bag and carried it out, locking the gas station behind us. Someone would come for their shift or something soon, and probably call an ambulance when the people didn't wake up. It wasn't ideal but it was the best I could do without a working phone.

"Why did that guy come after you?" Chet asked as I climbed into the middle seat.

"Maybe because I stopped his zombie last year, but you'd think he'd go after his ex first," I said, putting the bag down by Zach's feet and grinning as Gremlin ran up and jumped in the truck. He hopped over me, sprinkling water on my soaked skirt and turned a few circles in Zach's lap before shaking off and flopping down to clean himself.

"Did he still love her?" Chet hopped in and started the truck.

I shrugged. "Why?"

"Because you don't hurt someone you love. He went after her kid and then you, instead of her. Probably didn't want to hurt her. Probably wanted her back and thought he could blackmail her back to him by using the kid. You ruined it so he lashed out at you."

"Possible, but why now?"

"Maybe something happened to keep him busy till now. Or maybe he didn't have enough power till now."

"You're pretty smart, you know that?"

"Well, I am almost a doctor." He grinned and drove out of the gas station.

"I'm glad you're not freaking out about that guy being dead. Or magic existing."

"I think I might be in shock. Never seen a dead body outside a funeral before. But sounds like he deserved it. You don't mess with forces you don't understand."

"That's the way I see it."

"So, you gonna teach me some magic?"

I opened my mouth and closed it, glaring at him. "Oy vey! What did we just say! No. You don't mess with forces you don't understand."

"You could teach me to understand them."

I sighed, rubbing my forehead. "You… it's magic. It isn't something you can just learn. You have to have the power to begin with."

"Damn." He shrugged. "So, dinner's on you?"

I laughed. "Oh yeah. Dinner, drinks, gas, phones, and pretty much whatever else you want after I put you through this."

He looked at me for second before sliding his eyes back to the road, and put his hand on my knee. "You don't want to give me a blank check until you know what I'm going to ask for."

Tingles shivered through me and my belly jerked with the best kind of fear. "Oh really? You know that kind of trade is illegal in the US… at least outside of Nevada."

He winked at me. "It's a good thing I got me a lawyer then."

I laughed and pet Gremlin, staring out at the rain. "You know you shouldn't tease. I might think you're serious."

"Me? Serious? Never." Chet pulled over to the side of the highway, nailing me with a look that made me gulp.

My heart raced and my breathing picked up.

"Damn, Evie, if I didn't know better, I'd say you were scared." He unbuckled and slid an arm around my waist, looming over me.

"Terrified." I smiled, taking a deep breath of him and leaning in.

PART IV. EVIE JONES
AND THE SPIRIT STALKER

MONEY USED TO BE CONSIDERED the root of all evil. Now? I was pretty sure that title belonged to social media.

"Evie, breathe," Faye said over the phone.

I just shook my head, eyes glued to the ferkakta computer screen... and the picture on my ex's page of him and his wife holding a cutesy sign over her belly with a loading bar like on a computer screen that said, "33.33% Loaded."

After that was a status from her about how he'd been running out at all hours of the night for weeks to the market to get food for her cravings, and he couldn't tell anyone because she didn't want to tell people until the second trimester.

"I'm sorry," I said. "Evie's currently having an aneurism. This is her inner retard, laughing at her stupidity."

"You're not stupid."

"I... I let a putz string me along for months, stayed hung up on him even after he got the girl he actually wanted, and then I stayed friends with him online so I could stay in touch. You should *never* stay in touch with an ex! Especially an evil one!" I looked around the shoebox the hospital had the nerve to call an office.

"You have to forgive him eventually. It'll-"

"My hospital fired me. M… *the* hospital I've been at in one way or another since I was sixteen. The one I ran the fundraiser for every year since I was eighteen. I couldn't even get another job as an Assistant General Counsel because I only have a year's experience as a lawyer and most want at least five. I'm an Assistant Privacy Officer, making half of what I did. And now he's… He got promoted at his law firm and now they're having a baby. He gets everything and I've got nothing."

I sobbed and slapped a hand over my mouth, blinking to keep the tears back as my heart lurched. I wanted to curl up on the floor under my desk.

Or punch the wall. Or light the whole fucking room on fire.

Maybe all of the above.

"Is this where you want some tough love and me to tell you to suck it up?" Faye asked. "Or do you want to be an actual person with emotions and have me come over tonight with ice cream, blackberry liqueur, and DVDs?"

I sniffed, taking a deep breath. "I don't need… what DVDs?"

"The entire line of comedians. We're talking Christopher, Iliza, Jeff and Fluffy."

"Yeah, okay," I said. "I want *Love is Evol* first."

"Wow, you really are upset if you're agreeing to me comforting you. I'll be there at eight."

"George took Daphnie to his parents' for the week, right?"

"Yep. Halloween is mommy's week of freedom. He gets his in Spring."

"Okay, and we both have work off the rest of the week and are going to do our Halloween thing with the Coven this weekend. Life doesn't completely suck." I sighed. "Faye, can I cu…"

"No, you can't use the Samhain Festival power boost to curse your ex. You don't want to be like my ex, remember?"

"Yeah, yeah, yeah."

A knock at the door and an, "Excuse me?" made me jump and look up from the screen.

A girl stood in the doorway. She was maybe old enough to be at a college. She had a backpack and wore a little plaid skirt and plaid bows in her blond hair. Her pointy features were obnoxious and cheerleader-esque, and her pale green eyes had way too much makeup around them.

For some reason, I wanted to tear the plaid bows out… maybe take some hair with them.

"See you tonight," I said. Faye and I hung up, and I raised my eyebrows at the girl. "What can I do for you? Are you looking for admissions? Because you're at the medical center."

"No, yeah… I'm Mandy Taylor. I'm a student here… I mean undergrad, but I… I need your help." She pointed at the chair. "May I?"

I waved my hand and she closed the door behind her before taking the chair. She perched on the edge, chewing on her bottom lip and looking around my computer screen at me. I rolled myself to the side so I could look at her straight on.

"Okay," she said, smoothing her skirt down. "I… well… I don't know where to start."

"Is it anything to do with healthcare regulations? If not, I think you're in the wrong place." I forced a smile to undercut the harsh tone.

She looked behind her like she was checking the door was still closed. "I… no." She chewed on her bottom lip again for a second. "I think I'm being haunted."

"You mean by a ghost?" I froze, eyeing her with fear sliding icy fingers up my heart. Someone had ratted me out! The Council would be all over me. "Why do you think I could help with a haunting?"

"I talked to my professors and some of the graduate assistants who know about this stuff. And they said, you know, ghosts are possible. They show up all the time throughout history. And they had theories, but I could tell they didn't believe me. But after that, Chet said you might be able to help with more than just the theory stuff the professors know."

"Chet? Ohhhhh, you're taking anthropology?"

She nodded. "I'm a freshman. Chet's my TA; he said you could help. He said I had to keep it under wraps. Couldn't tell anyone because you could get in trouble if people know you… *know* something about this stuff?" Her voice went up, making it a question.

I rubbed my forehead. *Oy vey, I'm going to kill him.*

Chet had seen magic at work when we were attacked a few months ago, and I'd sworn him to secrecy. We'd dated, but after I lost my job, I told him I needed some time to figure out where I was in my life and we were better going back to friends for now. He'd been the one to tell me about the job at the U of U Hospital and put in a good word for me, but other than that, we hadn't talked in two months.

I missed him, but I just couldn't deal with anything after I lost my job and my world fell apart

I took a deep breath. "Why do you think you're being haunted?"

"I don't think I am. I know I am."

I resisted the urge to roll my eyes. I was the adult here after all. "Okay?"

She nodded again. "It started maybe a week ago. I'm not sure because it was so gradual. You know when something feels *wrong* and you just shake it off? Like you had a bad dream or the place is too cold so you're on edge and shivery?"

I waved a hand and nodded. *Come on, kid. I've got real work to do here…*

well, kind of.

I blinked and realized she was still talking. My forehead was starting to tighten and ache in the middle.

"...so I just shook it off. You know?"

Apparently I hadn't missed anything important.

"Yeah," I said.

"But the cold kept getting worse, and my roommate couldn't feel it, and then my laptop disappeared."

"Someone stole it?"

"No. I put it in my backpack, went straight home, and it was gone when I opened it, right after I got home."

"But you didn't notice the change in weight?"

"Well, I mean, I ride a bike and put it in the basket. It's heavy. You know?"

I rubbed the center of my forehead. "Okay. What else?"

"Two nights ago, I heard something in the bathroom. It was sort of a thump?"

I wanted to say, "Asking or telling, kid?" I kept my mouth closed. So sometimes I had tact.

"I got out of bed, went in there, and the faucet was on. I went to turn it off, and it was, like, pouring blood."

I sat up straighter. Okay, that was definitely a sign of a ghost. A pissed off one, and powerful at that. Meant either a poltergeist or a dead witch. Either way, she could be in serious trouble.

"And then I turned on the light and the blood was gone," she said.

I fell back against my chair.

Or she could be a kid with an overactive imagination fried from the bleach she took to her head, and a TA who was all too ready to fall over himself to help her. Oy vey, I was in a pissy mood. Still, I was *so* going to get Chet back for this.

"I tried telling myself it wasn't real," she said. "It was my imagination. I was freaking out from the noises in the dorms. But my laptop popped up this morning. I pulled it up and the screen saver was a picture of my family, with my eyes crossed out."

I shivered. "Okay, that's creepy. Do you have the laptop?"

"No. I screamed and ran to the common room to get my roommates. When I got back, the laptop was gone again."

"I know the professors probably already asked you this, but are you sure you're not seeing things? Halloween's on Saturday, creepy decorations are up, there's horror movies in theaters. You don't have any proof. Nothing has stuck. If it was a ghost, wouldn't he leave stuff around for you to show others so you'd get really worked up?"

"Do ghosts like it when people know about them?"

54

"A ghost pissed and powerful enough to mess with things on our plane wants chaos. Fear. They can't move on for whatever reason, so they start to lose it, and want to take others down with them."

"Then wouldn't he keep making only me see things so I'd think I was going crazy? If there was proof, I'd know I wasn't."

I shrugged one shoulder. "True, but ghosts aren't coherent. They aren't sentient the way we think of it. They're an echo. A memory. They just react." I leaned my elbows on the desk, pressing my fingers together in front of me. "Though, if it's not a ghost, but a trapped spirit, it'd still be coherent. That requires some serious power… and the proper rituals before death to pull it off."

"You do know about this stuff," she breathed, grinning. "I knew it!"

Oy vey.

"Do I need to say what I'll do to you if this gets out?" I asked dryly.

"Whatever you're already going to do to poor Chet?"

"Yep… only he's getting the dull hedge clippers because he's older, and owed me keeping my secret."

"I'll owe you forever if you can make this thing go away."

I pointed at her. "*Never* say that. I mean it. To anyone, but especially anyone…" I bit my tongue.

"Were you going to say magical? Anyone magical?" She grinned.

"What else has happened, if anything?"

She told me of the bad feeling building up, swearing she was being watched when she was alone, someone peeking into the window when she was at her boyfriend's place, the cold spots.

"And…" She finally paused for breath. "I've been hearing things from other people after I talked to the professors today. I walk past someone, and a voice hisses at me. It's happened a few times and it's only been like two hours."

"What does the voice say?"

"It says…" She looked down and when she met my eyes again, hers were filled with pure terror. "It says if I want to play it that way, I won't live through the night."

I grabbed my necklace, letting the stored magic wash through me and back out in a calming wave.

"Okay. My dad is… like me. He knows a lot more about this area. You okay with a sleepover? I swear my dad is a gentleman, and the only danger you'll be in is of being force fed kugel and cocoa."

She smiled, so bright and genuine I forgave the bows in her hair. "Really?"

"Yeah. If there's a ghost, or even a spirit, it'll be bound to an area or an item. My dad lives in Park City. No ghost is going that far. If it's a spirit, as in back from the dead and having powers, but corporeal, it's still bound to something, but it might be able to get out that far. That's what my dad's for. Nothing is getting into his house without a bind-breaking spell, twenty guns, and a federal warrant."

She creased her forehead and I shook my head. "Sorry, sometimes I'm under the impression I'm funny. My dad's is the safest place I can think to put you until we figure this out. I do want you to keep in mind this could be in your head." I held up a hand at her open mouth. "Hear me out.

"It could be stress. It's your first time away from your parents, I'm assuming getting wild… well, as wild as any freshman at the University of Utah can get, and it's your first college midterms. It's a lot to take.

"That being said, it could also be a flesh and blood person trying to get to you. Sneaking the laptop out may have seemed impossible, but you can pull off a lot with sleight of hand. Dorm doors are unlocked half the time. He sneaks in, drops it, knows you'll run, so grabs it then. Puts some kind of recording on you to hiss at you, turns up the AC, and anyone could be peeking through windows if there aren't curtains or blinds. Who's your boyfriend?"

She paled and jerked back. "Why?"

I raised my eyebrows. "Because I'm going to need to talk to everyone around you. Anyone who could be involved, know something, and no offense, but tell me more about you."

"I… I can't say."

I stared at her.

She looked down. "It's a professor here."

"Oy vey. Are you kidding me? *Kid.*"

She straightened, eyes flashing. "I'm eighteen. Not a kid. And he's not like whatever you're thinking. He's…" She sighed. "Brilliant, and kind, and yeah, he's older than me, but so what?"

I ignored that. "Who is it? I'll keep my mouth shut. It's *not* my business *and* not my job to report anything on that, I work for the hospital, not the university… exactly. But I need to know."

"It's Doctor Carl Kane."

There my eyebrows went, reaching for the stratosphere again. "Chet's boss? Mr. Ivy League?"

She giggled. "Is that what Chet calls him?" She held up her hand. "I won't say anything to Carl about it. He can be pompous."

"*Can be?*" I smiled and she did too. "Well, at least I know he's a good guy… basically." She tilted her head with a quizzical look guys probably found adorable. "We've gone shooting a few times. Hit dinner and drinks after, too. Can you run any firearms?"

"Run?"

"Use one proficiently. So I'm guessing that's a no. I'll have a talk with Kane later about making sure his girl can defend herself, but for now, we've got to focus on keeping you safe. Do you have a car?"

She shook her head. "I bike, and you can get anywhere in Salt Lake with Trax."

"Can you miss classes tomorrow, maybe Friday too?"

She nodded. "Yeah, I can get notes from my friends and the only professor I have who takes attendance is Carl, and I think he'll understand."

"Okay. If this is a real haunting, I'm betting it's going to hit its peak on Halloween. I'm off the rest of the week, and I don't think anybody will care if I leave early today. Hang out here for the next hour? I mean, literally stay in my sight at all times. We'll hit your place for stuff and I'll drive you to my dad's."

"Okay." She wiggled like a puppy and pulled a textbook and some highlighters out of her backpack.

Good, we had a plan.

If only I knew how to investigate.

I BUMPED THE ICE CREAM and comedian watching with Faye, and she tagged along with me to play Nancy Drew instead. It was better for both of us. Less calories this way, and it gave me something more important than my pathetic life versus my ex's perfect one to focus on.

"And my dad said it sounds like a ghost, but also kind of sounds like a stressed-out college student, or a putz messing with the girl sleeping with the professor," I said as I turned onto Kane's street.

Mandy had called him and said we'd be dropping by to talk to him about her ghost. I could tell from the way she smiled she was honestly smitten. I hoped the thirty-five-year old professor wasn't just having his fun with the hot undergrad.

"What do you think?" Faye asked.

I shrugged. "I'm going back and forth. She's a teenage girl, and I don't know, not someone I quite trust."

"You think she's hiding something?"

"No, I mean, I wouldn't leave her alone with my boyfriend. Or a college professor…"

"I thought a few minutes ago you were worried he was taking advantage of her?"

"I switch. Never claimed to be sane. Besides, I'm a lawyer, we're supposed to see things from all sides."

"Yeah, try being married to one of you." She grinned, looking down at her phone.

Thank the Goddess she looked away.

Because my face was probably showing how much that tossed off comment hurt since I'd wanted to be married to another lawyer. Who was now married and expecting a baby.

I wonder if it'll look like him?

"Okay," Faye said, and I forced my face into a blank expression as she looked up and pointed, "Kane's house is the last on the left."

We pulled into the driveway of a large stone house. Pretty snazzy for a state school professor.

"I don't know if she's seeing things, if it's some putz playing with her head, or if it's actually something supernatural," I said as we climbed out of the car.

"What do your instincts say?" Faye asked.

I snorted. "My instincts? You've seen my taste in men, and you actually believe I have anything resembling instincts?"

Faye gave me a look I couldn't read, and I rolled my eyes as we mounted the front steps.

I knocked on the door and Kane answered immediately, like he'd been waiting for us. He was long and lean, with dark blond hair he wore slicked back, and thin glasses perched on the slender nose that emphasized his high cheekbones. He was pretty, well dressed, and pompous. The definition of a freshman's crush.

"Hello, Evie. Mandy said…" He froze, fixing his eyes on Faye as his mouth pursed. "You brought a friend."

"Faye, Kane," I said, waving a hand between them. They hurry shook hands. "She'll be as discreet as me. But yeah, I wanted backup. Just in case Mandy's right about the ghost." We walked in and he showed us to a barn sized living room. "What can you tell us about all that?"

He shrugged. "I felt a little like we were being watched the other night. I looked outside, no one there. Obviously, I'm a bit on edge, considering the delicate position I've put myself in."

I snorted. "That's one way of putting it. So you're jumpy because you're screwing a barely legal student, which is strictly against the rules and you would lose your job." It wasn't a question.

"I like you better on the shooting range," he said, trying to smile.

"Sorry, Kane. You're in a tricky situation. What else can you tell us? Anything on this?"

"Why are you looking into this? You're a lawyer, not an investigator. You don't study the paranormal or psychic events. You laughed when I explained what my doctoral dissertation topic was."

"You were arguing some of the psychics on TV were real! You were begging to be mocked."

"No." He held up a finger. "I was arguing some events around them support their claims of being real psychics. And what would you do if you were psychic?"

"Not tell the whole world." I raised an eyebrow at him, staring him down.

His eyes flew wide and his tuchus hit the chair behind him. "Oh my god. You're one. That's why you're looking into this. You're the real deal."

I held up a hand and pointed a finger at him. "I never said that. Got it?"

"Right. I have so many questions. Is it a real haunting? How do you measure these things?"

"You *don't*. You stop them. We don't know anything yet. We stopped at Mandy's dorm and I didn't pick up anything there. If there was something ghostly, it wasn't hanging around when I was there. That doesn't mean anything except if it is a ghost, it isn't bound there. Does she have any kind of history of seeing things?"

"I've only known her about two and a half months. It hasn't been long, but I know her. No history of mental disease in her family. Certainly not in her. She's very stable. Mature."

"Yeah, yeah, yeah." I waved a hand. Faye shot me a look. Right. Be quiet, let them talk. That's how you got info. There was a reason I didn't go into litigation.

WE RAN THROUGH OUR QUESTIONS... what ones we had anyway. Faye asked more than me, but even a therapist couldn't know everything an investigator or a cop would ask. Mandy was a normal Freshman, besides dating the professor. Good family, lots of friends, played softball, painted, and wanted to be a pharmacist.

I looked at Faye. "Well, I'm not sure where to go from here."

"Can you pick anything up from Mandy's belongings? A vision or something?" Kane asked.

I opened my mouth but Kane held up a hand. "Hey Sebastian!" he said loud enough to make it clear he was warning me to stop talking, nodding over my shoulder.

I turned; a mini giant stood in Kane's doorway. He had to be at least six foot four with a broad back you could show a movie on, and with his square jaw, cupid's bow lips and salt and pepper hair, he looked even more like a freshman's crush than Kane.

I grinned, heart rate picking up and lips tingling. The smile had to be as dopey as it felt because Faye gave me a look.

"Sorry to interrupt. I came down for a drink," Sebastian said, his voice clipped and vaguely musical. Close to a British accent, but not quite.

"Ladies," Kane said, "this is my friend Sebastian Blake. He's a new professor at the U, and staying with me until he finds his own place."

"You have treated me with such hospitality, you are making me not want to leave." Sebastian smiled, fixing light eyes on me. "And your friends are?"

"Ah, Evie Jones, she's a hell of a shot... and a lawyer, but we forgive her for that."

"Ha," I said, holding out my hand to the professor. He took it and turned it over, brushing a kiss across the knuckles. I bit back a grin. That wasn't charming, it was hokey and old fashioned. I was sure of it.

Still, after the news I got today, I could use a new guy.

Whoa, don't get ahead of yourself.

"And I don't believe I caught your last name," Kane said to Faye.

"Doctor Faye Renaud," Faye said. She shook Sebastian's hand. "Are you an anthropology professor as well?"

"Yes, my specialty is Native American religions. I'm part Cherokee and felt it would help me get in touch with that side of my heritage, and it kind of stuck."

I expected Faye to jump in and talk about her Native American heritage too, but she just nodded and smiled.

"You sound almost British though," I said.

"I was raised in New Hampshire. I have heard I sound British before. Apparently the New England accent and British are closer than TV leads people to believe." He smiled and I smiled back.

Is he flirting?

"I heard a little bit on the stairs," he said. "You are investigating a haunting? And you are a real live psychic?"

"Yes and no." I gave him the same pointed glare I gave Kane. "Got it?"

"Fascinating. I would love to pick your brain. For your knowledge of the purely theoretical, of course."

"What a coincidence, I was about to ask to pick yours."

He met my eyes and held them, staring like he could see straight into my mind for the answers he wanted. Green eyes. I loved green eyes.

"Well, I was in search of a nightcap," he said, still staring. "Would you mind greatly joining me for a drink? There is a lovely little bar mere seconds away." He swept an arm towards the kitchen and I grinned and followed.

Faye tapped my arm and I paused as the guys walked into the kitchen. "He's flirting with you," she whispered.

"So it's not just me?"

"Nope."

"What do you think of him?"

She shook her head. "I can't get a read on him. He's... intriguing. But I don't like people I can't get a handle on."

"Makes you think they're hiding something, or at least that they're capable of it?"

"Exactly."

We walked into the kitchen and joined the men at the island counter. Kane was already pulling bottles out of a cabinet above the fridge and lining them on the counter.

"I think I'm going to like this bar," I said, grabbing the first bottle and turning it to read the label. "Twenty-five-year-old scotch. Sold."

"You have fantastic taste," Sebastian said.

"She has expensive taste," Kane said, pulling short crystal glasses out of the cupboard. "Can you still afford those fancy drinks on your salary now?" He poured a healthy dose into three glasses and Faye shook her head as he went for the fourth. He shrugged and put the bottle down on the counter.

I wrinkled my nose at him. "See, this is why we only get along when we're shooting. Otherwise, I have to hear you talk and you say stuff like that. Don't rub my nose in the job. And I do just fine with the cut pay. I have savings… so far."

"You have rich parents."

"Have you seen this house? So do you, obviously."

"What happened?" Sebastian asked, fixing his stare on me again. My heart hiccupped and took my stomach with it.

"The short answer is politics," I said.

He leaned in. "What's the long answer?"

"I don't think these guys want to hang around for that story. Faye's already heard it."

"Yeah," Faye said. "And we should be going soon. I have a house to clean."

"Where do you live?" Sebastian asked me. "I could drive you home if it's not too far."

"That's not necessary. There's a Trax station two blocks away and one near my apartment. I can catch that as long as I'm out of here before—"I checked my phone's clock—"two hours. I think I'll be okay."

"You sure?" Faye asked, raised eyebrows packing so much more into that question.

"Yes." I left off the "Mom" I wanted to shoot at her.

Faye left, Kane went upstairs to call Mandy and I turned my chair to face the professor as I sipped my scotch.

"So," he said, lifting his scotch to his pretty lips. "You want to go first?"

"OH DEAR," SEBASTIAN SAID, pouring me another glass. "So after all that, they fired you?"

"Yep," I took a long sip. "What can I say? Don't piss off the new CEO."

"Yes." He swirled the scotch in his glass, staring at it in the light. "I made the mistake of going up against my department head in a run for local political office."

"Oy vey!" I flinched. "Even I know better than that. What were you thinking?"

We'd been talking for I didn't know how long. We ran through his knowledge on ghosts, nothing I didn't already know, except for the stuff so far out in left field from the real supernatural I'd never even heard of it, my firing, and some of his firing.

"I…" He took a drink. "I was trying to impress a woman."

"Ohhh, now it's getting good." I leaned forward on the counter. "Tell tell."

"We were in love; she was the only woman I ever loved besides my wife."

"Divorced?" I asked.

He shook his head. "She died of cancer."

My face fell. "I'm so sorry!"

He shrugged. "It was a long time ago. I promised her I would keep living, because she didn't want me to die with her. So I kept going with my life, I dated, and I just… waited for death to come for me naturally. This other woman got me first. I never thought I'd love again, and then I did."

"But she left you?"

"She was dating me and another man at the time. She wasn't hiding it from either of us or anything, made it clear she liked her options open. But she said she loved me. And then he proposed. He came from a family with money. I was a professor at a university making a decent living, but that was it. So when it came time to make a choice, she chose him."

"You think it's because of the money."

He downed the glass. "Oh, I know it was because of the money. She told me as much. Said she wished she could choose me, but we'd never have the life she wanted. And that life was more important to her than our love. And she loved him too, so it wasn't a great sacrifice to choose him over me."

"Wow. At least she's honest?"

He stared at me. "Something tells me you've had your share of heartbreak."

"Only one… and yeah, it was bad."

He raised his eyebrows, still staring, like he had all the time in the world to wait my answer out.

I blew out air. "You and Faye, man, you guys have got to teach me that trick of staring until someone answers you."

"The key is to be comfortable with silence."

"Yeah. I'm not."

He stared.

"Fine!" I said. "I'll spill. It was the first year of law school. I met the guy, I fell for the guy, thought he liked me too. We dated, he was dating other people and did *not* tell me, but we also never said we were exclusive. And when I was completely in love and I told him that, he said he wasn't there yet, and stopped coming around, stopped calling, basically pulled the fade out."

I took a long sip. "A putz and a *coward*. He finally told me we should stop seeing each other, and then he popped up on Facebook with a new girlfriend the next day."

"Oh dear."

"Yeah, he apologized later, said he didn't mean to lead me on, didn't realize I was that serious. Blah, blah, blah. He married her last year and now they have a baby on the way."

"Are you two still friends?"

"No."

"Then how do you kn-"

"The evil that is social media," I cut him off.

He pointed at me. "I have been saying it's evil, nobody else seems to agree with me."

"I do." We shared a smile and he walked around the counter to sit next to me.

"Well, I am looking at the clock, and I do believe Trax stopped running about an hour ago."

I looked behind me and flinched at the time. "Yep. I'll call a Lyft."

"I could drive you."

"Are you sure? Haven't you had a few?"

"Over a few hours and after a big dinner. I believe I'm fine. But, if you're unsure, you could stay here. There's another guest room."

He searched my eyes and leaned in.

I jerked away. "What are you doing?"

His eyes flew wide and he sat straight. "I'm sorry, I'm sorry. I thought I was getting a vibe from you. I shouldn't-"

"No, no. I'm not complaining. I think there's a vibe too. You just caught me off guard. I mean, I was recently dating Chet. We're on a break, kind of, and maybe going back to just being friends. But I don't think I can go around kissing people in his department."

"Who's Chet?"

"Kane's TA?"

"Ohhhh." His eyes flew wide. "The young man with the rocker hair and the biceps. Ah, I can see I am not your type. I'm sorry; I'll drive you home."

"Hey." I caught his sleeve, grinning when he met my eyes. "My type is tall, intelligent men with great smiles who can cook. Other than that, I've dated across the board on types when it comes to looks. Okay? This is not me blowing you off. This is me saying I don't want to do something I'll regret."

"What if we do something we might regret but risk it?" He grinned, almost shyly, and leaned in.

I tilted my head up and his lips met mine in a soft kiss. He pulled back before it could get deeper, but just the quick, sweet peck made me blush and look down.

"I…" He chuckled and tried again. "Would you like to go out to dinner?"

I couldn't help but grin. "Do you know how rare it is for a guy to ask a girl out on an actual date these days? Most of the time it's, 'do you want to hang out?' It's really nice to run into a guy who still asks a girl out like a man. I'd love to. When?"

"Tomorrow at six? There's a new sushi place I want to try."

"I love sushi. I'm in."

HE DROVE ME HOME, walked me to my door and kissed me again. I dreamed of dancing marshmallow babies riding ponies with glasses. It was a good dream.

I put on Bach and made coffee and eggs for breakfast, dancing around my kitchen like a loon… or a twelve-year-old. Sebastian couldn't have popped into my life at a better time.

I pulled out my computer and checked Facebook, staying the hell off my ex's page.

And I googled Sebastian. He was a professor at Stanford until his run for mayor ended with a close call and his department conveniently lost money and had to cut people after that. He was unemployed for nearly a year until the position at the U opened up for this semester and he moved to Utah.

The phone rang as I was on to my second cup of coffee and the local news, and I sighed. Probably Dad or Mandy calling to report on last night. I'd told them to call when she got up.

We could start investigating today. Though I didn't have the foggiest idea where to start an investigation.

Maybe with a general supernatural sensing spell? Some kind of information pull, maybe? Or a good ol' fashioned séance. I'd never tried one of those, but Faye could walk me through it.

I grabbed the phone. "Hello?"

"Hey Sweetie."

"Morning Dad. You're off today too, right? You and Mandy want to grab lunch?"

"Um, Sweetie… we… Mandy's…"

My blood froze and my tuchus hit tile before I registered falling. "No."

"I found her outside. She either jumped off the roof or was pushed. She's still alive. We're at the hospital. She's in critical care… they don't know how much damage there's been. They're taking her into surgery. We need to contact her parents. The hospital can't-" Dad gulped like I did when I was trying not to cry.

"Yeah, HIPAA. They can't tell you anything." I sniffed, wiping my burning eyes. "I'll come to you and call her parents and… oh god, Kane. I have to tell Kane. Which hospital?"

"HEY." MY DAD PULLED ME into a tight hug when I got to the ICU, smoothing my hair down like he was imagining how he'd feel if it were me in the hospital bed.

"What happened?" I asked when we pulled apart and looked up at him. I was the spitting image of my dad. He was long and lean, with balding curly brown hair, but we had the same nose, cheekbones, and eyes.

He walked me into the ICU room. Mandy didn't resemble the perky cheerleader I'd met yesterday. Her blond hair was matted and half hidden under her, and she look drawn and pale in the bed. Half her face looked like someone took a cheese grater to it, and the rest of it was scratched up.

"I got up around eight," Dad said, putting an arm around my shoulders. "I thought she was sleeping and wasn't going to barge in on her. I made breakfast and coffee and went outside to have it on the patio. I could feel something was off. I brushed it off as a stranger's energy in the house. But… She was lying half over the rocks around the garden. Her skull… they're taking her into surgery soon to patch her up, but they aren't sure if she has brain damage."

I snuggled into his side. "The garden? That's too far for somebody to land if they jumped unless they got a running start. Do the cops think she was thrown?"

He nodded. "They've asked me a few questions. I called you when they took a break. But there's one posted at the front of the ICU. They didn't say anything, but he's here to watch me."

"They think you did it?"

"They'd be idiots not to. An eighteen-year-old I have no obvious connection to staying at my place and then ending up thrown off a roof. They probably think I was sleeping with her or trying to, and we fought."

"What did you tell them?"

Dad rubbed his face with both hands, looking like he grew new wrinkles around his eyes overnight. "I told them the truth. She thought she was being haunted, so she asked a friend for help, and that friend sent her to you because you dabble in the occult. And then she stayed with me mostly to appease her since she wouldn't let the ghost thing go."

"Oh, *that* version of the truth. Good thinking."

My dad gave me a look. "Thank you, daughter of mine." He stuck his tongue out at me, making me half smile. "When did you start to think I didn't know how to handle these things?"

"When I graduated with a higher degree than you have." I stuck my tongue out at him, pretending just for a second there wasn't a girl in the bed fighting for her life.

I sighed and Dad said, "I told the cops we didn't believe her, obviously, and were just trying to make her feel better, but now I think whoever's been haunting her is a real person and he's been messing with her mind."

"That was one possibility I mentioned. With this? He's either a spirit, meaning he knew magic enough to keep him here and corporeal past death, or it's a person who knew how to get past your defenses."

Dad shook his head. "I had a protection spell around the place to keep anything corporeal out. He would've had to get her to the roof and go up there himself. It reeks of magic. Spirit or living, it's magic."

"Tracking spell?" I asked.

"You'll have to do it while I make sure no cops are there. We can't have the Council on us for an exposure risk."

"We already have a risk. Under their rules, we should be reporting it now." I shrugged. "Since when do we play by their rules?"

"You are so my daughter." He hugged me tight to his side before letting me go. "You think you can do the spell by yourself?"

"I'll call Faye just to make sure. I called Kane. When he gets here, tell him what you told the cops, she thought she was being haunted, but don't tell him you told the cops it could be a real person who's been messing with her."

He stood in front of me and stared down. "Why?"

I shook my head. "Because it's always the boyfriend."

I SAT ON DAD'S ROOFTOP patio and sighed at the beauty of the valley and mountains. He had a multilayered house. The upper floor opened out onto the flat roof of the lower one, making a giant terrace. He decorated with cushioned chairs, a matching glass topped table, and tons of plants. It'd been my favorite place to study during law school.

Faye and I had already brought the candles out, so I set them up facing the four directions while I waited for her to get back with her witch bag and grounding elements.

It felt great out here to me, but Faye was a wind witch. Being this high while she did magic could risk her taking off, drunk on the power, so she used water and earth to ground her. As a fire witch, I wasn't really at risk around anything, not even my element; things were at risk around *me*.

I pulled out my spelling knife, a long, pure silver beauty with a specially made bone hilt decorated with emeralds. Dad bought it for me when my powers first started blooming, the witch version of a girl getting her period. I'd set the ugly curtains Dad's third wife picked out on fire. Strangely enough, they got divorced soon after.

I grinned as I kneeled on the ground in front of the furniture, as close to the patio's bars as I could get and still be able to draw a circle big enough for me and Faye, and put knife to brick, drawing a line around myself, and turning to make a full one with a prayer to the goddess.

With my Druid and Jewish blood, I could pick out of either tradition's magic. Druid was better for contacting the dead and tracking spells. Jewish was better for building offensive spells, like golems.

Once I drew the circle, I lit the candles, naming each direction as an element as I went. If you wanted to track a spell, using air as north was best since you could follow the magic on the air easier than anything else. I'd leave Faye to do that part.

Faye stepped out onto the roof, sliding the door closed behind her. The October wind blew her blond hair around, tugging strands from its ponytail, and she brushed them back with a hand before setting the bag on the ground.

"It's going to be up to you to keep me grounded," she said, pulling her blanket and bowl out of her bag. She technically had Navajo blood, despite the naturally blond hair, and found a stronger affinity to that magic than to her genetically stronger heritages of Nordic and Druid.

I was equally powerful with my bloodlines, but most witches tended towards one stronger than others, not necessarily the one that was genetically predominant.

Faye put the woven blue and white blanket down. She picked it up from one of the many sellers of Native American arts in Southern Utah, nothing more than a cheap, pretty decoration, but in hands with someone with power, it worked as an altar cloth.

She pulled out herbs I couldn't begin to guess about, and mixed them in a plain clay bowl. Navajo's weren't supposed do anything dealing with death unless they'd been properly warded, so she had to make sure the spirit, if that's what it was, couldn't cling to her when she traced its magic back.

"Are you going to be okay doing this?" I asked. "I know you…"

She nodded, smiling. "I had some problems with this when I was younger, but I'm not a teenager anymore. I've learned from some of the best shamans in the world how to handle the death magic."

"None of them are as powerful with necromancy as you," I said. "I don't want you doing anything that will put you in danger."

She waved me off with a grin. "Aren't I supposed to be the mother in this relationship? I've got nine years on you; let me do the worrying."

"Alright." I held up my hands and let her finish. She placed the herb mix on her forehead, throat, heart, solar plexus, and lower abdomen. A mix of magic using chakras and Native American herbs.

She put the bowl outside the circle and knelt in front of me. I focused on Mandy. On that perky, upturned nose, bleached blond hair, and innocent smile, on her trapped in a broken body in the hospital, maybe never to wake again.

Faye closed her eyes and held out her hands, palms up. I mirrored her, touching our middle fingers together and closed my eyes too.

It took everything in me to keep myself focused on the roof and Mandy, so I could ground Faye, and not get swept away with tracking the magic with her. I wanted to drive, wanted to watch where the perversion riding the air took us. I couldn't.

Stay here. Stay here.

I focused on Mandy, on the blond, leggy girl dressing to look cute and even younger, but like she didn't realize it made her look like a pedophile's dream, because she was too young and innocent to know better. On Kane talking about her, worried and glowing at once.

It was always the boyfriend, but here, I couldn't see it. He seemed too enamored, too much bathing in her light. His aura glowed when he talked about her. He didn't have the reek of magic used for evil on him.

People didn't always have that, just like sociopaths could hide under a candy coating of charm, but everything in me screamed he didn't do this. And he'd been devastated when I'd called him and said what happened. He'd dropped the phone and Sebastian picked it up, saying he'd drive Kane to the hospital.

Why didn't I see Sebastian there? I shook my head. *Focus!*

Faye's magic flowed over me, warming the chilly mountain air, bringing the smell of gardenias and play-doh. Faye even smelled like a mom. I smiled. Her kid was a toddler and the most chill one I'd ever met. Nerves of steel, just like her mommy.

Oy vey, supposed to be focusing on Mandy.

I didn't know her that well, so I fixed my brain on the patio, imagining it even as my eyes strained to open to refresh my memory. Nope, not allowed. You didn't want your eyes open during a magic tracking spell. You never knew what you'd see.

Or what would see you.

Faye's whispers caught my ears and I strained to focus on anything else. If I focused on her, I could get swept up with her. And whatever it was had her, I was sure of it. The air moved across my skin like we were flying through it and I dug my knees into the brick, breathing in the smell of Dad's plants and straining my ears to listen to the real wind, and not to Faye's.

"Shit!" she yelled, fingers breaking away from mine. The feel of air fell away like silk.

My eyes popped open and she stared at me with wide baby blues.

"What? What'd you see?" I asked.

She shook her head, licking her lips. "It's a spirit, but it's... it doesn't feel right. I think... from what I can tell at least."

She shook her head, taking a deep breath. "It's someone who was trying to cast a spell to hang around after death as a corporeal spirit, but wasn't a trained witch. It was someone who knew barely what he was doing, and had just enough power to try it. So now he's trapped in this area by whatever he tethered the spell to.

"I couldn't see what object he used to focus it, but it's around the U. He's not sure how to get back out. So he's trying to loosen the spell by getting the thing he directed the spell at in the first place to use magic. He thinks if he could get her to use her powers, it'd loosen up his."

"Mandy?" I asked.

Faye shook her head again. "I don't think he was trying to hurt her. I think he was trying to scare her into using her powers to help loosen the spell because he has a connection to her."

"Powers?"

"Mandy's a born witch. She's just so weak, she didn't know it."

"But her parents would've told her, trained her."

"Unless..." Faye raised her eyebrows.

I shrugged. "What?"

"Unless she got the magic from her dad's side, and that's not the man who raised her, and he never told the mom he had magic."

"Her dad isn't her dad?"

"Yep. And if this spirit is clinging to her, I'm guessing there's a reason. Like maybe that's daddy."

My jaw dropped. "We need to talk to the mom!"

I CALLED DAD AND HE said Mandy's parents were at the hospital, so I met him there.

Faye had errands and chores to get done while the house was empty so she ran home, but said she'd come back to help later.

The cops were still talking to Dad and had pulled in Mandy's parents. Kane was sitting by Mandy's empty bed. She must've gone into surgery while we were gone. Kane didn't even look up when I walked in the room.

"Hey," I said. "I know this is a stupid question, but how are you?"

He shook his head, not looking up.

"Okay," I said. "The doctors going to put her back in here after surgery?"

He nodded.

"Okay." I turned.

"Without you," Kane said.

"What?" I turned.

He didn't look at me, but said, "She loved Rent. We watched it last week. She's seen it so much she knows all the songs, but the part where Angel dies still makes her cry. She… she said I better not die before her and put her through that when we're old. She was already planning to be mine. How…?" His voice broke and he bent his head, shoulders shaking silently.

I stood there. Did he want me to hug him or leave him be? If I was crying like that, I'd want to be left alone.

I walked out on cat feet and joined the group in the mini-waiting room with the cops. They were talking to Dad while Mandy's parents just sat there.

Mandy was the spitting image of her mom. Probably one reason nobody ever questioned whose daughter she was. Also, genetics were a funny thing. You could have green eyes from two blue eyed parents and people would just think it was a fluke of genetics, they wouldn't jump to the idea that she was somebody else's.

How could a dad scare his own daughter like that? Once he knew she was his kid, he could've just asked for her help.

Something told me this guy wasn't playing with a full deck.

"Ms. Taylor?" I said, coming up behind her. She jumped and turned in her seat. "Sorry, hi, I'm a friend of Mandy's. Can we talk for a minute?"

The cops eyed us as she got up but kept talking to Dad. Good, I'd hate to have to whip out a mind-altering spell on the spot.

Yeah, yeah, it was wrong to do that to cops.

You know what, they were interrogating my dad, I wasn't too worried about hurting whatever brains they had.

I rubbed my forehead. I was being bitchy. They were just doing their jobs. If I didn't know the whole story, I'd suspect my dad too.

We walked a bit down the hall and I said, "I'm Evie Jones."

"Oh, the woman Mandy said was going to help her?"

"Yes. In my investigation, I've come across some interesting information." I took a deep breath. *Play this tough, like I already know the answers and I'm just looking for her to confirm them.* "I know your husband isn't Mandy's biological father. I think whoever's doing this is. So I need to know who that is."

Her mouth worked. "How… my daughter is in surgery! She may not live, or she'll be in a coma, or a vegetable! How *dare you*!"

People and cops came out of the waiting room, eyeing us, and I held up my hands. "Nothing to see here. She's upset."

The cops said something to each other and one peeled off to join us as the others went back into the room.

"You should leave," he said, towering over me.

My blood went cold so fast I got freezer burn. "Excuse you? I know my rights. I have every right to be here and I'm not hindering your investigation. I'm a lawyer, don't you dare pull that, 'You will respect my authority' bullshit with me. I will sue you and your department."

Okay, so I had no clue what I could actually sue for. I was in health law, not civil rights or litigation. He didn't need to know that.

He pulled himself up, the devil flashing in his eyes.

Oy vey. Smart, Evie, pissing off the cops during the investigation. Real smart.

Ms. Taylor looked at me with wide eyes and I smiled at her. "Sorry, ma'am. One moment."

I focused on the cop. No choice now. *Here's hoping the Council doesn't catch wind of this.* I met his eyes and he rested his hand on the butt of his gun. Ha, all my guns were better quality than that hunk of rust.

I pulled magic from my belly, from the fire that fueled good arguments and better sex. I twisted it in my brain, imagining the spell shooting out from my eyes to his. Twin fire beams left my eyes and hit his. Ms. Taylor gasped and the cop shook his head, dropping his hand.

"She's okay, officer," I said with a sweet smile. "Thank you so much for coming out here to check on her."

He shook his head again. "Of… of course, ma'am." He turned and walked back into the room, and Ms. Taylor turned on me.

"You… you… didn't."

I crossed my arms. "Yeah, I did. And I can do that to you, too. Start talking. Who's Mandy's real father?"

She crumpled to the ground like paper, dissolving into tears and pulling her knees to her chest like a little kid.

My heart twinged and I kneeled next to her. "I'm sorry. I thought… I was trying to be a hard-ass to get you to talk. Please stop crying. It's okay. Mandy's going to be okay."

"I can't deal with this," she sobbed into her knees. "He said… but magic isn't real. It can't be. I can't deal with this."

"He said?"

She lifted her face, her perfect makeup running down her cheeks. "My ex. We stayed friends, but feelings were still there even after I got married. My husband and I got in a fight one night. I left and I was angry, so I…"

"You called your ex," I said.

"Yes. It was only one night, and we used protection. When I found out I was pregnant, I assumed it was my husband's. Because what were the odds? What were the odds the time the condom broke or didn't work for whatever reason, it was that once instead of the dozens of times around then I was with my husband?"

"What happened to your ex?"

She looked down. "He… he dabbled in the occult. He was a good man. He was just curious."

I raised my eyebrows and bit my tongue. Yeah, because using magic implied you were a bad person.

"Last time we talked was right after I found out I was pregnant. He thought he found a spell to make someone immortal, and more powerful. He said he was going to try it if I didn't go back to him, because he'd have no reason not to try."

She buried her face in her knees again. "I didn't believe him. It was magic, it wasn't *real*! He… he was found dead in his office the next day, surrounded by crystals and candles, and in front of some kind of altar. He'd eaten poison. I guess as part of the ritual. Cops ruled it a suicide."

"Where was his office?"

"At the U, he was a chemistry professor."

"What was his name? I'll look into him."

"Christopher Springfield. Why do you think it's him?" She looked up at me.

"You'll just have to trust me on this one."

I put my arm down to push myself up and she grabbed it. "Can you fix my daughter? Can you… with your magic. Can you help her?"

I shook my head. "To heal, you have to know the body, know physiology, and be able to do work as delicately as a surgeon, to mess with the human body. I was risking serious damage just wiping a few seconds from that cop's mind. I'm a lawyer, not a doctor. I'd do more damage in there. It's like asking a lay person to diagnose and treat cancer. Also, you never know what energies you could unbalance in there."

"This is real, isn't it? It's really happening?"

I nodded.

"How could he do this?" she asked. "He loved me. And if she's his daughter, how could he do that to his own daughter?"

"Spirits get twisted when they're trapped. He's been around since you were a few months pregnant, so for what, nineteen years? Trapped in-between. Something got him out enough to affect this world, but he's still trapped, and that can make good people do *horrible* things. But here? From what Fa…"

I coughed. "From what *I* could tell, he was trying to scare her to get her to tap into her magic. Extreme emotion usually will trigger a young witch's powers. He was hoping her using her powers would get him unstuck. Probably hoping the extra power from Halloween would give her enough juice to get him out. I don't know why he thinks her power can get him out, or even if he's right."

"You could tell that, but not who or where he is?"

I shook my head. Faye had already tried to trace it back. It was too fragmented. Clearly a spirit jumping around without being held to the physical plane while still being able to touch it. We'd have to do the spell when it was within range and holding still, unless he stopped popping up wherever the hell he wanted.

Rumbling met my ears and the ground shifted under us. Ms. Taylor shrieked and I grabbed her and dragged her to the nearest doorway, shoving her against one side before I plastered myself against the other.

The lights flickered above us, and everyone else scrambled for cover.

The earthquake was only a few seconds and I looked around. "Wow, where did that come from?"

"It's Utah?" Ms. Taylor said, straightening her jacket.

I rubbed my forehead and rested my hand over my heart and my necklace. "I don't know… Where were we? Oh yeah, we also can't tell why now. What got your ex out now? Has anything big happened?"

Ms. Taylor wrapped her arms around herself. "Mandy started at the U. Could that have been it?"

"No. Her being there probably has something to do with it. But for a spirit to bust out of limbo, it had to be something big. Something emotional and life altering…"

I froze.

"What!"

"Oy vey. I think I know."

"KANE," I SAID AT THE doorway after I got past the cops in the waiting room. The one I'd taken those few seconds of memory from gave me a look like he couldn't quite place me but other than that no one noticed little ol' me walking by. The trick was to walk with purpose.

Kane didn't look up, and I closed the door behind me.

"Carl," I said softer, "I think I've figured out what popped the spirit out, and why now. But I need you to answer some questions honestly. Even if they're uncomfortable."

He didn't do anything.

"Carl, it could help her."

He nodded, not even questioning the lie. I was a *heel*.

"Have you and Mandy had sex?"

He nodded.

"Was she a virgin before that?"

His shoulders hunched and he didn't say anything.

"Carl, I can't assume anything here. I need a yes or no."

"Yes." His voice came out rough and harsher than before, like his pipes had been dipped in whiskey.

"Did she bleed?"

"I… I don't remember."

"Was it at your house or her dorm? Did you see the sheets in the morning?"

"It was in the office. We didn't mean to. We were just talking and kissing, and it kind of happened."

I nodded. Of course it was in his office. And the spirit had been tied to the university because that's where he'd died. But because she'd been going through something huge and emotional, and probably painful and bloody, her magic had spiked, and it pulled the spirit out.

High emotions and blood, you couldn't get a more powerful spell.

That's why the spirit thought her emotion fueled magic could get him out completely, because her boyfriend popping her cork had popped her dad's too.

"Oy vey, that sounds bad," I said out loud.

Carl barely twitched. "What does?"

"I was thinking and something came out in my brain sounding just *wrong*. When did you guys first have sex?"

"In August. I mean, we'd barely met. I'd never felt that way about someone I barely knew. Especially not a girl, practically a child. I didn't mean… You think that's what did this?" He rested his hands on the bed, clasped together, and rested his head between his arms, mumbling under his breath.

I caught enough to realize he was praying. I left and closed the door again behind me.

If that'd been the event, then the ghost had been around for two months. Which meant he'd started the haunting now to get Mandy to use her powers around Halloween, when the veil between living and dead was weakest, and our powers hit their peaks. And since he'd tossed her, he probably got what he needed.

If I couldn't find and stop him by Saturday, a month's salary said he'd be able to free himself Halloween night.

It was time to learn more about Mr. Christopher Springfield.

I HEADED HOME AND HIT the net. I found the article on Springfield's suicide online, and the records of his death. The article had a picture. He looked like a nice man around forty. I called Ms. Taylor to see if there was anything else she could tell me. She didn't answer so I left a message.

I'd hit a wall, so I got ready for my date. Wasn't much I could do until I got more info or got Faye back to help me try tracking the magics again. We could go to Kane's office and try to see what magic happened there… actual magic, not sex magic. Neither of us wanted to see that.

Sebastian picked me up, opened the door to the car for me, and took me a nice restaurant. We had a good date, a great bottle of wine, and I couldn't enjoy it.

"What's wrong?" he asked as we pulled into my apartment's parking garage.

I sighed. "I want to tell you, to get your input. I'm not supposed to. I could get in big trouble."

"What if you trusted me, and if you get in trouble, you can point them at me and say I made you tell me?"

"Wouldn't help." But I smiled. "You want to come in?"

"Sure"

We went inside and my stomach fluttered. I wasn't inviting him in for anything more than talking and maybe a drink, but still, inviting a guy into your place sent a message, and at the very least *could* lead to something.

Gremlin ran to the door and twined around my legs, purring his demands for his nightly serving of wet food. He always had dry food, but I regulated his wet so he didn't gorge himself and get a stomachache or get fat. He was a giant Maine Coon, twenty pounds if he was two, but it was all length and muscle.

I put a blob of wet food down and Gremlin abandoned my side for the food bowl in a hot second.

"Why don't you tell me what's going on, all of it, and we'll go from there?" Sebastian said, crouching down to pet Gremlin. Gremlin glanced over his shoulder at him then went back to eating. "I don't know how much help I'll be, but what if I know something?"

"You're just hoping I'll teach you something interesting," I said, grinning at him. "Do you want a drink? I make a mean dirty martini."

"Vodka or gin?"

I fake gasped. "Gin, of course."

"A woman after my own heart."

I went into the kitchen and he sat at the island counter separating it from the living room. Gremlin jumped on the island and sat in front of Sebastian, his back to the man in a clear demand for the pets to resume.

"I like your place," Sebastian said, petting Gremlin with long strokes as I pulled out the gin and vermouth.

"Thanks. Kane wasn't kidding when he said I might not be able to afford it much longer though. With my salary now, I'll have to dip into my trust fund. I didn't want to do that. Using my family's money to pay for law school is one thing, using it just to live though? I'm supposed to make my own way in this world, you know?" I poured the ingredients into the martini shaker and shook them with ice.

"I don't, but I will take your word for it," Sebastian said as I poured his drink out.

I made one for myself and slid his over to him with two olives resting in the glass. "Anyway, you really want to know what's going on?"

He turned his chair to face me and leaned forward as I sat next to him. "Yes."

I EXPLAINED IT ALL AND finished my drink, staring at him.

"Why do you think her losing her virginity is what sparked this?" Sebastian asked.

"I…" I blew out a huff of air. "Sex is all about two people connecting. It's a type of communication. It holds as much power as a spell, it's just not usually directed. Sex is already an outpouring of power and emotion."

I coughed. "If a young witch who doesn't know about her powers goes through something as big and emotional as losing her virginity, magic probably burst out. Sex is already a huge exposure risk, which is why witches are so careful about who they have sex with, usually."

"Because they could expose what they are to their partner?" He met my eyes and my heart rate picked up as my belly jerked.

I hadn't had sex in over two years.

"Yeah," I said, voice breathy. "But it's also because we can see energies. When you see how much is actually shared during sex, how much energy and parts of yourself you pour into the other person, and they pour into you, you have respect for it. You don't take it as lightly as some people, even if you've taken all the proper precautions to make sure no magic, um, erupts during."

He licked his lips and I did too, trying to keep my breathing even.

"So," he said, voice huskier than just a moment ago, "it's not something you enter into casually. How many men have you been with?"

"Three. College sweetheart, the guy who broke my heart in law school, and a boyfriend after him." My breath was too shallow and I took a deep drag of air, trying to get enough oxygen to my brain to get it to talk some sense into my genitals.

"I've been with two women," he said. "My wife and the woman I wanted to be my wife."

"Sebastian." I shook my head, voice dropping. "We can't."

"Can't what?" He leaned in, sliding a hand around my back.

"We can't have sex. We barely know each other."

"I know." He kissed me, deeper and harder than yesterday, urgency making him feel hungry.

Skin hunger.

He had it pouring off him. The ache people got when they hadn't been touched. Not just sexually, but at all.

Men got it easier than women because they didn't touch as often as they needed to to feed their need for human contact. They didn't hug, touch or play with hair as much as women. It was one of the prevailing theories in the witch world as to why men sought sex so much more than women.

Of course, we couldn't discount biology.

Sebastian stood and picked me up, his height and long limbs lifting me as easily as anyone with twice his muscle. He placed me on the counter and I wrapped my legs around him, my dress riding up like no lady's should.

But I never claimed to be a lady.

Sebastian bent, laying me on the counter, long enough to half lay on me as he remained standing. We kissed forever before he lifted me up and walked us into the bedroom, kicking the door closed behind him.

He dropped me on the bed and loosened his tie, his hands fumbling and clumsy. "Grrrr."

I sat up. "I got it." I loosened it, pulling it off over his head with urgent hands. "If we're going to do this, can I..." I licked my lips and went to work on the buttons on his shirt. "Can I use the energy for a spell? We're trying to find out more about what happened to Mandy."

He shrugged off his shirt and pulled off the undershirt and groped under my dress, hand sliding up and down my inner thigh making me shiver.

"Yes. I'd be honored to see you work, to be a part of it. Will we have to stop for you to set it up?"

"Not for long." I hopped off the bed and grabbed my amethyst off my dresser. "This'll store the energy. I can use it in a spell later."

I put the crystal under the bed, grabbed my knife and drew a circle on the floor around the bed and up the wall, walking on the bed around Sebastian. I finished the circle, sealing it with a blessing, put away the knife, and ran into the bathroom. I pulled open the drawer where I used to keep the condoms.

I hadn't had sex since law school. What were the odds they were still good?

I ripped through that drawer and couldn't find them, dropped to my knees and dug through the cupboard like a squirrel digging for nuts. No pun intended.

"Ah-ha!" I pulled the box out and checked the expiration date. "Oy vey!"

"What?"

"Ah!" I turned and Sebastian was in the doorway as suddenly as my cat could appear.

"Condoms expired. Told you it's been awhile."

"I, um." He looked down. "I brought a few. I wasn't… not to presume…"

I stood and grabbed him by his hips, pulling him into me. "It's fine. I won't hold you being prepared just in case against you."

"Oh good." He picked me up Gone with the Wind style and put me back on the bed, pulling my legs apart.

"Professor," I said in my sultriest voice, "your mild-mannered scholarly veneer's hiding someone who likes it a little rough."

"Just a little." He grinned, grabbing my panties and pulling them off over my heels. I reached for my foot to undo the clasp on the heel and he caught my hand. "I like women who know how to dress well. Leave the heels and the dress on."

I grinned and lay back, lifting my arms. He came into them and I held him to me as he rubbed against my front, kissing me again, obviously a man who liked to take his time.

Oh, this was going to be good.

"MEROW, MEROW, MEROWWWWWWW!" broke through my sleep.

"Gremlin, zip it!" I yelled on reflex, rolling to my side and reaching over. No one was there.

I sat up fast, looking around. The bedroom door was closed, Sebastian's clothes were gone.

"No way! Come on!" I said, pushing my hair off my face. How could I have been so stupid?

"Sorry." Sebastian opened the door and a black fluff ball shot between his feet, making him stumble, and the coffee in the mugs he held slosh over the sides.

I giggled, relief rushing through me. He didn't use me and leave. He wasn't a brash mistake I made because I was wallowing in my ex's perfect life compared to my pathetic one.

Gremlin jumped on the bed and nuzzled my naked chest, meowing his disappointment that I was still in bed when the sun was up.

"I was trying to let you sleep in." Sebastian sat next to me, handing me a mug.

"Yeah, the Grem monster has different plans. He wants to go outside." I scratched Gremlin's black fuzzy head and he purred, sitting in my lap and staring at Sebastian. I laughed. "Or he wants to keep another man away from me."

"Hmmmm." Sebastian leaned over the cat, kissing me lightly on the lips. "He's not doing a very good job if he's trying to be a gargoyle, guarding the beautiful princess."

"You talk so pretty." I took a long sip of coffee and sighed with the simple pleasure of that first cup of Joe. "How did you know I took milk and sugar?"

"You ordered coffee last night after dinner. You got milk and sugar then."

"You pay attention. I'm impressed."

"My gender in your generation has truly dropped the ball if asking you out on a date and paying attention to you is impressive these days."

"They really have. Which is why I got a cat and date older men."

He laughed, bright and cheery, and making him look ten years younger. "Are you going to do the spell today? Can I help?"

"Oy vey. I don't… I'm not supposed to… you know what, sure. Screw it. You can at least watch. I'm going to try it in Kane's office. Figure that's where the spirit was set free."

"I thought you said you thought her having sex is what caused that."

"Yeah." I grinned. "Guess where that happened?"

He pursed his lips like he sucked a lemon. "That is not how a girl should lose her virginity. It's *cheap*."

"I know, that's what I was thinking, but it sounds like it was spontaneous. And it's not like he doesn't care about her. I think that's the important part." I smiled at him. "Breakfast, then we can summon a spirit."

"Summon?" His eyebrows shot up.

"Yeah, we want to know who this guy is and how to stop him, that's the next step."

"Is it dangerous?"

"Ehhhh, probably. Yeah." I nodded. "Yeah, it really is, but I don't have much of a choice at this point. I've got till tomorrow night to find this guy if I'm right. You don't have to come."

"I'm not leaving you to put yourself in danger alone."

"Aw, what a gentleman."

"I'LL LIGHT THE CANDLES, naming each as an element," I said. "Since we're summoning a spirit, we'll go with my element, fire, first. Have to go with my strengths. If Faye were here, we'd do air first."

"And she couldn't make it because…?" Sebastian asked.

"Her kid's sick. Her husband drove back with her this morning. And she thinks I can handle this."

I wasn't sure she was right, but hey.

"I'll draw a circle around us with my knife," I said, "and then, *no matter what*, you stay in the circle. The spirit can't get to us through the circle."

"How do you know?" Sebastian looked around Kane's office like he was afraid the spirit would pop up behind him any second.

"You really don't need to be here for this."

"No." He put his arms around my back and pulled me in for a quick kiss. "I'm not leaving you," he said, looking into my eyes. "Besides, I want to learn about the reality behind the mysticism."

"Okay, you're about to get a big dose of reality. Once we sit, don't open your eyes. Again, no matter what. You don't know what can see you. I'm not joking."

I drew the circle in the middle of Kane's tiny office. There was barely enough room for me and Sebastian to sit cross legged between Kane's desk and the closed door.

I lit the candles, whispering my prayers under my breath as I went. I sat, and Sebastian followed suit, careful to stay well within the candles. Smart man.

I held my hands out palms up, the amethyst holding our energy in front of me. "I call on the fires of my heritage, the fire in my blood. I call on the spirit bound to the earth to answer or be burned. Christopher Springfield. Christopher Springfield. Christopher Springfield. Thrice said and done, I summon thee."

"Who dares!" burst around me, washing over my face like spring tinted with coffee breath breeze. "This is none of your business," the voice continued. It echoed through the room, harsh and deep. Not even human.

"I've got a girl in the hospital and a broken-hearted friend that says otherwise," I said, drawing on the crystal. The power flowed through me like a lava stream, and I thrust it at him with a flash of orange. It was almost sexual with the power's pulsating. "Who are you on this plane? Where have you been hiding?"

"No," the spirit said, forcing the power back into me, making me gasp and my head toss back. I shoved it back at him and he pushed back, the tug of war tugging things low in my belly, like the sex last night awakened a beast within me. The magic push felt too good. I'd never tried this with anyone who could push back.

"How are you doing that?" I gasped, blood pooling down low. "You shouldn't be able to, it's not your power."

"Can you free me?" The spirit's voice was softer now. "The power in here, with Halloween it's enough. Give it to me!" The spirit pulled power from my belly, tightening everything from my knees to my breasts with one violent motion, and I moaned.

I pulled out, eyes popping open and candles falling dead.

Before I could react, Sebastian was on me. He grabbed my leg and flattened me to the ground, hard and as ready to go as I was.

I LAY GASPING, HEAD ON Sebastian's chest. It was sprinkled with hair and covered with a thin sheen of sweat. His heart raced under my ear, and he stroked my arm as we caught our breaths.

"How did the ghost do that?" He finally broke the silence.

"Spirit. There's a difference, and I have no clue," I said, turning and kissing the pec under my cheek before laying my head down again. "He shouldn't have been able to take my magic and use it. I must've done the circle wrong."

I sat up with a jerk. "Or he was in it already!"

"What?" Sebastian sat up with wide eyes.

"He was already in here with us. That's the only explanation. He's a spirit, he can make himself non-corporeal and invisible at will."

"So he could still be here?"

"I'm betting he is, or at least was for that show. He wanted my magic. I mean, that was some great sex, but he sparked it. He wanted us to make more of that magic for him."

I grabbed the amethyst and plunged my magic into it. Empty. Shit! "Yeah, it's got bupkis. He took the power with him. With that and the power tomorrow, he'll be able to free himself."

"What happens if he gets free?"

I shrugged. "Faye thought he did the spell wrong. Thought he was trying to make himself immortal, botched it, and got stuck. Right now, he's on the planet like he wanted, so I think now he's either trapped and not quite corporeal like he wants to be, or he's trapped in a certain geographic area, or he realizes he doesn't want to be immortal and would rather be dead like he's supposed to be. No matter what it is, he's stuck in some way he does not like, and he wants out."

"So, it's not horrible if he gets out? It's not the end of the world?"

"Not from him specifically. But… it's against nature to have a spirit running around like this. The longer he's here, the more things will go off, like the laws of physics. Oy!" I smacked my forehead. "That's what happened to her."

"What?" Sebastian asked.

"The spirit was probably with Mandy, hanging out with his kid or just seeing if he could get her to use her powers, and his presence sent her flying. He didn't mean to! It's the laws of psychics going off. That's usually why spirits are so dangerous. Usually they're not bad people, they're witches who thought they could outsmart nature. I kept wondering why, why would he hurt his own daughter. He didn't mean to!"

I closed my eyes and slapped my forehead again. "That's what the earthquake was! I knew it felt wrong. His wrongness is picking up speed."

I dropped my hand to my necklace. "Oy gevalt. Tomorrow's Halloween. If he tries to get himself out… Who knows what could happen next? I've heard of blizzards, earthquakes, hurricanes. And that's just natural disasters we figured out were tied to unbalanced energies. Doesn't even take into account what people hit with the unbalanced energy could do to each other."

"Okay." Sebastian pulled on his pants and looked around. "Where did my shirt go?"

I giggled, looking around. "Ummm. There!" I pointed up. His shirt lay over one of the unmoving fan blades and Sebastian burst out laughing and reached up to grab it, chest muscles doing interesting things in the light.

"Now what do we do?" he asked, handing me my shirt, then plucking my skirt from the desk and handing that to me too. He paused at my belt and the holster with my gun in it. I picked that up, raising my eyebrows at him. He shrugged, giving me an apologetic smile.

I shook my head. "I don't know." I got dressed, blushing as I put the clothes back in order because he watched every move with sharp, unabashed eyes.

We grabbed my candles and put them back in their box. "I think we should do some more old-fashioned detective work. Check her dorm, her computer and phone, see what else we can dig up about this guy, and keep bugging her mom until she answers."

"Alright." He opened the door for me, waving his arm for me to go first.

I grinned. "See? Gentleman."

IT WAS THE MIDDLE OF the day, and luckily Mandy's roommates were out. We broke into her dorm suite, went to her room and shuffled through her stuff. I pulled up her desktop computer, laughing that she still had a desktop, and got in without a problem because she didn't have a password.

"Alright." I cracked my knuckles, wiggling my fingers and bouncing my eyebrows at Sebastian.

He smiled, but it was weak. He didn't have to say he wasn't comfortable in a girl's room, his crossed arms and the ramrod shoved up his tuchus said it for him.

"I've got a teenage girl with an older, forbidden boyfriend, and a spirit for a daddy," I said. "She's got to have some of this mishegoss on social media."

I pulled up her Facebook, Twitter, Instagram, and Blog. She talked about her parents and her artwork on her blog, school and friends on the other platforms, but nothing really personal.

"Oy vey, an eighteen-year-old smart enough not to advertise her entire life online? How am I supposed to find out anything useful?"

"I'm just as surprised as you," Sebastian said.

He looked over my shoulder as I pulled up her Facebook and clicked on her pictures.

Dodododahdodo, my phone sang the old Nintendo song and I clicked it on. "Hello?"

"She's awake," Kane said. "Mandy's awake!"

I sagged in the chair. "Oh thank the goddess. How is she? Is there any brain damage?"

"She's perfect," he said, voice choked up with obvious tears. "She's bruised and it's going to take surgery to fix the damage to her face, but as far as they can tell, her brain's fine."

We exchanged a few more words, but it was obvious he wanted to get back to her. "Okay, tell her I'll be there later," I said, hanging up and turning around. "Mandy's awake."

Sebastian sat on the floor, head in his hands. "I heard."

"Are you okay?" I got up and kneeled next to him. "Wow, didn't know you and Kane were that close. Well, I guess, since you've been living with him."

"I'm just so relieved." He looked up, meeting my eyes. His light green eyes were so pretty with tears filling them.

Oy gevalt.

It clicked. That knowledge women sometimes have, that epiphany that changes everything. I'd had it a few times in my adult life.

And now? Somehow looking into his eyes, I knew.

MY HEART DROPPED TO MY FEET. *No,* I thought. *How? I googled him! He's real and has a history online and…*

I tried to keep it off my face, but there was a reason I didn't play poker.

Sebastian's eyes flew wide. "Evie, no." He reached for me and I scrambled up to my feet and back.

"It's you!" I yelled, shrill and near hysterical. "Of course it's you! That's why the spirit could control the magic earlier, because he was in the circle too and he helped *fucking* make it. Pun intended!"

"Evie." He stood, holding his hands out. "I didn't mean to hurt Mandy. You were right, I was just trying to scare her into using her powers. When she flew off the roof, I couldn't figure out why or what happened."

"I know." I forced myself to take a deep breath. I'd shtupped a spirit, an actual dead man, no matter how corporeal he was. A walking, talking crime against nature and magic. "It's okay, I get you didn't mean to."

"Then why are you backing away?"

"Because you're a hazard. You caused an earthquake. You are carrying around a hell of a lot of unbalanced energy. You won't hurt me on purpose, I get that, but you will upset everything around you. We have to figure out how to put you back."

"You mean kill me." It wasn't a question.

"Seb… I mean Christopher, it is Christopher, right? I don't want to, believe me. But I don't know how to keep you here and balance out the world. Accidents will keep happening around you. Natural disasters will keep happening. They could get worse. We're lucky nothing happened during sex."

"The crystal must've captured it."

"No, the crystal captures magic, but a negative type of energy? No. That's what you *are*. You are a walking black hole in magic. A thing that messes with the rules of the world. You will put everyone around you in danger. You don't want that. Your *daughter* was thrown off a roof because of this. She could've died. You don't want to put her at risk again."

He looked down, searching the floor, his daughter's floor, like it held the answers. He met my eyes and my intestines went cold at the look in them. "You said yourself, I can be free tomorrow. I won't be a crime against nature then. I'll be a man again."

"That's not how it works! You try to free yourself, you'll be increasing the energy exponentially! You don't understand how bad this could get."

"Could!" he yelled back, hot as me now, and jabbed a finger at me. "Not will. You can protect the world from me. You can use your magic and keep my negative energy from hurting anyone else until I do the spell tomorrow."

"No, I can't, Sebastian." I rubbed my forehead. "You don't get it. If you do manage the spell, you will be *releasing* your negative energy. There's no way around it. That's what you *are*. That's what your magic is. You use it, you send out negative energy. Bad things happen. The last time a spirit tried this on Halloween, it set off a huge blizzard in Minnesota that killed *twenty people*. You've already set off an earthquake, and that's just from your existence. You can't do this. End of story."

He nodded along and met my eyes. "I won't let you kill me."

He held up the amethyst (when did he get it away from me!) and I barely had time to scramble over the bed and drop behind it before energy sliced through the air. It would've burned me, possibly taken a body part if I hadn't moved.

I grabbed my necklace and focused, thrusting magic into him like I had during the séance. Only then, I hadn't known it was him. How could I be so *stupid*? So blind?

Easy, I'd slept with him. It created trust, a bond, or so I'd thought.

Spirits always had to be tied to something. There had to be something in this world keeping him locked to it. Faye said it was something near the U. It had to be something of Mandy's, didn't it? Or maybe something left in his old office?

I pulled my gun from its holster and got up on my knees behind the bed, resting my arms on it to steady the weapon.

Seb… Christopher dodged to the side and out the door before I could focus on him enough to get a shot off that I could guarantee would go into him and not possibly punch through the thin walls and get someone else.

I could run after him and keep fighting, or I could try to figure out what he was tied to and destroy it while he wasn't in the way.

Door number two. Definitely.

Everything in me went numb and clinical. No emotions allowed.

I flipped through Mandy's books, dug through her clothes, her jewelry box, her drawers, looking for anything that screamed twenty-years-old. Nothing jumped out at me. Some of her clothes could've been more of an eighties' style, but they seemed more came back into style pieces than retro ones.

Christopher popped in front of me in the middle of the room.

"Ah!" I screamed.

He waved a hand and a force lifted my feet and slammed me into the wall. An air witch, of course. Breath burst out of my lungs like a shot, and my knees hit carpet. I couldn't suck in enough air to breathe.

Air feeds fire, you snake, I thought since I couldn't speak yet. I stood, lifted my hands, and blasted a wave of flames at his sorry, lying ass.

He blocked them, clutching the crystal in his hand like it was an erection, clearly drawing the power from it. The power I'd given him.

The power we'd made.

He shot a bolt of fired up air at me, and I barely had time to draw a shield before it hit. He threw another and another, so fast I couldn't even duck.

The bursts sucked energy from my shield and I shoved more in, dropping to my knees. I grabbed my necklace and threw fire back, struggling to breathe. If the shield fell…

The room shook and Christopher tripped. I jumped up and dove behind the bed as the computer flew off the desk and slammed into the closet door.

Anger burned a hole in my stomach and I drew that up.

"I am so sorry," I muttered to the owners of the dorm.

I lit the place on fire. Flames burst up on the door, the curtains, and the bedding first. I focused, making them spread.

"No!" Christopher yelled. "I didn't want to hurt you. Don't do this."

I closed my eyes, letting the heat wash over me, feed into my system to be spit out again in more flames. He may not have wanted to hurt me, but he'd been trying to.

The crackling died down as a force sucked my magic away from the flames. My crystal! He was using my own crystal against me.

I shot a stream of magic at him, growling with the effort of lifting twenty pounders above your head while you ran. And I ran straight at him.

He had a foot and nearly a hundred pounds on me. He wasn't going over easily.

I slammed into him, pulling the crystal from his hand. He shook me off and I hit the ground with my shoulder. It exploded in pain and I held up the crystal as he lunged at me, forcing everything out at once.

The power, the magic, the passion we'd shared gushed out like I turned over a bucket, and the room exploded, a ball of fire the size of that bolder that chased Indian Jones taking the room in one swallow.

My powers protected me from the blast. Christopher rose in front of me. Smoke clogged my lungs. I had to get out of here. I stumbled back towards the window and he grabbed my shoulder.

I met his eyes as his feet faded away.

The tether's in here.

I tried to tell him I was sorry, but I erupted in coughs. I sucked in a deep breath of tainted air and flinched. The heat couldn't sear my lungs, but I was going to need a doctor for all the smoke and soot.

Christopher's legs, torso, arms, and finally head followed his feet into oblivion. "I'm sorry," he said, still holding my eyes. "I panicked. I'm so sorry I attacked you."

Then he was gone.

THE FIRETRUCKS WERE ALREADY on their way when I scrambled out through the window and collapsed on the grass.

I watched the dorms burn from the gurney the EMTs pushed me onto in front of the building. Luckily, most of the kids were in class or out enjoying the weather, and the ones that were home got their butts out of there before they got any lung damage.

Hell of a lot of property damage, but at least no one was hurt.

The paramedics rushed me to the hospital and I didn't remember the next few hours. They must've taken good care of me because when I woke up, I felt much better.

Physically at least.

I'd looked up Sebastian Blake online. Christopher looked just like the pictures I'd found of the man. He must've figured out enough magic to pull a glamour and taken on the guise of someone who hadn't been in town long enough for anyone to really know him. Except for his eyes. It was hard for anyone to change their eyes because of the beliefs about the eyes being the windows to the soul. People didn't want to believe they could mask that, so they couldn't.

I was pretty sure I knew what happened to the real Sebastian Blake. There was only one way Christopher could've taken over his life that completely, but he'd probably go down in records as a missing person.

"You okay?" Faye asked from the hospital room doorway.

"Yeah." I waved her in and she sat in the chair next to my bed. "Why aren't you at the festival?"

She gave me a look.

I shook my head. "Is this going to be a pattern, Faye? Good guy, evil guy, good guy, evil guy?"

"At least that means the next one will be a good guy. And you know he wasn't evil."

"I know. He was just a guy with a little bit of power, and too much theoretical knowledge without enough practical. He made a mistake in a fit of a broken heart and trapped himself between worlds. He just wanted to fix his mistake. He didn't want to die. I can't blame him for that. One mistake took his whole life. That was it."

Faye took my hand. "Stop whatever you're thinking. You've made mistakes. Yes, you lost your job because of one, but it's nothing like his. You haven't ruined your whole life. You haven't murdered someone and taken over their life. You just suffered a setback."

Tears filled my eyes and I smiled. "That's not what I was thinking, actually."

"What were you thinking?"

I met her eyes. "That my dad is pretty amazing. And he's been a good dad, so when he gets back here with lunch, I should say thanks. And that I should call my biggest mistake and tell him congratulations on the baby."

"Really? Why?"

"Because even though he was bad to me, he's been wonderful to his wife, and he's already bending over backwards for his baby. He's going to be a good dad. And that's not a given. The last thing I said to him was something along the lines of, 'Bye putz.' Figure I don't want that to be our last conversation ever."

I took a deep breath. "I slept with Sebastian, Christopher, whatever." I shook my head. "Because I liked him, but also because I was upset over my ex's perfect life. He's still affecting me. And I don't think he'll stop until I get some closure. I don't want to make a mistake like Sebastian again. That was… I should've known. And if I hadn't been so desperate to feel wanted because I'm so wounded, I think I would have. Hand me my phone?"

She handed it over, grinning so big, the pride spilling out of her obvious as the sun.

"Oy vey," I said. "Just let me do this without the gloating, okay?"

She just kept grinning.

The phone rang three times before he picked up. "Evie? It's so good to hear from you!"

My heart rate picked up and my blood pressure skyrocketed at his voice.

I took a deep breath. "Hey Kieren. I just saw your Facebook status. Congrats on the baby!"

PART V. EVIE JONES
AND THE SHADOW OF CHAOS

"ARE YOU FUCKING KIDDING ME!" I clenched my fists to keep from shouting at work. "Why is he coming here? And why now?"

"He's coming to ski," Faye said, pushing her blond hair back and gathering it into a ponytail like she always did when she was about to pull her psychiatrist voodoo to calm me down. She tied it off with the scrunchy on her wrist like the nineties' teenager she had been. "And he wants to hang out. Evie, I think-"

"Oy vey. Hang out, sure, but you guys are letting him stay with you!" My voice hit highs only dogs could hear and Faye flinched.

I looked around the shoebox the hospital had the nerve to call an office before turning my chair to face the wall. The University Med Center was situated on the top of a hill overlooking the Salt Lake Valley, and had hallways made of glass and giant windows in patients' rooms so people could marvel at the view.

But peons in administration got interior offices little better than cubicles because it's not like we'd earned daylight or anything.

I took a deep breath and tried again now that I wasn't looking at my friend. It helped. It's why patients in therapy lay on couches or facing away from their doctors.

"We have a Council rep in town this week. That's bad enough. I feel like I can't so much as light a candle in my own home without them feeling it and coming to investigate. And now *he's* here and staying with you? What if the rep checks in on you guys to make sure you're not showing George your magic?"

I rested my hand on the gun under my jacket at my side like a kid grabbing her blankie. "I mean, I'm fine shooting a Council rep if I need to, but that's for you guys, not *him*. George can lie, but that putz won't know to if there's something that'd tip the Council off in there. He can afford a hotel room. He's a big fancy Senior Associate."

"There's nothing magical lying around the house he could see. It'll be fine. He said he wants to stay with friends because it gives him more time with them and that's the main point of the trip. He and George are close, and we haven't seen him since the weekend of his wedding."

"Yeah." I nodded, biting my lip. "But, this feels like a betrayal. I get he's George's friend, but you're *mine*. You're supposed to be on my side. And my side people don't let my evil ex stay with them for a ski weekend."

"I thought you two were talking again."

I tossed my hands up. "We talked once, for me to congratulate him on the baby and he hasn't called since. I opened the door; he didn't go through it."

"That's kind of what I was trying to do with this weekend."

I whirled my chair around and Kieran stood in the doorway, a carry-on sized wheeled suitcase next to him.

My stomach seized for a second before jumping into my chest, and my blood pressure skyrocketed right alongside it.

I looked at Faye, eyes wide. She just shrugged.

Yeah, real fucking helpful.

I rolled my eyes at her before turning them back on Kieran. He barely fit in the doorway, his head so close to the top I always wondered how he didn't get more concussions, especially whenever he visited New York City where the old buildings had low ceilings and lower doorways.

I knew he went down there with his wife about once a month because I Facebook stalked him, even more so since I reestablished contact.

Pathetic, I know.

He was six five and skinny. I'd always liked tall, and skinny just matched his personality. He was adorkable with his big hazel eyes, sharp features, love of law and politics and geeky north eastern accent.

He was from Maine and joked once he applied to Utah because he liked the skiing, and he chose that school over the other frontrunner with a coin toss.

Of all the gin joints in all the world had never made sense to me until I met him first year of law school.

He swiped the wool hat off his head, revealing the blond hair he kept short because he thought it made him look too young. He grew the stupid goatee for the same reason, trying to look like a man in his thirties and not a college kid.

"You've been quiet for like a minute," he said. "Should I go, try that again?" He grinned, wide and sweet and *him*. "I mean, I don't have to be here. I can be a figment of your imagination, and we can get together tonight for dinner?"

I laughed, looking down at my desk. "Kieran, you know I never know what to say to you. I don't think I'll ever know what to say to you."

Oops, usually it took two martinis to get me that honest. Speaking of, I could seriously use one now. Or three.

"Well, you could say yes because you know I'm a diabetic and I have to be fed." He grinned and shrugged off his thick black coat and put it on the coat rack, sitting next to Faye without asking.

"I don't really know what to say to you either." He shrugged. "That's why I never called. I didn't want to bother you."

"You're the one that dumped me. It's your job to reach out. I can't, unless I have a good reason, like to tell you congrats on the baby. Come on, you'd been dating how long? You know the rules." I tried to smile and it fell so flat I could hear the whomp whomp whomp echoing in my brain.

"I'm…" He sighed and met my eyes, making my heart seize. "I'm sorry, Evie."

"For what? For five years ago or for surprising me today?"

"Both."

I searched his eyes. I hadn't seen him in almost four years. He'd graduated the year before me and moved to New York, and I hadn't seen him since.

"I don't believe you," I said. "I haven't seen you in forever, haven't heard from you. You obviously do not care; you never really did. I get it. I was a girl you screwed around with, and then you were done with me. You know what? I release you. You did your due diligence, you said hi, you pretended you care. Good for you. You're done. You've done what any guy would do to try and make up for being a dick. Good for you. Now go away."

His mouth worked and he looked at Faye. "Can you give us a minute?"

"No." I stood before she could say anything. "I'm not going to have a heart to heart where you say the exact right thing to make me think you give a damn because you don't want other people to think you're an ass. Band-Aid, bullet hole."

I walked around the desk, looking at Faye. "Tell me when he leaves."

I walked out of my office, ceding territory. But it's not like it was actually mine. I was fired from the hospital that was *mine*. This one was just a job, a place to kill time and build experience until I could get a real lawyer job again. I wasn't exactly making a go at life, and now my ex, who had it all, was back.

It was too much.

I ran into the bathroom and shoved my way into a stall, tears coming out hard and hot before I got the damn door closed.

His big eyes stabbed through my mind's eye, and I clutched at my chest. It was like I was back in first year, hearing him tell me it was over. He'd broken up with me right before finals because the other girl he'd been seeing had put her foot down. Either they stopped being casual, or she walked. And he picked her.

I cried, whispering, "It's his fault."

I grabbed tissues and wiped under my eyes. "It's all his fault."

I walked out and froze at the mirror. The mascara was half under my eyes. I grabbed a towel and went to work, getting the makeup off so I didn't look like the mess I was. My suit skirt and button-down blouse were at least nice, but my plain black flats didn't do much for the outfit. My skin didn't look great after the crying, but it wasn't terrible. My light brown hair sparkled with fresh highlights and curled nicely over my shoulders today. Overall, I was looking decent considering I wasn't expecting to see my ex.

Was I actually worried about how I looked for him!

I punched the wall, pain from the slam stabbing through my knuckles. I didn't hit hard enough to break open skin or anything. I wasn't that good at punching. Much more the weapons girl than the fist fighter.

I rested a hand on the gun and grabbed my necklace with the other. It was my wand for lack of a better term. It stored and focused my magic. I didn't want to use either on him. Not really. No matter how bitchy and childish I was acting, I didn't want to hurt him.

I wanted to hug him, to ask him about his life since he left, to stay up talking until two a.m. like we used to do. Even if I couldn't have him, kiss him or do more. I wanted to be able to talk.

I *wanted* to be friends.

I pulled my phone out of my pocket and saw I'd missed five calls from Chet in the last three minutes. "Goddess, did Faye tell you to check on me?" I shook my head and called Chet back.

"Chet, hey," I said.

"Evie! Thank god," he said, voice pinched with panic.

"What, what's wrong?"

"There's a shooter in the hospital!"

THE BLOOD FROZE IN MY VEINS, and I turned to the door in what felt like slow motion. I waved my hand and sealed the door with a push of sloppy magic. No time for finesse if there was a crazy guy out there.

What about Kieren?

"Some nut walked into the lobby and opened fire a few minutes ago," Chet said. "A guy pulled out his weapon and shot back, covered the lobby and kept the guy, I mean the first guy, pinned while people ran out. The shooter got two people before the guy started shooting back. Then the shooter got on the elevator. No one knows where he is or what he wants. They've got the injured into rooms to treat them but everyone's scared and locking themselves in patients' rooms. The cops are on the way. I was trying to call you!"

"I'm on fourth. Are you outside? Stay there."

"Evie, I'm-"

"*No.* You're not going to play hero and come in guns blazing. I've got this. I'll find him and take him out. I don't want anyone else in the line of fire."

"I'm already here. Faye text me you were upset and I came over to cheer you up."

"Oy gevalt! Where are you?"

"I'm in the lobby. I was down the hall when he came in, otherwise I would've been the guy shooting at him and taken him out then."

"Tell me you're behind cover."

"Of course. I'm behind the front desk. What kind of firepower do you have on you?"

"Just my revolver. Anyone say what kind of gun or how many bullets he's got?"

"Don't know. Let's just assume a lot. Any other gunnies there?"

"Not that I know of." I took a deep breath. "We're babbling because we're panicking. You do know that?"

"Yeah."

"So I've only got my revolver with six rounds, but I have magic. It's not really going to be a problem once I find him… oh *shit!*"

"What?"

"The Council's in town. If I use magic, they'll be able to sense it. Something like sealing a door won't register very high because it's a little magic, but a big spell? Or if I light anything on fire? Everyone's laying low this week. The last thing we need is a formal investigation."

"Why? It's not like you all do black bad magic or anything."

"That's not what the Council cares about. They care about keeping witches and magic secret, and they're tyrants. No one actually lives by their rules. We just try not to call attention to ourselves. Right now though, I don't think we have a choice. I'll just have to hope I can get the guy without using magic."

"Evie, if it comes down to it, take him out however you need to. You can always explain it to the Council later."

"I don't think you get how tyrannical they are about their rules. They won't care if I had a good reason, won't care if my life was on the line, just that I broke the rules. Rule number one is you don't use magic to kill. Because then it leaves some very confused and pissed off humans who want to figure out why someone's dead through means they don't understand."

"So just knock him out."

"I can try." I stared at the bathroom door. "I'm scared, Chet."

"Can you get a knockout spell going fast, and make it so they can't sense it?"

"Not really. I'll have to duck and get it ready. Or make it now and keep it charged. I can't afford to waste that kind of energy. You see why just turning him into a crispy critter is easier, right?"

"It's your call, girl."

"I'm heading out now. Stay where you are. I'll be down in a minute. *Run* if you hear shots, okay?"

"Okay."

"I mean run *away* from the shots."

He'd already hung up.

I can't believe this is happening.

I pulled up a shield and poked my head into the hall. If the Council rep sensed the shield and came to see what was going on, things could get uglier than they already were.

Admin looked like any other office life-sucking hallway, with little offices and cubicles, and the bigger dogs with big offices around the outside. I slipped past the first opening into the cubical bullpen, keeping my gun up and looking around, ears straining for steps. I paused at the stairs. I could go down… or I could go left, back to my office.

Kieren was with Faye. She'd keep him safe. She wasn't a shooter or great with offensive magic, but way better at shields than me.

I turned left. If anything happened to either Kieren or Chet, I'd never forgive myself, but Chet had a defense. For all I knew, Kieren and Faye split up after I stormed out.

Please let him be out of the building.

I walked down the hall on light feet, grateful I'd worn flats now. My steps echoed lightly on the linoleum floors, but nothing compared to the clacking of heels.

I hit my office so fast, I knew I was in shock, everything moving too quickly. I got in and closed the door behind me as quietly as I could. We didn't know where the guy was, and precautions couldn't hurt.

"Evie," came from behind my desk in a hiss. The surprise didn't even make me jump. Kieran poked his head up and waved me over. "Get down. There's a shooter. There's an emergency email that told everyone to get out if they were near an exit or hide."

"Yeah." I kneeled down next to him. "I heard."

He creased his forehead. "Then why the hell did you come back here? What are…" I met his eyes and his widened, mouth going slack.

I looked away. "We need to get out of here. I've got my gun on me, so I'll go first. Keep quiet, and stay down. Once you're outside you should be safe."

"Once *I'm* outside? You're *not* staying in here."

"The cops aren't here yet. For all we know, they'll take their dear sweet time setting up a perimeter or something instead of just running in. And that crazy guy is here for a reason. Hopefully his reason got the hell out of the building, but if not." I shrugged. "He opened fire on the lobby. No provocation. No warning. I can't leave."

"You're not a cop." He grabbed my chin, yanking it up so I'd look at him. "You know how you told me I always had the perfect thing to say?" He searched my eyes. "Right now, I don't. Tell me what I need to say to convince you to get the hell out and not be crazy. Tell me what to say and I'll say it, just please get out with me and let the cops handle it."

I sniffed, water works swelling in my eyes and ruining the badass chick image I had going. "See." I smiled. "There you go again, saying the perfect thing."

If he was anyone else, I would've grabbed his hand and yanked to get him moving. Instead, I jerked my head towards the door. "Come on. I didn't hear the original shots, so that means he has a suppressor. Or the hospital has thicker walls than I thought. Either way, I can't guarantee he's not still shooting or not nearby, but he's not doing both."

We slouched to the door and I shook my head when he grabbed the doorknob. I waved and he backed up so I could open it.

I opened the door slowly and poked my head out, assessing the hall with a few quick jerks of my head. I kept my gun low but finger next to the trigger and jerked my head again at Kieren to get him to follow me.

We slunk down the hall like cats, Kieren pretty quiet for a beanpole. We hit the stairs and I eased the door open, putting my gun up and keeping it pointed out just in case the shooter had the same idea.

The stairs were like a lot of big buildings' stairs, solid and echoey. I held still and listened for a minute. I couldn't hear anything besides my stupid heart hammering and Kieren's breathing.

We got down the steps as quick as we could while keeping our steps light and quiet, and burst out into the lobby a minute later.

Chet's head appeared behind the desk and my heart loosened a bit. Chet and I weren't an item, we'd tried and it didn't go anywhere, but our friendship had survived after a few months' break and I couldn't believe how grateful I was for that.

He waved us over and I broke and ran for him, paranoia the only thing keeping my arms out and down instead of thrown around his neck.

"Okay, you get him out, make sure no one's taking shots from a window or something," I whispered.

"No," Chet said. "You're not doing this alone. You need someone to watch your back."

"You two both need to stop acting crazy and come out with me," Kieren said. "I'm serious. This isn't a game."

"Yeah, we got that," Chet said before I could. "We're armed, you're not. Get outside."

"Kieren," I said before he could argue. "I'm not going to be able to do this if I'm worried about you. Do you get that?"

"Good. Then you won't do it."

"Dammit, Kieren, people could die."

"That's what I'm worried about."

"I'm armed."

"So is he." Kieren clenched his teeth and met my eyes. "Evie, I get you have this vision of yourself as brave in the face of danger, great, you proved it's true. Now get over it. You aren't equipped to handle a madman like this."

"Yes, I am."

He tossed up his hands and turned away. "I can't... do either of you have an extra gun?"

"Whoa, *no*," I said.

"I do," Chet said, pulling his spare from the belt under his shirt. "It's a double action revolver like Evie's. All you gotta do is pull the trigger. It means you-"

"I know." Kieren checked the back to see the bullets. "I wouldn't ask for one if I didn't know how to use it. How do we find this guy?"

"Kieren, no," I said.

"*You're* the one that was saying people could be dying and you have to stop this man now. We can't wait for the police. Do you really have time to argue with me?"

"Stupid, testosterone filled dumbass."

"Yeah, I care about you too."

"If you're doing this because I said you don't care, I take it back. I was trying to hurt you and get a rise out of you. Okay? You don't have to prove anything."

"*I'm* not trying to prove anything." He stared me down and I looked away first.

Chet kept his eyes peeled and looking above us and around the lobby in case the shooter tried to get the drop on us, but he paused to give me a look and mouthed, "Ex?"

I shrugged and nodded.

Chet nodded once at the elevators on the right. "He went that way."

"ICU's on that side. You think he lost someone?" I said.

"Or he's just a crazy guy who watches bad doctor shows because that's the *only* place someone shoots up a hospital."

"Bite your tongue, that was a good doctor show."

The boys fell in around me, Chet in front and Kieren in back. I didn't fail to notice they put me in the middle, but I didn't have time to complain.

I focused, pulling my magic up, sensing the world, trusting the guys to keep an eye out. *Oy vey, I'm trusting Kieren to watch my back… literally.*

The hospital hummed, electronics in every room setting the world on edge, and making my teeth hurt. This was easier to do outside when all I had to sense was nature and what was wrong in it. With the electronics and chrome and glass around me, it got a lot harder to feel out any specific person or thing.

I sent my mind out, "sniffing," for lack of a better term, for a person with ill intent, malicious aforethought, mind on murder.

Nada.

"Oy vey," I said under my breath.

"What?" Kieren asked.

I shook my head. "I'd explain if I could."

We kept creeping and I zoned out, focusing on the world again.

Okay, if there's not someone trying to actively commit evil, what about mental illness?

I sent my brain skipping through the hospital, searching for telltale signs of a brain slightly off from the rest of the world. This was easier. Emotions didn't always give off the sense of wrongness, because emotions were part of all humans, even blinding rage or grief. But someone with a brain left of sane? That one would stand out against the crowd.

Red throbbing hit my senses upstairs. I couldn't tell what floor, but it was definitely this wing.

"Upstairs," I said.

"How do you know?" Kieren asked.

I didn't look at him. "I think he might be going for the ICU. That's upstairs. On third."

"Okay."

Chet looked back at me, raising his eyebrows. I nodded, slight and slow. If Kieren noticed, he didn't say anything.

We snuck up the stairs at the end of the hall, all of us so on edge that it began to seep into my consciousness and block out the sense of wrongness the shooter gave off.

I held up a hand and got in front of Chet when we hit the third floor. He opened his mouth and I wiggled my fingers, hoping he'd get it.

He shook his head. I met his eyes and wiggled my fingers again.

"Whatever it is, just say it," Kieren hissed. "I don't know what you're trying to keep from me, but this isn't the time."

"It's always the time. Stay behind me, I'm going first."

"No," Kieren and Chet said together and I pushed open the door, shield up and pushed in front of us like half a bubble. Imperceptible to the human eye, but hopefully strong enough to stop a bullet.

Bullets rained down the hallway and smacked into my shield with meaty *thwaps*, cluttering to the ground a second later.

I screamed and Kieren grabbed my arms, pulling me down and behind a nurse's cart. Yeah, like that was bullet proof.

His eyes widened and he looked from the bullets on the ground to me. His mouth worked and I smiled. "Surprise."

"How…"

"Now you know why I wanted to go first." I stood, gun up and at the ready. The bullets stopped as fast as they'd started and I looked around. He definitely had a suppressor, otherwise we'd all be deaf right now. But where was he?

Patient rooms lined the hallway, and no movement of shadows or form said what room he was hiding in.

"Evie, can you tell what room he's in?" Chet asked.

I squinted my physical eyes, the motion focusing my magic by proxy. I felt for the wrongness, the crazy seeping into the world like an oil spill. Illness speckled the rooms, blurring the senses. He was here, and *different*, it's how I'd found him in a hospital full of sick people, but I couldn't just pinpoint him like a metal detector. Maybe someone like Faye with more finesse could, but not me.

"No," I said. "Kieren, any idea where Faye went?"

"I think she was going back to work. She left right after you. I said I was going to wait for you and she said she thought that was a good idea."

I sighed. *Of course she did.* "She's better at sensing out people than I am. I was going to say we could call her up here if she was still around."

"You were going to bring our friend into…" Kieren paused. "She's like you, isn't she? M… um, something."

"The term is magic. We're witches, Kieren. And yes. She's better at delicate work like sensing and shields than I am."

"What are you good at?"

"Lighting crap up." I bit my lip. "Except, we're in a hospital, with oxygen tanks and stuff, and for all I know I could throw a fireball and get something really important."

"Okay," I said. "I put up a shield, we go down the hall, checking room by room. Once we find him, you guys light him up. I'm going to be drained if I have to keep a shield up more than a minute so it'll be up to you."

"I think he was close," Chet said. "It happened so fast I didn't get a good look, but I remember seeing his face, so I think he's closer, like the first few rooms."

Dear goddess, we were stalling. We were scared and stalling while the crazy guy did who knew what.

"Can you take energy from either of us?" Kieren asked.

I snorted and covered my nose with my hands. "Sorry, I realize you don't know what you're asking, but oy vey."

"What?"

"The short answer is yes, but taking energy from another person is extremely intimate. I mean, we're talking levels that go beyond even sex. And sex is a good way to get that energy out. If you do the spells first and set up something to collect the energy, like a crystal. I've only tried it once." I flushed as a stab rang through my heart.

"I have a feeling that ended badly," Kieren said.

"Not as badly as *you*, but it was up there." I shook my head. "You guys know we're stalling, right?"

"Yeah," Chet said. "Let's go." He tapped my shoulder and I took a deep breath, raising my hands to visualize raising the shield, careful to keep the gun pointing out.

Air molecules solidified in front of us as a convex lens. The shape was more energy efficient than a straight wall, but still, I wouldn't be able to keep the air this hard for long.

I kicked off my shoes and stepped forward, taking a deep breath, and again and again. I walked down the hall on tiptoes, light as my cat when he stalked me through the apartment. I'd been through tougher spots than this. I'd fought a summoned water demon, a witch from my own coven who was being a bitch, a zombie, and a solidified spirit.

But none of them had been trying to kill me, not really. Now? This guy wasn't just out for blood, he was nuts, which made him even more dangerous. The crazy didn't usually have a sense of self-preservation that'd make them back off when you pointed a gun at them.

Then what does that say about us?

I hit the first room and poked my head in. Nothing obvious.

I focused and wrapped the shield around us. I went in and looked in the bathroom first. Nobody. I could tell nobody was hiding behind the bed since it was off the ground and you could see under and behind it.

I backed out and we proceeded to the next room. The guys shifted on their feet, almost in sync.

Shots ripped through the hallway, hitting my shield with enough force to make me feel the bullets like baby bee stings. The shield tried to fall and I held it tight, focusing and pouring out magic like puke, head exploding with the shove.

The guys shot back, the blasts so painfully loud they left my ears ringing before the deafness of ears protecting themselves from horribly loud things shut the sound off. The lights flickering through the rain of bullets told me I was going to have a migraine after this if we couldn't end it soon.

My shield wavered and I grunted. Had to tell them to get behind cover. The words wouldn't come. Not like they'd hear me anyway. I took a deep breath and shoved more energy into it, praying it held.

The boys stopped shooting and I didn't have to ask why. We only had six to nine bullets each. They were out. Chet reached for my gun and I nodded, grinding my teeth together. The gunman stepped into the hall and I could see it was some stringy haired kid, maybe old enough to drink. Black lines ran up his arms and his head fought with itself, lighting up my senses like neon, shooting my head with pain as intense as any bullet.

I tried to close him out, but he focused on me, like he was trying to shove his thoughts at me, trying to hurt me with his mind.

He's a witch too. Schizo, but a witch. Probably had the condition exasperated by magic.

There just weren't strong enough words for a situation like this.

Chet grabbed my gun and pulled it out of my locked hand. The gunman grinned, shoving brainwaves at me.

The shield fell.

He raised the gun almost in slow motion. His finger tightened on the trigger and he pulled.

I put up a shield, focusing on reflection.

The bullets hit and ricocheted, pounding into the crazy man, at least five hitting him before he loosened his grip and collapsed to the ground.

Black silk slithered out of the man's skull, condensing on the floor into a black shadowy bunny and hopped away.

"Huh," I said, dropping the shield and crashing to my knees, not even feeling them eat linoleum before I passed out.

"EVIE?" A VOICE ASKED, so quiet I could barely hear it. I took a deep breath and smelled sweet skin and sweat. I wanted to lick it. He always smelled so good.

"I love your smell," I said, eyes flickering open.

"Um…" Chet's eyes went wide and he smiled. "Thanks?"

"It's a compliment," Kieren said from the other side. "She's big on smell."

"She ever tell you how good you smelled?"

"Every time she drank. Two margaritas and she was smelling my neck and rubbing against me like a cat. It was cute."

"You." I pointed at him. "Stop talking. I like this guy. Don't scare him off."

Kieren tapped his ear. "Can't hear you."

They're probably yelling for us all to hear each other. I repeated, practically yelling.

"You do?" Chet asked. "You said we should just be friends."

"Oh, um, I may have a concussion making me honest. I just saw a shadow bunny, obviously I'm out of it."

Chet held my arm and head as I eased myself up to sitting. My head threatened to split itself open and I rubbed it, staring at the dead body.

"Cops are coming. You were only out for a second," Chet said.

"Oh, feels longer." I rubbed my head some more.

"What do we tell them?" Kieren asked.

"Oy vey." I would've shaken my head if I wasn't scared I'd shake my brains out. "I don't know. We can say you guys shot in self-defense, but if they look into it, they'll be able to tell the bullets don't match your guns."

"So we just hope they don't look into it since it's obvious what happened?" Chet asked.

Kieren and I looked at each other. Neither of us did criminal law, but we knew more about it than Chet. Kieren raised his eyebrows, and I shrugged.

"Yeah, I guess," I finally said. "I mean, there's no reason to look into it if there's nothing to investigate. He was a crazy guy who shot up the place. You guys hunted him down."

"Us?" Kieren asked.

"Oh yeah, you guys are going to put me in a dark room and not tell the cops I was involved, because my head's killing me and I'm going to puke if I'm out in the lights one more minute."

"Yes ma'am," Chet said, laying on the fake southern drawl. He scooped me up Scarlett O'Hara style. The bones in my skull slid, and I buried my head in his shirt as he walked me back to the first room. He lay me on the bed and brushed my hair from my face.

"Bring my shoes in here?" I asked. "If they try to question me, I'll tell them I work here and had a migraine, so I came to lie down, fell asleep, and didn't hear much beyond a scuffle and then really loud shots."

I closed my eyes and lips brushed my forehead.

"I CAN'T BELIEVE ALL THAT TIME I didn't know," Kieren said, sipping his whiskey.

I leaned back as much as I could in the stiff kitchen chair and put my feet up on Chet's lap under the table.

Chet shot me a look and rolled his eyes.

Faye put the port on the table and went back in the kitchen to grab glasses.

It'd taken me sleeping to get rid of the migraine and the boys came back to check on me in the morning after the cops finally let them go. They weren't in trouble, they were heroes.

The cops were pissed they had to follow protocol: set up a perimeter and go in carefully when a crazy gunman was on the loose, so the fact that civilians stopped the madman before he could kill anyone was cool in their book; they'd just had to get through paperwork and question the guys to make sure it was self-defense.

The guys were already getting calls for interviews. Kieren thought I'd want in on the action, get my share of the fame. Chet knew I was cool staying out of the limelight.

Faye made a potion to fix our ears and we took it the second we got here. I was enjoying being able to hear fully again.

"I can't believe I missed all that," Faye said, putting the glasses down. "I must've walked right past him on my way out."

"Good thing you weren't there," I said. "You *know* the Council sensed all that magic. They're going to investigate."

"You think they'll figure out it was you?"

I shrugged. "People around here know where I work. All the Council has to do is start questioning people. You know some of them would give me up in a heartbeat."

"But if the humans aren't looking into it…"

"Then there's a chance the Council won't look too far since there wasn't any exposure, and no reason to think the guy was killed by magic. All I did were shields, which are invisible. They'll sense that and think it was a witch behind a shield, invisible and hiding so nobody saw her."

Faye poured the port. "We hope."

"And pray," I said, picking up my glass and holding it out over the table. "To pulling a fast one on crazy people and crazier governments."

"Hear, hear," Kieren said, clinking my glass. Faye and Chet followed suit.

I took a long drag of port.

Movement out through the sliding glass door caught my eye and I waved my hand, using the motion to focus my magic and flick the back-porch lights on.

The shadow bunny stared in at us through the glass, so dark it was like he sucked the lights into himself. A black hole in the shape of a cute, fluffy bunny about the size of a house cat.

"What's wrong?" Chet asked, looking at the door.

"You don't see that?"

"See what?" Faye stood to see over the guys' heads and her hand flew to her heart. "Oh dear."

"What are we looking at?" Kieren asked.

"Okay, the guys can't see it. Definitely a witch thing," I said. "Faye, I think I saw that thing come out of the shooter."

"You think?"

"I was passing out from magic drain. I assumed I'd imagined it."

The blackhole bunny smiled, mouth somehow twisting up at the corners like a human's. Its teeth glinted under the lights like black needles.

How could I even see details like that?

"Chet, shadow monster thing that can distort reality?" I asked.

He shook his head. "Um, um, what culture?"

"I don't know. I can tell you it's right outside the door."

The bunny hopped through the glass like it wasn't there.

"And now it's inside!" I grabbed Chet's arm and hit Kieren's shoulder. "Run. Run!"

"From an invisible shadow bunny?" Chet lurched to his feet and Kieren was seconds behind.

"Yes, from an invisible shadow bunny!" We ran upstairs, Faye first and me taking up the rear.

We ran into the master bedroom and George looked up from the book he was reading to a half asleep Daphnie in bed.

"What the…!" George jumped off the bed and dove under it as I slammed the door behind us.

George pulled out a black box and opened it just as Faye reached him, like they'd practiced it in a drill.

Hell, they probably had.

I giggled and covered my mouth. A magic attack drill. Oy vey, that was funny.

Faye tossed me her spelling dagger and I unsheathed it, drawing a line in front of the door with a prayer while Faye set up the candles in a circle around the bed.

"Wow," Kieren said. "You guys have this *down*."

"Someone tries to kidnap your baby with a zombie, you set up precaution drills," George said, handing his wife a lighter out of the box.

"Whoa, what?" Chet asked.

"Guys, shush." I drew a circle around us and the bed, encircling Faye's candles too. If the thing came in, at least I'd have something drawn to hold it off with while she finished the real barricade.

The bunny came out of the wall next to the door, making me jump.

Daphnie giggled and waved. "Bunny."

"Wait, she can see that?" I asked. "How?"

"You said it was a witch thing," Kieren said.

"Yeah, but she's too young to have powers. She's not a witch yet."

"But genetically-"

"It doesn't work that way. You're not a witch till the powers turn on around puberty. If this is something only magic people can see, then she shouldn't."

"She!" Chet said. "You're all girls. Maybe only girls can see it."

"Anything you know of that is female specific?" I asked as the bunny hopped up to my invisible line, stopping right in front of it and sniffing.

"Bunny!" Daphnie screamed, clapping her hands.

The bunny jumped, bouncing off the line I'd drawn. At least the line was doing something.

Fog grew from the floor, swirling up and out like a smoke machine. It swelled and took the air up to my knees in five seconds. I jumped onto the bed, George close behind. He scooped up Daphnie as Faye disappeared under the cloud, still making the candle circle despite the interruptions.

Daphnie giggled and clapped again as the fog swirled around my ankles and I met Kieren's eyes over the wave. His big eyes were positively anime-esque with fear, and his mouth worked as the grey grew over it.

"Faye, get that circle up, now!" My voice hitched up at least two octaves and I sucked in air like an asthmatic.

I turned, looking for Chet. He was long buried. The wave grew over my head and I took a deep breath, holding it against the intrusion just in case. The world was dark, and my heart ached with an echo of the day Kieren broke up with me, like I was flashing back or watching a movie without actually seeing the scene.

What the hell?

The world blinked back on like someone turning on a TV and I looked around. Faye's candles were up and on. She looked over her shoulder at us and sighed, hand flying to chest when she saw her baby and husband were fine.

"So the candles got rid of the fog?" I asked.

"Yeah," Faye said, "Turned off the second I said the spell to light them."

The guys looked around too, all three of them looking confused but fine.

I did a doubletake.

Three!

Two Kierens stood in the room, Chet off to the side, mouth hanging open.

The Kierens turned and saw each other at the same time, jerking in the same way. They looked at each other, then at me, almost in unison.

"Evie?" both asked.

The one on the left glared at his twin then met my eyes as I jumped off the bed. "What's going on?"

"Well," I said. "The fog could've been a spell to make two of you, but I'm betting since I'm not seeing the bunny that one of you is actually the bunny in disguise. I'm just not sure why."

"And you don't know which one of us is the imposter?" the Kieren on the right asked, looking from him to the twin, grinning so wide and nervous I was half convinced he was the real one now. "Shit."

"Would he be able to read minds?" the left one asked. "Maybe you could ask us questions."

"Does it matter?" Chet asked, making me jump. "Whichever one's the fake, he's not hurting anything."

"Yet," I said. "But good point. If you aren't trying to hurt anyone, and you aren't a *killer* shadow bunny, um, creature. I can't believe I'm saying that with a straight face."

The Kierens sniggered, the way he always did. Oy vey.

"Then stop pretending and just tell us what you want," I said. "We're all reasonable here, and if you don't mean us harm, well, I don't see the point of hiding."

The Kierens looked at each other, raising their eyebrows and staring the other one down.

"Stop the staring contest," I said, waving my arms and stepping between them like they didn't have a foot on me and could see right over my head. "Alright, what day did we meet?"

"Um," Left Kieren said.

"I'm not sure what guy could tell you that, Evie," Right Kieren said. "Didn't you always complain about that? I never could remember important dates."

"Like your birthday," Left Kieren said.

"Oy vey." I looked between them.

"Ohhhhh," Left Kieren said, grinning. "It was a trick question. You were waiting to see which one of us tried to guess?"

"Clever," Right Kieren said.

"Come on, bunny man, just give it up. There's no point to this. Obviously you don't want to hurt us, otherwise you would have. Faye's circle isn't keeping you out. So what do you want?"

The looked at each other again and I slapped my forehead.

"This is getting us nowhere," George said. "Dude, who won the Superbowl this year?"

"You know I don't follow football," Right Kieren said. "Ask me who won the last World Cup."

George sighed, bouncing Daphnie in his arms. "Yeah, this isn't going to work. The thing must be able to read minds."

"Or at least the mind of the person whose form it took," Faye said.

"But how did it take his form?" Chet asked. "And why him? Wouldn't becoming one of the witches be more helpful?"

I pointed at him. "*That* is an excellent question. Why Kieren?" The Kierens looked at me and I rolled my eyes. "Of course that didn't work."

"Evie," Left Kieren said, stepping closer to me. "I'm me. Can't you look into my eyes and know that?"

"I would think so," Right Kieren said, stepping closer too. "I can tell you certain things you probably wouldn't appreciate being said in front of mixed company to prove it's me. One thing about the Halloween party?" He cocked his head

I blushed and pointed at him. "You be quiet."

"Back room," Left Kieren said. "I can play this game, too." He glared at the other him. "But I would never offer to spill such intimate details. Evie knows that."

I took a deep breath.

And froze.

"I have an idea," I said, waving Right Kieren to me. "You come here and give me a hug."

"Um, okay?" he came up and hugged me, bending down, squeezing me just like he always did, holding me up on my tiptoes and close to his body. I took a deep drag off his neck.

I'd remember Kieren's scent till the day I died. If there was one thing this thing couldn't mimic, okay, it'd be the eyes, and those he had down. But if there was a *second* thing he couldn't mimic, it'd be smell. Everyone had their own, and most people didn't think about it.

I turned to the other Kieren and held out my arms. He rushed in, hugging me tight against him, just like the other one. Only he smelled completely different, a musk with hints of the weird fruity shampoo he liked and something salty that was probably sweat but always reminded me of sex.

I sunk into the smell, memories popping in my brain like snot bubbles, and hugged him tighter. I let him go, meeting his eyes as I backed up. He smiled. He got it.

He held my eyes and my heart rate picked up again for a completely different reason now. We'd had something. And it'd been real.

And it hadn't mattered to him. At least not as much as the woman

THE MAGICAL ADVENTURES OF EVIE JONES

who'd become his wife.

My heart ached and I whirled, pulling my gun out with one motion and pointing it at the imposter.

"Okay, now that we know it's you, why don't you do us all a favor and start talking?"

It grinned, still so Kieren, but without that extra zing of pheromones, or whatever it was on guys that made girls go gaga when they smelled them, it was just a smile. "How did you know? The way we hugged you? I was paying attention; I had that down."

I shook my head, a small smile inching onto my face. "That'd be telling. How about you answer my questions, and I'll answer yours if I like the answer?"

"Now," it said in my voice, making me jerk.

"Yikes," Chet said.

"That'd be telling," it said. "And I'm not close to done with you yet." It melted away like cotton candy in the rain, disintegrating in front of us in bits so fast it was gone in a few seconds.

"Well, shit," Kieren said. "That was brilliant."

"Yep," I said. "Don't say what. It's probably still listening and if it tries that again, I'd like to be able to use that trick again."

"What if it turns into you or him again and reads his mind to figure out what it was?" Chet asked.

"Then hope it can't really read minds?"

"What now?" Faye asked. "I don't think it's gone. We can't leave the candles without its magic affecting us. And…"

"What?" I asked.

"The fog went away when I got the circle up, but it was still in here with us. In the circle and using magic. How? The candles either keep magic out or they don't."

"Good point," I said. "None of this makes sense. It turned a schitzo into a gunman, or pushed him and just watched from a front row seat. We don't know."

I took a deep breath. "Anyway, it was fine with killing then, and now it was in here, had us all covered, and all it did was take the form of one of us. Why? It could've killed us, taken off with us, basically had its way with us if it'd wanted while that fog was up."

"We're assuming something then," George said.

"What?" I asked.

He shook his head. "No clue. But if things aren't making sense, we're assuming something."

Chet opened his mouth, looked around and said to Faye, "I just realized we're surrounded by lawyers."

"You just realized that?" she asked, raising her eyebrows. "Let's get moving before they start debating."

"Move where?" I asked. "The thing's just hanging, it hasn't done anything to hurt us."

"Yet," George said, holding Daphnie closer.

"If it's responsible for the mad man in the hospital, I'd say it's trying to hurt us," Kieren said. "Whatever that was doing by impersonating me…" He wrinkled his forehead. "I don't know, but it was trying to pull something there."

"Annnnnd, that's why I said we needed to move," Faye said as I opened my mouth. "They'll argue this to death with that thing out there doing who knows what."

I shot her a look. "We're not that bad."

"Please. I spent how many Friday nights watching you three go at it your first year of law school?"

I looked at Kieren, eyes going to him like they were magnetized. "We did have some fun debates." Some fun other things too. I clapped my hands together and shook my head. "Oy. We know the thing is here, and it doesn't follow any magic rules we can tell."

"And it wants to mess with us," Chet said, full lips pursed like he was sucking a lemon and trying to hide it.

"What's with the face?" I asked.

"Holy." Faye muttered something under her breath and drew a symbol in the air, her face paler than usual. I didn't do Native American magic like she did, but I recognized it as one of her tradition's symbols.

I turned, following her wide eyes.

Black moved down the wall in a wave, like little droplets of water moving independently… and a little jerky.

Spiders. Little brownish ones. Hundreds of them. Faye whimpered. She was so arachnophobic she couldn't even see a clip from the movie.

"Oh, hell no!" I blasted the wall with the hottest fire my hands could conjure, frying the itty-bitty bastards.

The wall went up with a whoosh, sending smoke dancing in the air for real this time.

Reeee, reee, reee, the fire alarm screeched, making me clamp my hands over my ears and drop the flames. I pointed at it with a quick squirt of flames, flinching at the noise for a moment before it died with a last pathetic beep.

"Run!" George grabbed his frozen wife's arm and dragged her out of the bedroom.

I ran out with the boys behind me, Chet with his gun up and pointed back at the wall.

"Why'd it have to be spiders," he whispered, so quiet he probably thought I couldn't hear him.

I snuffed out the flames still dancing on the walls with a blink before they could eat the house, and Chet slammed the door behind us.

We thundered down the stairs after Faye's family.

"Where to?" I asked as we hit the living room.

George already had Daphnie's baby bag slung over his shoulder, and Faye clutched her box of magic items to her chest like a teddy bear.

"Out of the house, get away from this thing, regroup, go from there," George said, hints of his army days before law school crackling through. He shifted Daphnie to his other arm and nodded at us. "Move out."

Faye went first, getting the door. And stopped. She twisted and pushed, but the door didn't open.

"Faye?" I asked.

"I think we're trapped in here," she said, voice so light I had to strain to hear it.

"Okay, nobody panic," George said, squeezing his wife's shoulder.

"Who's panicking?" Faye asked, voice still high and squeaky as mine had gotten after she said Kieren was coming for the weekend.

"So we're trapped," I started, "and it's gone from cute and fluffy to turning the bedroom into a rap video, to-"

"Huh?" Kieren interrupted me.

"Fog machine," I said. "And then it turned into him, and scared the crap out of Faye. Why? There's no sense, no *reason*. It's like it just wants to cause trouble."

Faye's jaw dropped. "Oh my god. I think I know what it is. If I'm right, I know how to get rid of it!"

My heart jumped. *Finally* we were getting somewhere. "Share with the class."

Black walls like something out of a video game slammed up around Faye, George and Daphnie, and disappeared, taking the family with them so fast, I couldn't even blink before they were gone.

"Um," Chet said. "I'm guessing it didn't want her sharing with the class."

"Ya think!" I rubbed my arms. "If Faye knows what it is then theoretically I can figure it out." I searched my brain.

"You've got nothing, huh?" Chet asked.

"I've got bupkis. Actually, I've got what aspires to be bupkis when it grows up!"

Kieren looked around. "What now?"

"Until it attacks? We grab the books, Chet gets on the net, and we research, try to figure out what the hell this thing is."

"The hell I am is a bunny," the thing said in a cute, child-like voice.

I jumped and looked around. "Where are you?"

"What?" Chet asked.

"Oh god! Can you not perceive it again? This is getting old, Shadow."

"Shadow?" it asked.

"I figure you should have a name."

"That's so sweet of you. I figure you should have a scream." Its giggle ran down my spine like a loose bead of sweat, and I shivered.

"Only way I like my screams is with an orgasm," I said, flipping my hair off my shoulder and raising my eyebrows at the world. "And if you're offering, well, it's been a few months."

The black walls slammed up again.

Around me!

"NO!" I BIT DOWN ON the scream, taking a deep breath.

The world came back, and Kieren and I were in Faye's guest room.

"Ummmmm," I said, walking to the door. I turned the knob and of course it didn't give. I pulled on the door and nothing. I grabbed my phone out of my pocket and hit the on button. Of course it stayed dark and dead.

"It's separating us," Kieren said.

"Thank-you, Captain Obvious." I shook my head and shoved the phone back in my pocket. "Why? And why take groups of us?"

"Right now, it has Chet alone."

I met his eyes and the blood flowed out of my head so fast I slumped against the wall. Kieren rushed to my side and grabbed my arm a second later, and I gave him a weak smile.

Musk, cologne, and salty sex smells filled the room. Sexy man scent, only like it'd been bottled… and then the bottle had been shattered on the floor.

"Do you smell that?" he asked.

I nodded, licking my lips and breathing through my mouth.

"It's delicious," he said, licking his lips too. He looked around and I tried to breathe without tasting the air or smelling it. "It's like vanilla and something almost like a pie cooking."

I blinked. "Really? Smells like… well, kind of like you, and Chet. Smells like sex and man, and I'm getting turned on."

He met my eyes. "You did say you would take screaming with an orgasm. Maybe the bunny took you literally."

My stomach erupted with flutters like bats out of hell… or a brothel, and I lunged for the door, turning and pulling on the knob like… oh dear, even my thoughts were going down the gutter.

"We need to get out of here," I screamed. "Now!"

"Evie, breathe."

"That's exactly what I'm trying not to do."

"Nothing's going to happen." But his voice dropped, and the low notes tugged at things even lower in me.

"Really? Because right now I'm wet, and I can feel my vagina trying to crawl down my legs to get to you. If it makes it over there, toss it back."

He threw his head back and laughed. "Oh dear god, there's an image."

"I'm trying really hard to say things that could in no way be sexy."

He laughed again. "Mission accomplished. I don't know about you, but I'm not inclined to get it on even with the wonderful smells."

"Well I don't *want* to get it on." I took a deep breath and slapped a hand over my mouth as chocolate invaded it. "And now there's chocolate. What next? Oysters! Red wine? Oy vey, I'm giving it ideas."

"Evie." Kieren walked over and grabbed my shoulders.

His touch zinged through my body and my knees gave out. He held me against his chest, and I rubbed into him.

"Remember how you said I used to purr like a kitten?" I whispered. "Right now, my body wants to do that and a whole hell of a lot more."

He pushed me back to arm's length, erection obvious through his loose slacks. "Down girl. You're a prude, shouldn't you have more self-control than this?"

"I think something about being a prude makes me more vulnerable to this kind of attack actually. Makes it so I don't get some nearly as often as a slut, so I want it more."

"Maybe you should be more slutty."

"Says the whore of Salt Lake City," I said, trying to force some attitude into my voice.

His eyes widened. "I never took money, thank you very much."

"Sorry. I meant man-whore, aka a slut. Because you weren't particularly discerning about what you screwed. I'm surprised you just stuck to girls."

He blinked, confusion painting his pretty pretty face. "I think you're trying to insult me. I'm not sure why."

"So I can get us mad at each other and in no way feeling sexy or like we want to get it on. Because I'm this close to jumping you."

"Remember I dumped you right before finals, got married to the woman I left you for, and you told me tonight that back then you wanted to curse my penis."

I narrowed my eyes and growled. "Well *that* worked."

He spread his hands, grinning. "See?"

"Yeah, yeah, yeah." I froze. "Wait, I'm horny but I don't want to jump you. I'm fighting it." I grinned. "Kieren, I don't want you anymore! If I did, I would be rubbing up against you. I even have the perfect excuse for it. This stuff is better than alcohol for that. But I'm not. I don't want you!"

"Um, good?"

I danced in place. "Give me a second. I'm going to see if I can channel this energy into something productive." I shook out my hands and held them up, palms pointed at the door. I took a deep breath through my nose, letting the sex scents burn their way down my synapses and light the fuel under my fire.

I blasted the door and it went up in flames, smoking more than Bob Marley on holiday. Kieren backpedaled, coughing hard enough to make him shake. I kicked the door at the jam, powers protecting me from my flames, and it burst out in a cloud of smoke and cinder.

Kieren collapsed, and the bunny hopped on top of him like it was playing king of the hill.

"Nice," the bunny said. "I didn't even have to do anything to get that. You're *fun!*" He disappeared with Kieren.

"No! What do you want!" I yelled before running out the door, flicking my wrist to smother the flames. I ran downstairs, and Chet threw his hands up at the bottom of the stairs when he saw me.

"What is that thing pulling now?" he asked. "Wait. How do I know you're you?"

"Right back at ya," I said, waving him over. "Hug me."

He wrapped me in his arms, hugging me harder than a kid leaving his stuffed animal behind on the first day of kindergarten. I took a deep breath, sucking in the scent of man that smelled a lot like what was going on upstairs, just more natural.

"Unless he caught on, you're you," I said.

"Yeah." Chet rubbed my back, keeping me pinned against him. "But I want to make sure. Where did you go?"

"Bedroom. He threw me and Kieren in there and apparently was trying to get us to sleep together."

That made him let me go, but he grabbed my arms on the way out. "What!"

"Calm down. Nothing happened, but the bunny took off with Kieren after he collapsed... I'm assuming from the smoke, but I don't think it'd take him out that fast. *What* is going on?"

"This is getting old."

"Yeah. And I'm getting pissed."

The air in front of the couch swirled with blue sparkles like a water whirlwind in a kids' book. A man not much taller than me and so slender you just knew he got beat up as a kid stepped out of the whooshing thing and blinked at me.

"Evie Jones," he said in a thick South Boston accent, sighing and shaking his head. "I should've known if anyone was going to give me trouble this week, it'd be a Jones. I'm the Council representative."

There weren't enough curse words in the English and Yiddish languages for this.

THE MAN WALKED TOWARDS CHET. "And you are?"

I jumped, moving to his side so fast the man flailed his arms in weak defense. I grabbed him by the shoulders and thrust him into the wall.

"We need to know you're real and not that shadow thing," I said, voice stone cold calm. "I suggest you hold still."

His eyes were wide behind his glasses and he nodded. "You're stronger than you look."

I shrugged. "I'm sexy, I know it."

The bafflement on his face was priceless, and it just got better as Chet burst out laughing.

"Huh?" the rep asked.

"She works out," Chet said.

"I don't get it."

"You don't need to," I said. "What's your name?"

"Ryan O'Shay."

I raised my eyebrows, looking him up and down. "You're a little dark for somebody named O'Shay."

He scowled at me. "African mother, Irish father. Can we *please* move this along?"

I could see it. The full lips and skull tight curly hair were paired with light blue eyes and delicate features you got from the Irish.

"How'd you know my name?" I asked.

"We get dossiers on everyone in the coven we're visiting. And they point out the troublemakers for us to memorize. You and your father are in the top ten to pay extra attention to."

So much for thinking I was keeping a low profile. I growled under my breath and pulled out my pocket knife, slashing a slit no deeper than a paper cut on his arm.

He yelped and jerked away as ice slapped my hands down with bitter sting. Of course he was a water witch. Just my luck.

I glanced at Chet. He opened his mouth and I shook my head slightly, bulging my eyes at him.

Don't say anything. Don't give away you're a human. Please understand this and shut up.

He looked confused but kept his mouth shut.

I sighed and turned back to our *guest*. Blood as red and thick as normal welled up, and he held his hand over the cut. The skin grew over it like a fast-timed video of a wound healing and a few seconds later it was a day-old scab.

"Wow," I said. "How'd you do that?"

"I'm a doctor. If you understand the mechanisms the body uses to heal, you can figure out what processes to turn on to increase the healing process. It gets easier the more you practice, so I practice whenever I get the chance."

Or you're the damn bunny thing with a ton of magic to burn.

If only there was some way to tell Chet the trick with the knife wouldn't prove anything, and I was doing it to distract the man in case he really was with the Council.

"That's probably smart," I said. "But not right now. You're going to need all your magic. We all are. We've been trapped in here by some kind of shadow demon or something, with way too much magic and no apparent motive. It's gone between terrifying us, to taking some of us somewhere, to trying to seduce us."

"What do you mean too much magic?"

"He got into the house, past the barriers without an invite, no problem. He's gotten past drawn circles, changed shapes, teleported us, turned on who can perceive him when, made spiders come out of the wall, made a room smell really strong and different to different people. And he's not even breaking a little shadow sweat. What is this thing?"

O'Shay shook his head, eyes so big they looked like they'd pop out of his skull. "I don't know. Anything with that much power… I can't begin to guess."

"Well you're a ton of help. I'm *soooo* glad you came here to rescue us. I'm going to do a locator spell and find the others. Then you're getting us out of here. Save your magic for that. Got it?"

"You're not in charge here, Evie."

"We don't know each other. I'm Ms. Jones or just Jones to you." I grinned as he flinched. "Yeahhhhh, I know you old school putzes. You're not going to disrespect me or treat me like a child," I said more for Chet's benefit. "And I know I'm not in charge. That bunny thing is. Have you realized that yet? Give it a minute. I'm sure it'll pop back up."

I left off the, *Unless it's you.*

The bunny hopped out of the couch, landing in front of O'Shay. "Oh, a new plaything. It smells funny." It looked over its shoulder and winked at me.

Great, it'd caught on. I smiled sweetly and pulled out my gun, triple tapping the little jerk. The rounds went straight through it with the zing of suppressed bullets, thudding into the carpet, leaving wispy holes in the bunny's hide.

O'Shay dove behind the couch, a second too late if he'd thought I was going for him, and poked his head over it.

"Worth a shot," I said, the snort threatening to bubble up my throat in panicked giggles. "He's Council, play with him." I jerked my head at

O'Shay.

"That could be fun. They have so many rules. So many rules to *break!*" The bunny disappeared.

O'Shay met my eyes. "Ms. Jones, I believe I will defer to your expertise in troublemaking here."

Expertise? Me? I shrugged. "Okay. Keep an eye out for that thing while I try locating the others."

"How many are there?"

"Three adults and a baby. The human was knocked out near the beginning, no clue what's going on. But the bunny took off with him so who knows what's happening to him now."

"That's the only human here?"

"Yep," I said. "Well, the baby's not a witch yet, but she's two and she will be." I shrugged, struggling to keep my face blasé. I never was a great poker player. I pointed at him. "I mean it when I say keep an eye out. We have no clue what this thing could throw at us next."

He nodded, looking at Chet. "What type are you?"

Chet didn't even bat an eye. "My strongest magic's in my Indian heritage, and I'm an earth witch."

I bit back a grin. Smart boy. His doctoral dissertation was on ancient Indian religions. If there was anything he'd be able to pull off, it was Indian.

"What type of Indian? Cherokee?"

Chet looked down his nose at the little man. "That's Native American. I'm India Indian."

"Ohhhh. Any chance this is something from your tradition?"

Chet shook his head. "It could be a lot of things. But nothing I can say for sure covers what this thing is doing. Maybe a Rakshasa, one of Ravenna's creatures. But there's no record of them in real life, just human mythology."

My heart fluttered. Damn, he was *good*.

"My magic's drained," Chet continued. "I've got guns and knives, but they're not much use with this thing. I can help you look out, but I hope you've got more juice than you're showing."

"I do," O'Shay said, not arrogant, just fact.

Couldn't worry about that now. I closed my eyes and held up my hands, feeling out the world like I had at the hospital. Hard to believe that's where this all started. It seemed like months ago and not days. The world sparkled like onyx in my mind and I opened my eyes.

"Everything's drowning in magic right now," I said. "I can't differentiate anything."

"Then we look the human way," O'Shay said. "It's not a big house judging by the size of the living room."

"But that's only if they didn't get taken outside the house," Chet said.

I flinched. Hadn't let myself consider that possibility. Hadn't let myself consider the other, very probable possibility either.

Faye wasn't dead. I'd feel it.

"So, we check the house and if they're not here, we work on getting out. Figure it out from there."

"Can we call in reinforcements?" Chet asked. "He got inside, others should be able to, too."

"I can't get out," O'Shay said. "I tried."

"I already tried the phone upstairs," I said. "Not working."

"Why is the phone always not working?" Chet asked.

We shared a smile and O'Shay's head went back and forth between us. "This has happened before?" he asked.

"Water demon sicced on me by Faye's ex," I said.

"And you didn't report it!"

"Oy! I didn't know guys' voices could get that high without a knee to the balls. And no. The water demon killed him for us, saved us the paperwork."

His mouth worked. "You're supposed to report all magical attacks!"

"Really? You want to bust my balls about that *now*? Really?"

A sprinkle of something hit my shoulder and I wiped it away. Water? I followed the trickle up and a line ran through the ceiling, like walls damaged from a water main in the bathroom. *What the?*

The ceiling came down and I screamed, covering my head and running.

CHET GRABBED ME BY MY arms and pulled me into his chest and under the winding metal stairs for protection from the worst of it.

It didn't help.

Water poured out of the ceiling like someone put in a waterfall feature, and the water rushed through the living room, filling it faster than physically possible. It hit my ankles, was suddenly up to my knees, and then my waist. I pushed away from Chet, swimming backwards to the kitchen.

And hit a wall.

I turned, resting my hand on the air like a mime in an invisible box.

"Oh, hell no!" I screamed, bringing my hands up and slogging a few feet. "Get behind me, boys, it's about to get hot in here."

My heart raced and I used the fear to fuel the fire as I shot it out of my palms, hitting the water with as much heat as I could muster without passing out. The water steamed and hissed where the flames hit it, and I gritted my teeth, pouring more of myself into it, making the water sizzle and steam.

"Evie!" Chet grabbed me from behind, forcing my hands down. "Stop

116

it!"

"We're going to drown!" I fought against his arms, thrashing and bucking. "Stop the water."

Chet whirled me around and pulled me into him, kissing me so fast my arms were still up against his chest.

The kiss went from hard and panicked to soft as I sunk into it, and Chet pulled back too soon, looking me in the eyes when mine slid open.

"Okay, good, that worked," Chet said, grinning. "Evie, there's no water."

"What?" I turned, looking around the living room. The couch, chairs, TV, assorted toys, and books on their shelves were all perfectly dry, but a little singed. "Um. There was water. If the ceiling didn't collapse, why did you grab me and pull me under the stairs?"

His eyes widened. "I didn't."

O'Shay peaked his head over the side of the couch. "Is she done?"

"I think so," I said. "None of that happened? I imagined it?"

"All we saw was you scream, run, and start shooting fire at the living room. O'Shay put it out and was trying to talk to you, to get through to you."

I took a deep breath and smiled thin and tight at O'Shay. "Thanks for not assuming I was attacking you and attacking back."

"Based on what you've told me, I could tell you were seeing something and panicking, and figured this thing would think it funny to turn us against each other. Especially with your dislike of the Council."

I looked down, biting my lip. "Mr. O'Shay, you just proved by not assuming I was attacking you that you're not all douchebags looking for any excuse to throw witches in Oz. Some of you might have a brain. Thank you."

He drew his eyebrows together, making his forehead wrinkle up. "You're welcome, and I *think* there was a compliment to me buried somewhere in there."

I nodded. "Somewhere. You'll have to dig for it." He smiled at that. "Okay, so this thing can make us full on hallucinate. Technically right now this conversation could be fake then."

"How do we tell?" Chet asked.

I shook my head. "This just got a hell of a lot scarier because we can't. Faye said she knew what it was and how to get rid of it right before she disappeared. That means it's something on the books."

"Any clue?" I asked O'Shay.

"Fear demon again?" Chet asked.

"I don't think so," O'Shay and I said as one. We looked at each other and I grinned, waving at him to continue.

"It has gone after fears. But it's also done other things that, as far as I can tell, have nothing to do with fear."

"Something that feeds on emotions?" I asked. "It's tried fear and lust, but that doesn't explain it mimicking one of us. Well, confusion's an emotion. Right?" I rubbed my forehead. "I'm sorry, emotions aren't my thing, and I'm getting a headache. Someone help me out."

"We're forgetting what started all this," Chet said. "The hospital."

"Whoa." O'Shay waved a hand. "What happened at what hospital? Something happened before it came to the house?"

Chet and I looked at each other. He raised his eyebrows.

I widened my eyes and shook my head, a bare vibration.

"Oh, it's going to be like that?" O'Shay said. "I saw that. What are you hiding?"

I shook my head at him.

"It could help. It's my turn to say you're going to bust my balls right now? Really?" O'Shay flung his hands up. "I'm trying to help. I'm not the enemy."

"Yeah, but you kind of are," I said.

"Did you do something illegal?"

"I plead the fifth."

"We don't have the fifth amendment in our government."

"Or much of any rights once someone's accused. Which is why I'm keeping my mouth shut." I grinned at him, big and cheeky, my heart pounding so hard I was afraid it was going to pop a gasket.

"Let's say anything you tell me is off the record. I want out of here. Mostly because this thing hasn't singled me out yet, and it's probably about to."

"Evie?" Chet said.

"I can't trust the whole story with a Council rep, I'm sorry," I said, holding up a finger to cut O'Shay's open mouth off. "But, I can tell you the important part of it. Did you hear about the shooting at the university hospital the other day?"

"I think I heard something on the news. No one was killed besides the shooter, right?"

"Yeah. We're the ones who took out the shooter. I thought I saw the black shadow bunny jump out of the guy's head. Just assumed I was seeing things... from the stress."

"Oooookay." O'Shay squinted at me.

"That's the relevant part," I said.

O'Shay crossed his arms and gave me a long look.

"I think it followed us home," I said, freezing. "No. Because I was in the hospital with the migraine. Chet, you went home. We didn't come here for two days. So why...?"

"It followed Kieren back here?" Chet asked. "And then waited for all of us to be together again?"

"Technically it could have followed any of us and just waited for all of us to be together. But that begs the question of why again. It keeps separating us. Why not just go after us one by one before tonight?"

Chet shrugged. "Besides the fact that it's playing us off each other and we're apparently entertaining. It's like throwing dogs in a cage and waiting to see who fights, who fucks, and who becomes friends."

"The more you throw in there, the more possibilities. In chemistry the molecules with more atoms are considered to have more entropy because of the greater amount of pos... Oh dear goddess!" I slammed my palm to my forehead. "It's an entropy!"

O'Shay's mouth fell open. "That's why there's no obvious pattern or motive."

"It explains everything." I ticked them off on my fingers. "The power levels, attacking one minute and seducing the next, splitting us up, confusing us then terrifying us."

"Not killing any of you."

"The gunman not killing anyone else."

"It coming after *you* specifically."

"Hey! I am not that bad."

"You're practically an anarchist."

"Oh please, those are basically political hippies." I waved my finger at him. "I'm a libertarian. There's a huge difference. It means I believe in individual rights *and* bathing every day."

Chet's head bounced between us and his mouth worked like it was killing him not to ask.

"How do we get rid of it?" I asked. "Faye knew so it swiped her."

O'Shay shook his head, closing his eyes. "Ummmm."

I looked around, hand on my gun even though it wouldn't do me much good.

"What are you looking for?" O'Shay asked.

"That thing to come back. Now that we've figured it out, I'm assuming it's going to pop up and do something to us again. It's been letting us talk for a while."

"Maybe it's tormenting the others right now," Chet said.

"That's a cheery thought," I said.

"Why don't you run through what you know about them?" Chet asked. "Maybe it'll shake things loose."

I held back a smile. Bright boy. "Entropies were this myth about creatures between realities that could slip in through a hole in reality and feed on chaos.

"Until about ten years ago when actual documented cases started popping up all over the world, meaning around that time, somebody did something to rip a hole in reality, and at least one of them got through.

"So every once in a while, a little being that feeds on chaos pops up, causes problems, usually a lot of problems, but doesn't really kill anyone because people are more fun and have a lot more potential for entropy if they're alive because of the millions of different choices people make every day."

I looked at O'Shay. "Any of this sparking anything?"

He shook his head and closed his eyes. "There's something on the edge of my brain. I just can't catch it."

"All I've got is try to trap it, but I don't think we can."

"They thrive on chaos, so maybe impose some order?" Chet asked.

I shook my head. "No. If we're able to make decisions, able to react, it'll still have stuff to feed on. We have to figure out how to get it out of our reality."

"We could knock ourselves out so it has nothing to feed off of, gets bored and leaves," O'Shay said. "But then we'd have a problem of it going after other people. Possibly exposing magic."

"How have witches dealt with them in the past?" I asked.

"That's what I'm trying to remember. I know at least two cases where the witches put themselves under a sleeping spell, and the thing got bored and wandered off."

"Not an option," I said. "We can't risk it going after innocent people."

"Or exposing magic," Chet said, shooting me a smile.

I grinned and nodded. "Or that."

"There's another account where the witch moved the entropy back out of this reality, but I can't even begin to figure out how to get it to go through a hole."

My head snapped up. "But you know how to rip a hole in reality?"

"Yes. We had a seminar last year."

Chet shot him a look, but was smart enough not to ask.

"The one in Boston?" I asked. He nodded, and I snapped my fingers. "*That's* how Faye knew. She went to that. Okay, you open it, I'll get him out."

"How?"

"Not going to say it out loud because I'm betting he's listening."

"Wouldn't he want to go home?" Chet asked.

"No. I think we're far more entertaining for it than whatever darkness is outside reality," I said. "O'Shay, get the spell ready, I'll set the bait."

"OKAY," O'SHAY SAID, SITTING AT the kitchen table. "It's ready when you are."

I looked around the kitchen. The entropy had left us alone for over fifteen minutes. Made me think he was either contending with the others, or found us trying to get rid of him too entertaining to interrupt, and was watching with a little shadow smirk.

Chet watched from the archway leading from the kitchen to the living room, keeping his mouth shut and his eyes open. After years of studying other cultures, he knew to learn the most, you watched and listened.

So far, O'Shay didn't suspect a thing, thank the goddess. He hadn't even asked Chet's last name to look him up later. And since Chet was obviously a nickname, he wouldn't even be able to look on the registry and figure out Chet wasn't a witch if no one with that first name was there.

"Now what?" O'Shay asked, hands on his bowl. The dough inside was supposed to act almost like dynamite, splitting the reality open for a few seconds into the nothingness outside realities where entropies were born.

"I kind of expected the entropy to attack by now," I said. "He's being awfully quiet. But give me a second, and turn around."

"Why?" O'Shay asked, face closing off, suspicion building behind his eyes.

"Because I'm going to try to get the bunny out, and I don't want you to see me when I do." I raised my eyebrows and O'Shay blushed, turning around.

"Do you need me to-?" Chet asked.

"No," I cut him off. "I need you for this to work. Need you to be surprised too."

I unbuttoned my top and Chet gulped. "What are you doing?" he asked, voice as raspy as a man staring at water after a day on the salt flats.

"Trust me." I flicked the buttons open, slowly, letting my fingers linger on the shirt once it was undone, and Chet's eyes followed them up, past my stomach and to my breasts as I shrugged the top off, keeping a hold of it.

My red lace bra was meant to be seen, and I'd worn it to feel pretty tonight since I was seeing the guys, same reason I'd wore the silk eastern design shirt, but now I was glad I'd worn them both for completely different reasons as I unhooked the bra and let it fall down my arms and to the floor.

Chet stared at my chest and stepped closer, slow and jerky, like he was moving against his will, a bug drawn to light he was pretty sure would zap him but he couldn't stay away.

"Evie, what are you doing?" Chet's voice shook.

"Causing chaos," I whispered.

The bunny jumped between us, wiggling his tail puff and practically vibrating with excitement.

"O'Shay!" I yelled.

O'Shay whirled and threw the dough on the ground in front of me, barely missing the bunny.

Grrrrrrrrrrr, the world growled, shaking open at the seams. Cold winds of nothingness blew through the kitchen, and the rip in the floor glowed around the edges, showing darkness so complete it was the true representation of nothing, dark so complete light couldn't escape. A black hole without the gravitational pull.

I tossed one end of my shirt at Chet and he caught the long sleeve.

"What?" Chet asked, eyes flying wide. "Evie, no!"

"Put those big, strong arms to good use," I said, jumping into the hole. The bunny came after me a second before all I could see was the absolute darkness. I couldn't feel, see, smell. Rumbling met my ears, the only thing to keep me sane. There wasn't time out here. There wasn't anything.

Black hole, rippled through my brain. Fear boiled under my skin and my stomach lurched as sensation like something pounding through my entire body took me over, almost like a giant penis beating into a tunnel going from my groin to my brain.

I fell on my knees to the kitchen floor, the overhead lights blinding and harsh. The silk shirt I'd magically enhanced not to rip while O'Shay worked on his spell clutched in my hands. Chet grinned down at me and dropped to his knees, releasing the shirt and hugging me so tight I couldn't breathe.

"He's not a witch!" the bunny's voice came through the rip right before it snapped shut.

"What!" O'Shay yelped.

I pulled away from Chet and jumped to my feet, pulling out my gun and getting between the man and Chet before he could get his hands up.

Suddenly being topless in front of guys didn't seem like such a big deal.

"Freeze," I said. "So much as blink or say a syllable of a spell, and I'll shoot you."

"You know the rules. I'll erase his memory of tonight, he'll b-"

"You don't know what kind of brain damage that could cause. I get you're a doctor, so you're probably pretty good, but still, no one knows enough about the brain to tell exactly where memories are stored."

"Ms. Jones, I promise you, just taking out tonight-" He froze. "He knew about witches before this. You said you were attacked before." His mouth hardened and he looked at Chet.

I put my finger on the trigger and pointed the gun dead center on his chest. "I won't let you kill my friend."

"He knows about us!"

"And he hasn't told anyone. What does that tell you?"

"You know the rules."

"Goddess, stop saying that! *Fuck the rules!* You're the only one who knows. I kill you, or you sign a blood oath swearing you won't tell anyone that he knows."

"Blood oath?" Chet asked, almost too quiet to hear over the crackling of blood rushing to my brain.

"Forces you to keep your word," I said.

"Then have me sign one saying I won't tell anyone about you."

"Only works on witches," O'Shay said before flicking his eyes back to me. "You kill me and you'll have the entire Council combing your city looking for you."

"I'm not so sure about that." I shrugged. "I'm pretty good at making up evidence, false trails. Watched a lot of CSI type shows, so I can at least confuse them, make 'em think the bunny did it. They already knew something was off. Something powerful was attacking, right? You must've told them before you came to investigate."

He didn't answer, and I grinned. It couldn't possibly look as nasty as it felt. "That's what I thought."

"You're bluffing."

I met his eyes over my barrel. "You really think I have a problem killing you? You're Council. You started out as the enemy. I've been trusting you because you seemed like you were here to help, but now? You're back to being the enemy."

His fingers wiggled by his sides, barely visible and far too fast.

"Down!" I screamed, taking a shot before diving to the side behind the stairs.

Water crashed through the metal spiral stairs, blasting me in the face with the force of a speedboat shooting water behind it. I put my hands up, pushing out a weak shield.

We'd already been going against this thing for a while, how were we going to manage to take out a powerful witch from the Council? I'd been practicing battle magic since I was attacked by a zombie over a year ago, but that didn't mean I had the know how or juice to take on a Council member.

"Evie!" Chet's back appeared in front of me, and I took a deep breath as the water cut off. It sprayed around his body and moved up to his face as he protected me from the spray. He turned his head to the side and put his hands up in weak defense, but stayed steady even as his thick lips twisted in pain. "Light him up, girl!"

I popped out from behind the stairs with my gun up, trying to see through the water clogging my eyes.

O'Shay pulled up a shimmer in the air before I squeezed off the first shot, and the bullet hit a shield in mid-air, falling to the ground harmless.

"Where's a rifle with a fifty-round drum when you need one?" I said, ducking behind Chet. "Chet, down!"

He went down to his knees and I got one shot through the water before the wave hit my face with the force of a firehose and I flew back, smacking into the wall.

Chet pulled out his gun and squeezed off a shot from the bottom step. The roar of the water filled my ears, but even I heard the deafening pop from an unsuppressed gun.

If one of us had hit him, O'Shay wouldn't have been able to keep it up. I brought my hands up and flung fire out like I had when the bunny made me see the water. Only this time, everything was real. And O'Shay would kill Chet just as easily as the bunny had tormented us.

Fear clenched my heart and I pulled it up, shooting it out of my hands, willing flames hotter than I'd ever pulled off. The water attack fell off as steam filled the room, and Chet got up and rushed across the living room with speed usually reserved for sprinters, or at least football players when they were that big. Chet slammed the slender man to the ground, and I ran around the stairs just in time for O'Shay to magically fling Chet across the room.

Chet hit the flatscreen over the fireplace, cracking it like a boulder in a windshield. He dropped his gun and fell to the ground, barely catching himself with his hands and knees to keep his head from slamming into the floor.

The TV creaked a warning, and Chet scrambled out of the way as the monstrosity George insisted he had to have because *sports*, crashed to the tile in front of the fireplace.

The TV sizzled and sparked, and Chet rolled over, gasping as he stared at the thousand dollars' worth pile of rubble.

I looked over, and O'Shay stared at the scene wide-eyed, trained for violence but probably never actually in it. He was an investigator and a doctor.

"O'Shay," I said slowly, "I got an entropy out of here tonight. That'd earn me a Merlin under normal circumstances. The least you could do for me is take the credit for this in exchange for not telling anyone about Chet."

His mouth dropped. "You'd hand over your claim to a *Merlin*? You could ride that for favors for years."

"Yeah, and it can be yours for the low, low price of my friend's life. Say you got here, that thing was tormenting me. Everyone else was locked away, you saved my ass, and figured out how to get rid of it. I'm out of magic. You could kill Chet now. But you will spend the rest of your very short life looking over your shoulder for me."

"You can't beat me."

"Not in a fair fight, no. But I'm a woman, O'Shay. I don't give a *shit* about fair play, letting you taste fear before I kill you, or any of that honor *bullshit*. I care about winning. And I will put you and anyone who happens to be in the building I bomb, or in the way of a sniper's bullet, or anything else I will come up with to kill you from far *far* away, in the ground."

O'Shay paled, freckles showing through the light brown skin. "I could kill you, right now."

A smirk I knew was as ugly as it felt graced my face. "You could try. But wouldn't that be going against your precious rules? Can't kill a helpless witch who's not presenting an immediate danger."

"I could make an exception."

My hand curled around my gun tighter. I had one bullet left, and maybe two seconds to aim and shoot before he could put up a shield again. Chet had more in his gun, though. He'd maybe have a fighting chance if he were fast enough or I distracted O'Shay enough.

"No, you can't," Faye said.

My head snapped around so fast my neck popped. She stood on the stairs, the guys and baby nowhere in sight. She'd probably told them to stay wherever they were stashed until we cleared the Council rep out of here.

"I'm a highly respected member of the Salt Lake Representatives to the Council," Faye said.

She walked down, crossing her arms and fixing O'Shay with her mommy stare. "The Joneses may have a reputation that'd mean not many on the Council would care to look into her death. But my word is gold. I will testify you killed her when she was helpless and out of magic, and did it to take credit for her getting the entropy out of here. And if you kill her, you'll have the entire Jones clan quite literally gunning for you."

"You won't live through making an enemy of me or my family, O'Shay," I said. "*Or* you can take the deal and be a hero."

"I'll take door number two," he said, so fast I bet he would've agreed to it before Faye reminded him I had family who'd take his pansy ass down.

Three sighs hissed through the air, and I nodded. "I'll draw up the contract. Pleasure doing business with you."

"OH MY GOD," KIEREN SAID, taking a gulp of whiskey and shaking his head as he put it down on the table. "That's… how did I miss that!"

"Passing out from forgetting to eat and your insulin pump shorting out probably had something to do with it," I said, shaking my head right back at him. Chet rubbed my knee under the table and I rested my head on his shoulder.

"I was a little preoccupied," Kieren said. "What with the killer shadow bunny and everything."

I snorted. "There's really no way to say that without sounding sarcastic, is there?"

"No," Faye said, sitting next to me and resting her head in her hands. "Kieren, pour me some whiskey, please."

He poured her a shot, and without looking up she said, "More."

"She faced spiders tonight," I said. "Give her a triple... hell, a quadruple."

"Yes ma'am." Kieren poured enough whiskey to make an elephant happy and put the glass in front of Faye before sitting next to her and rubbing her arm.

"So you guys were in the baby's room the whole time?" I asked.

"Yeah, had us trapped. I could tell when he was gone because the spiders swarming my baby and husband disappeared, and they were fine and staring at me. Said I'd been hallucinating the whole time, and they couldn't get me out of it or get the door open. I'm surprised you didn't hear me screaming."

"Bunny probably kept us from hearing it," I said.

"Yeah." Faye's hands shook as she wrapped them around the whiskey and took a long drag.

My eyebrows shot up. "Oy. Normally you have to have a can of Coke for one shot."

"Tonight's not normal," Faye said, voice rough and straggly. "Whooooo! That's making my eyes water."

"Whiskey will do that," Chet said. "I've got to ask, what's a Merlin?"

"Merlin Medal," Faye and I said as one.

"It's like the Medal of Honor for witches," I said. "You flash it to a member of the Council, it's a free pass for small infractions. Maybe even big ones. You get favors, drinks, premade spells and potions. It's a sign to all the other witches that you either did something amazing and earned it, or, as is more and more common these days, you know somebody high up in the Council who gave you one for being a friend... or really good at sucking dick."

Kieren's mouth hung open in what I used to call his duck mouth because his lips went out when he did it like a ducky's. "I can't believe that just came out of your mouth."

Chet put his arm around me and I pointed over my shoulder at him. "I blame him. Bad influence."

Chet snuggled up to my neck, nuzzling it. "How about we let these guys go to bed, go back to your place and I be a really bad influence?"

I blushed and Faye managed a small smile as I looked at her. "Go, I'm okay."

"You're traumatized."

She nailed me with her mommy look. "I've got George upstairs ready to take care of me, and Kieren to back him up. I'll live. Go get yours."

Kieren chuckled, grinning.

I frowned at him. "Do I want to know?"

"No," he said. "I just... I want you to be happy and from what I've seen tonight, he's a good guy. He'll be good for you."

"That's kind of a creepy. This you giving us your blessing thing," I said.

"Evie." Kieren met my eyes, "I want you to be happy, and I know after me you didn't really trust guys, so take it from someone who admittedly was a dick to you. He's a good guy."

"Thanks man." Chet held up his hand and they fist bumped.

I looked between them. "You two bonded while I was unconscious at the hospital, didn't you?"

Chet nodded and Kieren shrugged and I shook my head.

"Faye?" I asked. "Am I being crazy here?"

"No, telling him you wanted to be friends when you didn't was crazy. Go, be happy. Get yours."

I blushed. "Are you sure you're going to be okay?"

"I swear, I'm good." She toasted us with her glass before taking another gulp. "Whooooo! Yeah, I'll live. You go do the same."

I stood, taking Chet's hand and he climbed to his feet. "Yes ma'am."

PART VI. EVIE JONES
AND THE ROCKY ROULETTE

"IT'S MY PLEASURE TO BURN," I said in a low growl, leveling my gun at my captive's chest.

"Damn, that's creepy coming from you," Chet said from behind me. "Why aren't you shooting him?"

Dr. Wolf kept his hands up, gun useless at his feet, eyes bouncing between us. Poor goof dropped it when I got the drop on him.

"We're taking him prisoner," I said.

"There are no prisoners in paintball, Evie," Chet said, walking past me, the plastic mask over his face not obscuring the giant grin.

I giggled. "There are when I play."

"I'm pretty sure he's right," Wolf said, light Serbian accent coloring the words. "It's not in the rules. You shoot, you get points; you get shot, you're out of the game. You get extra points for capturing the other teams' flags. Team with the most points at the end of the game wins. That's it."

I shrugged. "Says who? Not like there's a ref during paintball games."

Wolf snorted. "No wonder my wife likes you."

"Oh yeah, we love your wife up at the med center. Won't stop me from shooting you though. Chet, grab his arms, tie them behind his back with your belt."

Wolf grinned, shaking his head. "I *know* that's against the rules."

"I'm still fuzzy on why we're taking him prisoner," Chet said, pulling the belt off his camouflage suit.

"We're going to put him up on the bandstand in the middle of our territory with a sign, wait for the geologists to come investigate, half of us will ambush them and the other half will go into their territory and look for their flag."

"You are so sexy when you're diabolical," Chet said, tying up the doctor.

"Why were you quoting Bradbury?" Wolf asked.

"Our team's motto," I said, pumping the fist on my free hand. "Go Anthro-Fires."

We frog marched Wolf back to our side of the field. I sent a text explaining the plan to the rest of our team once we were safely under cover in our team's shed. The sheds were the home bases for teams, where they couldn't be shot… if everyone was following the rules at least.

"What makes you think putting Dr. Wolf up on a platform will make the geologists come for him?" Kane texted back. "I know this is faux-war, but I don't see people coming to rescue their Captain."

"I'm going to piss them off with a little help from Sheldon Cooper," I said out loud as I wrote it. "I think they'll at least want to come close enough to see, and get offended."

We put Wolf up on the platform and Chet covered me while I shot my gun on the giant slab of wood behind him to paint out a message.

We backed up once we were all ready and Chet burst out laughing, bumping me with his arm. "You are way too hot to be this dorky."

I snorted. I'd written, "Geology isn't a real science! Love Sheldon Cooper."

"TO EVIE, AND HER ABILITY to piss people off as only a lawyer can," Kane raised his drink over the table and his girlfriend Mandy giggled.

I held up my martini. Hey, it was five o'clock somewhere, and it was a weekend. "To beating the Geology, BioChem, Computer Science, and Physics departments in the U's fifth annual Science Bowl."

"To hot guns and the hotter women that shoot them," Chet said.

"Hear, hear," our team said, clinking glasses. Mandy and I grinned at each other. As the only girls on the team of ten, we knew who they were talking about. Even with scars lining half her face from being thrown off my dad's roof last Halloween, she was still beautiful.

To compete, the departments had to put together teams of ten with at least two girls. The Anthropology guys were led by their department head, Dr. Kane, who got a few other professors and doctoral candidates and filled out the group with one of the girl TA's husbands, me and Mandy. Apparently none of the women in the department wanted to run around on the field in the March chill, getting dirty and sweaty with the boys and getting shot with paintballs.

Didn't make sense to me. Paintball was a blast! As long as you didn't get shot by the other side. Those things *hurt*.

"Oh sure, rub it in," Wolf said, smiling wide and sweet. He and his wife Rose joined us for lunch, hard feelings nonexistent once the game was over.

"I still can't believe you tied my husband to a pole out in the open like that," Rose said, shaking her head. "You are a cold woman, Evie Jones."

"What?" I grinned. "The other teams were too confused to shoot at him. He wasn't even hurt."

She leaned over and kissed her husband before giving me a wink. "If they had, I could've patched him up. I would've still been pissed."

Rose was a dermatology attending at the University of Utah Med Center where I worked as an assistant privacy officer. I'd hated the job when I first got it because it was a step down from my past job as an assistant general counsel, but I'd met some truly awesome people working at the university.

"I am fine, lovely," Wolf stroked his wife's cheek, staring at her so intently it made me grin. "I would not object to being treated by my *doctor* tonight, though."

Rose and I both blushed and I turned to look at Chet. He took my hand, kissing the knuckles.

"I still need a cute pet name for you," Chet said. "How do you feel about marshmallow snuggle monkey?"

I burst out laughing and shook my head. "Way too long."

"Well I-"

Clink clink clink clink clink, the glasses clattered on the table as one. I jerked my hands away and stood up so fast I knocked my chair over. The table vibrated, shaking the drinks and plates of bread. Drinks fell and the others scrambled back from the table.

"Under the table," Wolf said, pulling his wife down. Chet and I followed, scuttling under.

The earthquake shook the world for a few seconds and crashes thundered through the restaurant.

I peeked out when the earth calmed, and it didn't look like too much damage, some broken glasses and plates, a mess sure, but nothing terrible.

Corey's cell phone went off near me and I looked at him. He was the husband of the girl TA. I couldn't remember her name since she never hung out with us. He was also a detective.

A detective's phone going off was about as bad as a doctor's.

I grabbed it off the floor and tossed it to him. He caught it midair on his knees.

"Yes sir?" He nodded a few times, muttered a few more, "Yes sirs," and hit the phone to turn it off.

"What it is?" I asked. "Did the earthquake cause more damage somewhere? Wait, there's no way they'd be able to get to the scene of whatever this fast."

He shook his head, eyes switching back and forth across the floor like he was in REM sleep. "No."

So why did he look so horrified?

"We have a dead body. He was found in his office at the U about an hour ago… still wearing his paintball suit."

I grabbed my necklace and a hand rested on my shoulder. I didn't have to look back to know it was Chet's. "Who?"

"Sean Quart." Corey's voice broke and he looked just south of my eyes, not enough to hide the shimmer over his. My heart sank.

No.

"Oh god," Chet said. "Man…"

"Do we know him?" Rose asked.

"He's one of Corey's best friends," I said when Corey didn't answer. "He's a friend… *was* a friend of a lot of us in this group. Paintball, poker, drinks after work. He fixed my car last month. Corey, you can't investigate your buddy's death."

"They don't want me to investigate," he said, voice even and flat as a pancake. "They want me to identify the body, if I can."

"If you can?" Rose asked.

Corey looked up with empty eyes. "He said he's missing his face and hands."

"YOU CAN'T COME INTO AN active crime scene," Corey said as we followed him onto the professors' offices' floor in the geology building.

"We'll stay outside the office," Chet said. "Just don't want you to be alone right now, man."

"We're going to a crime scene. I won't be alone. Tons of people at crime scenes. You'd be surprised how many of us they can fit into a tiny room." His voice echoed off the linoleum, making it hollower and emptier than it already was.

Shock. Had to be.

It wasn't hard to tell what office was Sean's. A group bunched at the end of the hall, standing on tiptoes and trying to see over each other.

Corey pulled out his badge and flashed it, ordering the crowd to move without a word. They parted for the badge and grief-stricken man like the Red Sea.

I pulled up a perception spell and scurried after him, keeping close to his back so I'd get through with him before the crowd closed again.

Chet made a sound and I glanced back at him, shaking my head and winking.

I wasn't truly invisible, just imperceptible. People would see me, but they wouldn't realize it. Far easier to bend people's perceptions around you than to make yourself invisible. That required a knowledge of light bending and physics I certainly didn't have.

I'm a lawyer, not a doctor, dammit.

The human brain is designed to filter, otherwise we'd be overwhelmed with sensory input. This spell told people's brains I was unimportant, and therefore it didn't need to waste time on me.

Which is why Chet still saw me. His brain was sure of the fact that I was important. I was okay with that.

The uniform at the door held up the yellow police tape for Corey and he walked under, eyes forward and face stony. Cop face, I guess. The body lay under a sheet next to the desk, too straight to have not been moved since he was found.

A dark woman wearing jeans and a silk top stood with her back to us off to the side with a detective; other than that, the room ran with blue. Cops, detectives, people who must've been CSI.

The detective pressed his hand to the woman's back and half shoved her out into the hall. I couldn't see her face but something seemed familiar about her swinging black hair and the way she stood.

What the?

I plastered myself against the wall next to the door, hoping I wasn't leaving anything forensic that'd throw them off, or direct them towards me.

Maybe entering an active crime scene wasn't my best idea, but if a friend, even a casual one, was dead, I wanted to know why.

And more importantly, *who*.

The cops exchanged words lost in the din of the active crime scene. Who knew they were so *loud*? A dozen people talking and moving in a small office was as loud as a law school house party, only without the music.

Corey kneeled by the body, and one of the others pulled the sheet back. I glanced around and darted across the room between groups of cops, pressing against the wall next to the them.

The body's face was gone, leaving a red mash of a mess, like someone had cut it off.

I gagged and clamped a hand over my mouth for a second, breathing through my nose.

Death clogged it and I gagged again, breathing through my mouth.

His suit jacket was off, leaving a black tee over strong arms. When he'd worked on my car, I'd teased him and Chet about geeks having such big guns. They'd worked out a few times together since our little clique formed last winter.

It was like the male version of shopping.

His hands were gone along with his face, like Corey said. How the hell was he supposed to identify this?

Dental records would probably do it, right?

Corey must've said something along the same lines because a gloved hand peeled back Sean's lips.

Revealing mangled gums where the teeth had obviously been pulled out quickly.

I gagged again and hauled ass out, shoving past the crowd and dropping the spell once I was in the middle of them. They were so fixated on the office, they'd probably think I had been in the little crowd the whole time.

I hit clear air and barreled into Chet. He caught my arms, rubbing them and kissing my head.

"Evie?" someone said from behind me.

I turned and froze.

"Ashley!"

My friend stared at me with wide eyes and an open mouth.

She'd had her hair smoothed and straightened since I saw her maybe two weeks ago, and she looked casual and young outside her usual work suits, but still.

"What were you doing in there?" I asked, rushing forward and hugging her.

"I..." she looked down. "I kind of shoved my way in. The cops wouldn't listen to me!"

"About what?"

"That's not Sean!"

I did a double take. "What! Wait." I held up a hand. "How do you know Sean?"

"Um." She looked down again, cheeks darkening.

Corey shuffled up to us, staring at the ground. "I couldn't. Let's go."

"Who are you?" Ashley asked.

"This is Corey. He's a friend of Sean's and ours," I said. "Ashley, what do you mean that's not Sean?"

"What?" Corey looked between us, hope shinning so bright from his eyes it was practically corporeal.

"I saw an arm when I pushed in there, before the cop shoved me out. It's not him," Ashley said.

Corey shook his head. "I don't... don't understand. Sean doesn't have any identifying marks. No tattoos or obvious birthmarks."

"Yeah, no marks, right?" Ashley said, the dark skin not masking the blushing.

"Right."

"So, it's not him."

Corey narrowed his eyes. "If you don't stop beating around the bush, I'm going to get seriously pissed off."

She looked at me and I shrugged. "Just say it. We've got a dead body. I think you can live with a little embarrassment."

"Okay, good point." Ashley sighed, looking back at the ground. "I know it's not him because I was with him last night. If there are no marks on his arms, it's not him. Trust me. I know how long my… marks last."

"Marks?' My eyebrows flew up. "Ohhhhh, *marks.*"

"They were fucking, I get it," Corey said, making Ashley flinch. "Nail marks don't last that long unless you really carved him up."

"Not nail marks," Ashley said. "I ummmm, I bite. And he, um, has a very high pain tolerance. He lets me bite as hard as I want. Trust me, he has marks. He'll probably still have them in two weeks, but he definitely has them right now."

Corey's mouth worked and he stared at her until she looked up.

"Are you sure?" he asked.

"Positive. I'd be a lot more upset if I weren't. That body isn't him."

Corey whooped and grabbed her, pulling her into a bear hug so hard I was afraid he'd break her beanpole body.

"Guys," Chet said. "I don't want to ruin this moment, but that does beg a serious question."

"Yeah," I said as Corey let Ashley go. "We have a dead man, with identifying marks removed, dressed in Sean's clothes, and close enough to his body type to make people think it's him."

Ashley's eyes grew wide again. "So, why?"

I nodded. "Yeah. If someone wants us to think Sean's dead, at least until the cops can get DNA results, then why? And where the hell is Sean?"

"WHAT DO WE KNOW?" I asked once we were all back to my place. "Sean's gone. Someone put a guy with a similar build in his clothes, in his office, and removed identifying body parts."

Ashley flopped down at the island counter and the guys flanked her like guards. I pulled a bottle of wine out of the fridge and held it up.

"Yes," Ashley said so emphatically it made me almost smile.

"Beer?" Corey asked.

"No beer, but I have harder stuff. Scotch, rum, vodka or gin?"

"I love you."

"Is I love you rum or scotch?"

"Scotch."

"They must've taken him," Ashley said, looking from the guys to me. "Right?"

"It's an assumption, but it makes sense," Corey said as I poured him a drink. He was the one who thought his friend had died, he got a drink first. "Otherwise, why place a decoy?"

"Do you know what Sean was working on?" Chet asked, hopping as my giant Maine Coon Gremlin jumped on the counter in front of him, sitting with his back to him in a clear demand for pets.

"His specialty was earthquake detection," Corey said, reaching over to pet Gremlin too. My cat pulled his head back before padding closer and rubbing Corey's hand with his head. "He was doing experiments with vibrations and movement."

"And we just had an earthquake," I said, pulling out wine glasses. "No way that's a coincidence."

"Um, unless they're using him to cause earthquakes, not sure how it could be anything else," Corey said. "That took some set up. They took him before that earthquake hit."

"What exactly was he working on to do earthquake detection?" I asked, pouring glasses of wine and pushing them to Ashley and Chet, careful to go around the twenty pounds of black fluff taking up the counter.

Gremlin meowed, and I smiled.

"Not sure, I'm a cop, not a scientist, but he did say he had a little machine that shook a small area to test his equipment."

"So an itty bitty earthquake generator?" I asked as I grabbed my baby's food, pouring him a cup. He abandoned the guys in favor of food and crunched away.

"No." Corey shook his head. "I asked him about that. It'd only shake models he made. Mostly he was studying the vibration and movements. He'd be more useful for studying than for causing anything."

I crouched by Gremlin, petting him. "Any way they could make it bigger to actually shake the earth?"

"No clue. We'd have to ask the geologists."

"Wh…" Ashley took a deep breath. "Is there any reason they'd want to shake the earth?"

"Stealing," I said. "You know, knock out power and electronics and stuff."

The guys stared at me with looks suggesting I watched too many movies.

"I know how it sounds," I said, holding up a hand. "But they do it in the movies. Maybe it's based in real science."

"But why would they need people to think he's dead?" Ashley asked. "And only for a few days? I mean, DNA is going to show that isn't him when they get the tests back."

"Maybe to make people think they stole his stuff and…." I sighed, shaking my head and standing. "Except it didn't look like anything was stolen and his real equipment was in his lab, not his office. I've got bupkis."

"We're going to have to pull the geology guys in," Corey said. "Not going to be able to figure out what's possible without them."

I pulled out my phone. "I'll call Wolf. I know his wife can be trusted. Hopefully he can be too."

Wolf picked up on the second ring, and I nutshelled it for him.

Wolf paused for a long moment before saying, "You're saying there's a dead body, made to look like Sean, but it's not him, and you think it's because thieves want to use an earthquake machine to knock out power grids like on Ocean's Eleven?" Wolf asked, accent thicker over the speakerphone.

"Or if you have another theory," I said. "Though, I think in Ocean's Eleven it was basically a nuclear bomb without the nuke, that knocked out electronics, not a little earthquake machine."

"Let's get this straight, it's not a little earthquake machine. It doesn't cause earthquakes. It causes motion that simulates earthquakes. Huge difference."

"See, this is why we need you," I said. "We don't know this stuff."

"An earthquake is the earth moving due to tectonic plate motions, not just shaking because of whatever is moving the surface. Sean had a machine that shook the surface, to study motion."

"Any reason you can think of why someone would want to kidnap him over that?" I asked.

"No. He was working on it. He wasn't close. He had no more knowledge of early detection than the scientific community in general."

"Dr. Wolf, is there any way this could be used for anything worth killing and kidnapping over?" Ashley asked, the two glasses of wine she'd already downed not shaking her legal brains at all.

"If he was onto something, theoretically, any technology he came up with to detect could be sold. But he didn't have anything profitable like that."

"Are you sure?" Chet asked.

"Positive."

"Was he working on anything else?" I asked. "Anything at all that'd give someone a reason to kidnap him? Maybe we're assuming it was earthquake related because this happened to be around a little earthquake. Maybe it *is* a coincidence. What else can a geologist do?"

"Study motion," Wolf said. "There are calculations we can do and predictions we can make, but that's it."

"Okay, thanks," I said. "Can I call you again if we brainstorm anything else?"

"Of course," he said.

"Thanks." I hung up.

"Predictions," Chet said. "Evie, anything you could do with predictions?"

"Me?"

"Yeah." He looked at the others. "I mean people like you."

"What are you talking about?" Corey asked.

Chet grinned and shrugged. "Evie?"

I sighed. "Yeah, okay. He's asking if this could be anything magical."

"Magic?" Corey's face locked up, telling me exactly what he thought of people who believed in magic.

"Evie thinks she's a witch," Ashley said. "She's not crazy, just a Wicca type."

"No, I'm not. Somehow I just know this is going to bite me on the tuchus." I held my hand out, palm up, and pulled fire from my belly, making a ball in my hand the size of a grapefruit.

"Shit!" Corey yelped, blinking and stumbling back. "What the fuck!"

Ashley dropped her drink, the glass shattering on the kitchen floor and sending little slivers flying.

I snuffed out the flames, and Chet held up a hand, gesturing he'd get the broom.

"Don't want you in there with no shoes," he said to me, gently pushing Ashley into the living room. "You either."

He went to work on the kitchen and Ashley stared at me. "How?"

"Ash, you going to be okay?"

Her mouth worked and she swallowed hard enough to see it. "I don't know."

My phone rang and I pulled it out of my pocket.

"Oy vey." My heart hit the carpet and I shook so hard I was afraid my bottom would be next. I walked over to the couch and sat, taking a deep breath before swiping the phone on.

"O'Shay," I said, keeping my voice pleasant, "to what do I owe this pleasure?"

Chet froze in the kitchen, staring across the island at me. "Council?" he mouthed.

I nodded.

"Jones," O'Shay said, "I've gotten reports of activity in the Salt Lake Valley. You wouldn't happen to know anything about that?"

My heart bounced back up, hammering so hard I was afraid it'd escape out of my chest like that thing in Alien. "What kind of activity?"

"Magical," he said in a duh voice.

"Yeah, I got that. What kind of magic? Anything that could be causing earthquakes?"

"Have you been having earthquakes?" he asked, surprise evident.

"Just a little one, but now you're asking me about magical activity, I'm worried. What have you been sensing?"

"That is not how this works. I represent the Council; I ask the questions."

I cocked my head, grinding my teeth before saying, "Say, how's that Merlin treating you?"

"Don't try pulling that card. Our deal was the claim to the Merlin for my silence, nothing more."

"Actually," I said. "You should read things more carefully before you sign them. How about you go grab your copy of the contract and call me back. Please." The please came out in a hiss.

He hung up.

"What the hell was that?" Corey asked.

"*That* was my government. They're called the Council," I said. "And they've sensed something going on around here. Not sure what, but there's a few too many things going on for me to think any of this is a coincidence."

"But what were you two talking about?"

"Yeah," Chet said. "What was that bit about he should've read the contract?"

I grinned. "Okay, to catch you guys up first. Our government doesn't allow humans to know about witches. When we had some trouble with a magical shadow bunny-"

Ashley snorted and I looked at her. "Oh, you're serious. Okay."

"Yeah," I said. "He was causing problems, and the Council rep, O'Shay, came to investigate. We lied and said Chet was a witch. We captured the shadow and sent him home, but he told O'Shay Chet wasn't a witch before he left. Rules say humans can't know. If you can erase their memories, then you do, but if you can't, like if the human has known for a while, then you have to kill them."

Ashley made a little noise.

I nodded. "Yeahhhhhh, he tried to kill Chet. Since I was the one who got the shadow out, I would theoretically be rewarded by the Council. I traded O'Shay the claim to the glory for him leaving Chet alone and for his silence on a human knowing about magic."

I paused as Chet walked over, apparently done with the sweeping. He handed Ashley a fresh glass with a wink and a, "Don't drop this one. These are nice glasses."

She forced a smile and I took his hand as he sat next to me.

"Now we get to the evil, underhanded lawyer part," I said. "I wrote the contract. It's a magic binding one. You literally have to do what you are bound to under the contract. He couldn't tell anyone about Chet if he wanted to. What he didn't notice in all the legalize is I added an addendum.

"Since a Merlin award gets you favors for years, possibly life, I included that I get favors from him, as long as I say please and it doesn't put him in immediate and present danger to do it, basically."

"Fuck girl, you're hot when you're diabolical," Chet said, kissing my cheek. "You're brilliant. How did you know he wouldn't read it all the way through?"

I shrugged. "How many people do you know read through the licensing agreements on software, the back of ticket stubs, or even their apartment leases? He may be a government rep, but that doesn't make him smart." I snorted. "Usually it's the opposite."

Chet chuckled too.

"You have to be very careful with magical contracts," I continued. "Can't just throw a ton of stuff in there for one thing. So mine is worded to say he owes me half as many favors, to the same degree, as what he gets from others using the Merlin. I'm betting he's not the conservative type and has been raking the favors in."

"Same degree?" Ashley asked.

"It's more magical math than anything I could really explain in human terms." I frowned. "Well, okay, the idea is based on the amount of energy that goes into his favors. So say he gets a candy bar, I'd be able to call in a favor for one of roughly half the calories, even if I wanted Skittles instead. Make sense?"

"Not even a little bit." She took a long drag of wine.

"The point is, there's a powerful member of my government that owes me, and he's about to figure it out and call me back."

"I don't get what's forcing him though."

"Magic. If I ordered him to tell me right then, he would have without wanting to. I told him he could read the contract first so he'd at least understand why, but magic will bind him to his word. I just have to… let it know, I guess, when it's time to get forceful."

"That has so many disturbing implications."

I nodded. "You don't want to know what these things have been used for in the past."

"Are we talking Rumpelstiltskin type deals or sex trade?"

"Both and worse."

She flinched. "I think I'm starting to understand your world view a little better."

I smiled. "Scary world when someone's actually expected to read a contract's fine print and is bound to it, isn't it? You learn to be careful and responsible for your own decisions real fast."

She took a longer drink of wine. "I'm a contract attorney and the idea of that scares the shit out of me."

"It shouldn't. The world would be a less complicated place if everyone read the fine print." I glanced at the phone in my hand. "He's taking his dear sweet time. I'm calling my dad. If we're going to need to pull out some magical tracking or if something magical is going on, I'm going to need help."

"What about Faye?" Chet asked.

I shook my head. "She's in England for the-" I froze.

"What?" Chet said.

"For the equinox," I said. "It's tomorrow!"

"So?" Ashley asked.

I didn't answer, mind batting around the possibilities.

"So the equinox is a powerful time for witches," Chet said after a moment. "Power is more concentrated, you can do more, right?"

I nodded. "It's like Halloween. We… if there's something magical going on, it'll be revolving around the equinox."

"HOW DO YOU GET YOURSELF into this stuff?" Dad asked when he got to my place.

"Hi Daddy." I hugged him, resting my ear against his steady heartbeat. I finally let him go and he came inside. "I have no clue."

"You're a Jones. It's in our blood."

"Oh, so this is your fault?"

"I will gladly take the credit for your troublemaking."

"Haha." I held a glass up and wiggled it.

Dad shook his head. "Has the Council rep gotten back to you?"

"Not yet. He's reading that contract *real* careful now." I smiled but it felt flat. "Dad, have you sensed anything off magically? I'm not even sure where to look for anything specific until O'Shay gets back to me."

"I haven't, but I'd have to know where to look, too."

"I know. Worth a shot."

We chattered, answering my friends' questions about magic for another few minutes until the phone finally rang.

I picked it up. "About time, O'Shay."

"You bitch." He let loose with a series of curses so bad they made me gasp even though I was expecting him to be pissed.

"Are you done?" I snapped when he finally paused for breath. "Oy vey, I've half a mind to fly out there and wash your mouth out with soap."

Dad snorted and I slapped a hand over the phone's speaker. "Oy, when did I start channeling Bubbe?"

O'Shay ran off on another tirade and I twisted the phone away from my ear.

"Keep it up," I said. "You've got another five horrible things to say before I cut you off and order you never to cuss at me again."

The squawking from the ear side cut off and I put it against my ear again. "What do you know, O'Shay?"

"There's a magical surge in your area," he growled, every word fighting its way out. "We thought it might be you or one of the other troublemakers in your area preparing a spell to unleash with the power of the equinox. With it tomorrow-"

"You're not going to be able to sense every little thing," I cut him off, "so it's a good time to pull something. I know. It's not me, but I'm definitely worried now. What have you sensed?"

"Magic. Unbalanced enough to set off alarms."

"And an earthquake." That meant the witch was either too sloppy to balance the energies, or they just didn't care. "Are we looking at one witch or a group?"

"This is a group. Based on the signature, it's probably four or five channeling the energy of the equinox through the earth."

"Can you send me the reading's you've gotten so far, O'Shay?" I asked. Wow, my voice stayed steady. No clue how.

"Yes."

"Do it."

"What do you think this is?"

I looked between my dad and my friends. Could giving him the info hurt us? Giving our government any info always had that risk, but here, it'd probably be better so he could tell me if anything else went with my theory.

"A friend of mine is missing," I said. "Whoever took him dumped a body with no identifying features but close enough to him in body type that the police think it's him. He's a geologist. He's been studying how to detect earthquakes."

"And you think it's related?" O'Shay cursed again.

"Is there a way for witches to use the power from the equinox to do something big and bad, if they know where energy is going to come from? Like in the form of an earthquake?"

"It's always possible, but that'd take more witches. We're talking a whole coven to pull that off, and they'd have to be on top of the fault line, putting them in danger as well. Whatever this is, I think it's something smaller," O'Shay said.

"What could we be looking at then?" I asked.

"At this point, I couldn't begin to guess, but I'm betting anyone willing to kill someone just to be able to take another without people looking for him, aren't going to be using this power for anything good."

That coming from you putzes who kill humans for just knowing about us?

I took a deep breath.

I can't believe I'm about to say this.

"Even if it's something smaller, it's still about four or five against two. O'Shay, I think you just won yourself a trip to beautiful Salt Lake City."

"I DON'T LIKE THIS," my dad said, shifting on his feet next to the baggage claim belt at the airport.

"Dad, you can leave," I said. "I don't want you caught up in all this."

Dad looked down at me. "I'm going to pretend you didn't just suggest I abandon my own daughter."

"Okay." I held up my hands and Chet grinned. "What?" I asked him.

"You two are so alike, it's hilarious. Most of the time, you know, girls are afraid of turning into their mothers."

"Haha, well I'm perfectly fine with turning into my father."

"Thank you," Dad said.

"I'm fine with that too," Chet said. "I like your dad, just keep your boobs."

Dad chuckled along with him and I rolled my eyes. "Okay guys. We-"

O'Shay walked out of the crowd and I propped my hands on my hips, walking up to meet him.

"Jones," O'Shay said, nodding without offering his hand.

"O'Shay." I nodded too.

He lifted a little rolling suitcase. "I didn't check a bag."

"Great. O'Shay, this is my dad."

Dad did hold out his hand, class outweighing disdain for everything Council related. O'Shay took it. "Ernest Jones. You can call me Ernie."

"Ryan O'Shay. Ryan."

We walked out of the airport and to the car parked at the curb.

O'Shay froze as Ashley waved from the driver's seat.

"Jones," O'Shay said as Dad opened the door, "please tell me that is not another human you've told about us."

"Ummmmmm." I twisted my mouth to the side, looking up and around as cartoonishly as I could. "I'm going to be calling in a lot of my favors this weekend."

"We may as well put up a sign," he said, walking around to put his suitcase in the trunk.

"Is letting him know there are more of us who know about magic a good idea?" Chet whispered.

"No, but you saw Ashley. She wasn't taking 'no, stay' for an answer."

We got in the car, Chet up front since he was the biggest, us witches in back.

"We're going to try tracking down Sean, that's the missing geologist, with some of his stuff," I said once we got going. "How are you with tracking spells?"

"Decent. Nothing spectacular. Are there other witches here we could press into service?"

Dad and I looked at each other.

"I don't think so," Dad said.

O'Shay's face creased up. "Why not?"

"Well," I said, "there is the issue of humans being in on this. Not a lot of them I'd trust enough to know something that could get my friends killed."

"And we aren't the only witches who have a problem with the Council," Dad said, keeping his tone as even and diplomatic as when he was making a presentation to a potential new client. "No one is going to want to put themselves on the Council's radar, not even to curry favor."

"Well, one or two might," I said. "But not the type of people any of us would want help from. If those types of witches get involved, they'll turn you in the second they find out you made a deal with me to save a human. Same reason you couldn't bring anyone else from the Council to help."

"Thanks for putting me in that position, by the way," O'Shay said dryly.

"Hey, you're the one who didn't read the contract. Can't really blame me for that."

"It was underhanded."

"I'm not arguing." I shrugged.

Dad snorted.

WE GOT BACK TO MY apartment and Corey said, "Now what?"

"We're going to try a locator spell to find Sean," Dad said. "O'Shay's going to drive. I'll anchor."

"No," I said. "I'll anchor."

"Ev-*ie*."

"Dad-*dy*."

I stared my dad down, but could see the humans looking between us out of the corner of my eye.

Chet was right, I was the female spitting image of my dad, and Mom always said I was his little clone in personality, too.

I crossed my arms, staring into my dad's eyes, golden brown just like mine.

"No," Dad finally said.

"What are we missing?" Ashley asked.

"To anchor someone, you have to form a bond. It's a very intimate act. I've only done this with family and close friends. It's letting them see a part of you. O'Shay owes me, Dad. I can order him to never speak of what he sees in my head."

"You can order him to do the same with what's in mine," my dad countered.

"Yeah, except that's going to take a hell of a lot more of the favors he owes me."

Dad flinched and I knew I had him.

"Why?" Chet asked.

"Because her father has more in his past to hide," Corey said, making Dad and me look at him. "I was born in Venezuela, we got out when I was seven, but the things I remember." He licked his lips. "I know the things men do to protect their families under an oppressive government."

I turned to O'Shay. He was too busy staring at my dad to notice.

"Don't ask, O'Shay," I said. "You *don't* want to know. Let's do this."

I put Gremlin in the bedroom so he wouldn't knock over the candles and break the circle, chuckled a little as he yowled and scratched under the door, got my spelling knife, and placed the candles as Dad disabled the smoke detectors. Couldn't have those things going off in the middle of a ritual and shattering our concentration.

"You've done this before?" O'Shay asked as I drew the circle with my spelling knife. It was a beauty with its bone handle and emerald inlays, and I caught O'Shay staring at it.

"I'm usually Faye's anchor," I said. "And you know how powerful she is with this stuff."

Faye was the go-to necromancer in the country. She had her position as a Council emissary because of it. It's why she was invited to Stonehenge as part of the American contingent to the summit there.

"Yes, but you like her," O'Shay said. "How do I know you won't let me fly into the ether?"

"We could do another contract, but that will leave us both even more tied. I don't think either of us wants that. You're just going to have to trust me."

"After that bit with the contract, I don't."

I looked him in the eyes. "O'Shay, my friend is missing for who knows what reason. You know the lengths I'll go to to protect a friend. I swear on his life, I will not let you fly off. I *need* you. Trust that."

He nodded, sitting cross legged on the carpet.

I sat in front of him. "What's your bloodline?"

"Druid and Hoodoo."

"I can say I don't know anything about Hoodoo. You're probably better off using Druid magic to track."

"But you work with Dr. Renaud and she uses Navajo to track?"

"Yeah, and I know how to anchor her for that through a lot of practice where we built it up. Unless Hoodoo is like Navajo, I don't want to risk it."

He shook his head and held out his hand, palms up. "It's not. Druid's better for tracking anyway."

"It is for me too."

"Yeah," he snorted. "The Jews are definitely good for battle magic. That has got to be where that fire and rebellion comes from."

"If your people were slaves for millennia, you'd take your freedom pretty damn serious too."

Ashley gasped and I grinned.

Yeah, I said it.

"I'm *black* and *Irish!*" O'Shay said, sputtering through laughter.

"Yeah, but in the course of history, who were slaves longer?"

He frowned. "History's not my strong point. I'm a doctor."

"Uh-huh, well, on behalf of all of our peoples, that's where the fire comes from. I can see you sputtering over there, Ashley," I said. I couldn't really, only hear the incomprehensible babbling.

"You can see behind you!" Ashley asked.

"Only when I turn my head, or when there's a mirror."

Dad laughed with me and I shook my head.

"I could hear you," I said.

"Are you stalling, Ms. Jones?" O'Shay said.

I shook my hands out. "I think so. This… well, you know."

He met my eyes and my heart rate picked up. "I never wanted to see a Council rep's soul."

"I think it'll be good for you then. Because I can tell you, not all of us are sullied."

I gulped and put my hands up too, touching my middle fingers to his.

"A fire anchoring a water," he whispered. "God help me."

"Amen."

I closed my eyes as his magic washed through my hands, cooling me from the inside out.

I'd done this so many times with Faye over the past few years, I didn't even notice her soul brushing against mine anymore. We knew each other so well, it wasn't a shock, it was as easy as a hug.

O'Shay's spirit crashed through me like a wave taking everything in its path, and I pushed it away on instinct. Water was dangerous, it crushed our magic and made us weak.

I took a deep breath as the water fled, fear riding its top like salt, and pulled the fire back, the apology as clear as I could make it.

The water eased forth, nicer, like it was asking, power obvious in the light touch. It took more power to hold yourself back than it ever did to throw in your all.

I shivered, squeezing my shoulders and letting them relax. A technique Faye taught me. You tensed up and released to give yourself a physical method of relaxing that'd take your brain with it. I followed it with my arms and legs.

The water came to my shores again, gently lapping instead of pounding.

My stomach clenched without my permission and I grunted.

The water crawled up the burning fires in my mind, steam hissing out. The power burned through me like cold flames, and I could hear my breath coming in jagged gasps in the real world as things low in me tightened.

I grabbed onto the water, light foam flooding through me. O'Shay's soul, opening itself up for me to see and judge.

Wanting me to see.

My walls fell and the water swirled around me, making steam as it touched me.

Darkness of a child who swore he'd never be helpless again touched my brain, a poor kid raised in the rough neighborhoods of South Boston by a mother who was too busy doing her next John for a bump to raise her son. A kid who jumped at the chance to serve when he found he had powers so he could get out of that life. Someone who knew with every piece of him the government that took him away from his mother was a good one because it was protecting people.

He actually believed with every inch of his glowing soul that the Council was good.

Ha.

The water pulled back, most washing into the sea, leaving me holding the end of it.

The power I held to anchor the rest twined around me, playful and cool, making my skin tingle with steam as it swarmed over me.

I shouldn't…

I couldn't help it.

I pushed the water off, leaving myself open. It took the invite, shoving itself back against me.

In me.

I bit my tongue, pressing my lips together in the real world before pushing back. It came again, plunging through my stomach, making it flutter and drop like it did on a roller-coaster.

I bit down harder.

If it kept this up…

My eyes snapped open just in time to see the flames on the candles kissing the ceiling before falling dead.

Now that was some serious power.

O'Shay's eyes popped open and I yanked my hands away, standing on shaking legs and walking to the bathroom as fast as I could without running.

I locked the door behind me and caught myself on the counter.

Chet yelled something about what the hell did O'Shay do, and I took a few deep breaths, staring at myself in the mirror.

The door clicked open and I whirled on it as O'Shay stepped inside, closing it behind him.

"What did you tell Chet?" I asked, voice rough.

"That I was powerful, and it was harder for you to hold than you thought it'd be," he said, keeping his voice low.

"Well, that was part of it."

"I didn't mean to-"

"I know." I couldn't look at him. "Hey, that was both of us."

"When you pushed me back, I shouldn't have shoved like that."

"You wanted to see if you could."

"No, I wanted to show you my power. I wanted to scare you."

I laughed. "You didn't scare me."

"No." He stepped closer and my knees shook. "I scared the hell out of myself though. You are everything I fight, your sure belief that the Council is wrong, and bad for witches, something to be destroyed if you could. You believe that as surely as I believe it is good and just, and what is necessary to protect witches."

He took another step and I put out a hand, pushing against his chest. "We're literal opposites in magic, O'Shay. That doesn't work. And we are opposites politically. You saw what happened, water and fire destroy each other."

"No." His voice dipped down lower but he stayed put. "They make something new. Steam. That combination. I've never felt anything like that from anyone I combined a spell with. You can't tell me you didn't feel that. I saw it. I *saw* you."

"You wanted me to take you," he whispered. "As much as I wanted it."

"I like power, O'Shay, as much as you. Your power called to me, that's it." I finally met his eyes. "You are the representation of everything I hate and will fight to my dying breath. The most we'd ever have would be some angry sex."

He smiled and it made my heart hiccup. Oy gevalt, what had I done when I agreed to do something so intimate with him?

"I'm taken," I said. "I'm taken by someone I respect. Right now, I want you, I do, but you're a coward. I could *never* have feelings for you."

I walked to the door.

O'Shay grabbed my arm and pulled me back, pinning me against the wall behind the door and pressing close, the erection obvious against me.

I growled, lighting his shirt on fire. He smacked it down and pushed water against me like he had in the mental world, thrusting into my magic, making me gasp.

He pulled back and licked his lips. "I'm not a coward. I'm pragmatic, just like you."

"You're a *coward*. I've seen it. You hiding behind a couch in Faye's living room when I shot at the entropy. Your first thought was to hide. You're a coward. I could never have anything with you."

He growled, slipping an arm behind my waist and kissing me, pouring power past my lips, begging for me to shove it back, to start the tug of war that'd felt so good again.

I pushed him away with my hands instead, cutting the power off.

"I don't know how things work in Boston," I said, drawing my gun and pointing it at him. "But you know we call that sexual assault here, right?"

"You wouldn't shoot me. Not after that." But fear creased his voice.

"You're scared of guns, aren't you, O'Shay?"

"I've never felt anything like that, and I'm betting you haven't either. How can you just toss it aside?"

I kept my gun on him as I eased to the side, grabbing the door handle. "Because I want more than the physical. And I have felt that before. Once."

He smiled, opening his mouth.

"And I destroyed him," I said.

His mouth snapped shut and doubt came through his eyes.

"He was a spirit and he pulled my powers just like you did," I said. "Goddess, it felt good. And in bed? Before I knew what he was? He was amazing, forceful. I respond to power, it turns me on. I'll still kill you if I need to. Just like I killed him."

"Last time you threatened to kill me, it scared me. Now? You're just turning me on. That gun, knowing you would kill me, it's exciting me. It's kind of disturbing."

"I'd look into therapy if I were you. Take a minute, get yourself together." I opened the door and closed it behind me, resisting the urge to light my bathroom on fire.

Chet stood across from the door, leaning against the hallway's wall between pictures of my family.

I blushed, looking down.

"Yeah," he said slowly. "I figured."

"Did you hear that?"

"No, that fucker put something on the door so I couldn't hear. Kept me out too."

"And you were worried? About me or that I'd do something?"

"Mostly the first, little bit of the second."

"I'm not going to lie and say I didn't feel anything. I am telling you he tried something and that's why my gun's out." I put the gun away.

"Do I need to kill him?"

I had to smile at that. When Chet said it, he meant it like normal people. Like did O'Shay do something Chet would *want* to kill him over, not that he'd actually do it.

"No, but *I* may."

He frowned because he knew I meant it.

"What did he do?"

"In the anchoring, our powers, our souls felt each other. He pushed and I pushed back. After that, he was playing. It's almost like our powers were having sex."

He nodded. "The sound you made. It was only for a second, but it was the same sound you make when I pin you to the bed."

"I didn't mean to."

He nodded. "I can't give you what someone like him can. I don't have that power. If you want that, tell me now."

"No!" I said, looking out at the living room.

"Your dad took them out to grab food," Chet said. "I think he knew how intimate it was getting and didn't want to see."

I sighed. "Yeah, that would've been awkward."

"Evie-"

"I want you. I *choose* you. Yes, that felt good, but I said no, and I stopped him. Because I don't like him. Because I have you. And I don't want anyone else."

"Okay," he said after a moment. "I'm feeling a little insecure so you're going to have to forgive this."

Chet grabbed me, pinning me against the wall almost like O'Shay had, giant body pressing me down as he kissed me hard. He picked me up and my legs went around his waist.

"Um," I said, pulling my mouth away from his. "When?"

"At least twenty minutes, and I'm not feeling patient. We'll be done by then."

He walked us into the bedroom and kicked the door closed, dropping me on the bed and climbing on top before I could even think about undressing myself.

"WE'RE BACK!" DAD YELLED from the living room.

I opened my eyes, pushing up off Chet's chest and looking around. My shirt hung open on me, at least two buttons broken, my pants were on the floor, and my cute lacy panties were nowhere to be seen.

Chet was completely naked, and he looked good that way.

Gremlin slept splayed out on the loveseat under the window and I blushed. "I just had sex in front of my baby, that's got to be animal cruelty or something."

"Especially since he's fixed so he never gets any himself. I need a nap," Chet said, sitting up and stretching.

I giggled, kissing his chin. "Yeah, you were getting a good workout there."

"Evie." His voice turned serious. "I don't like feeling that way. Inadequate. Don't put me in that position again."

I nodded. "I won't. But, is it too soon to make a joke about this?"

"No." His beautiful full lips finally broke into a smile. "Go ahead."

"That was so good, I'm tempted to flirt with guys in front of you just so you feel the need to claim me like that on a regular basis."

"That doesn't sound like a joke. It sounds like a suggestion. What if I claim you like that on a regular basis so you never *want* to flirt with anyone else?"

"Deal."

We shook on it and he laughed, kissing my forehead before I jumped out of bed, grabbing fresh clothes and pulling them on.

"I hope that prick heard us," Chet said. "Really pound it home."

"Pun intended?"

"You know it."

"You know I'm not interested in him. His power did it for me, yes, but he's a coward, I really don't like him, and I told him as much."

"Okay." Chet leaned back against the wall, smiling like the cat that ate the canary.

"You're really proud of yourself, aren't you?" I asked, pulling on a fresh top.

"Yep. I can't do that powers sex thing with you, but I can make you whimper. Still haven't made you scream. Yet." He winked.

"At least you have a goal."

I slipped out, closing the door behind me so Chet could get dressed without giving a peep show.

O'Shay was sitting on the couch, reading something on his phone. He looked up when I walked in, the blush obvious.

I smiled at him. "Oh, you found something to entertain yourself while we were busy. Good. I felt like a bad hostess, but well, a girl doesn't turn a man like that down."

He looked down as he stood, and I smiled bigger.

"Everything okay, sweetie?" my dad asked, keeping his voice even as he pulled the Chinese takeout from the box. My stomach growled, reminding me we left the restaurant before we'd gotten lunch.

"We're good. O'Shay, you figure out where Sean is?"

"Yes," he said. "I have a general area in west Nevada, maybe two hours from here, and we can track more precisely when we get closer."

"Good, so we eat and go. At least now we know he's alive."

Chet walked out of the room, fully dressed, eyes still glittering, and I had to grin.

He walked up to O'Shay and cold-clocked him right in the jaw, dropping the slight man like a bag of bricks.

"You touch my girl again," Chet said with a low growl, "remember, she's not the only one with a long-range rifle. And I'm a better shot than her."

O'Shay stood, rubbing his jaw. "Don't make threats you don't mean to keep. I know you wouldn't actually take a life. The reason she's so scary is because she would."

"Fine, I'll just beat the shit out of you while she holds your magic down. Fair?"

O'Shay smirked. "T-"

"What is it with Jews and Chinese food?" Ashley said loudly. "I never got that."

"It's something we've always done," I said, grinning at my dad.

We raised our arms at the same time, singing out, "Tradition!"

The guys burst out laughing and we sat down to chow.

"Thank you," I mouthed at Ashley.

"You're welcome," she mouthed back.

Something told me O'Shay wasn't done being a testosterone filled putz though.

WE ATE, PACKED UP, Chet complaining about how heavy my bag was as he hauled it downstairs to the car, and piled into Dad's SUV. Dad drove with O'Shay giving directions. Dad's car had more room so it was the obvious choice. And the three rows meant I could be in the back with Chet while O'Shay gave directions, and Ashley and Corey sat in the middle seats.

A few too many people who knew about us according to O'Shay, but oh well.

Maybe that's the best way to fight the Council? Tell humans about us, one by one, until there's so many who know about us that witches become common knowledge and this whole protecting us through ignorance thing doesn't work anymore.

"What are you thinking about so hard?" Chet asked, leaning over to take my hand and kiss my knuckles.

"I have an idea," I said. "I'll tell you later when we don't have an audience."

"Oh?" He grinned. "This have anything to do with what happened about five minutes before those guys came back with food?"

I chuckled. "No, but I can come up with some ideas along those lines, too."

"If you're going to think that hard, I'd hope so."

"What makes you think I was thinking hard?"

"The look on your face. It's serious Evie. You only get that look when you're plotting something. It's why I see it so often."

I had to smile. "Do you remember the night we met?"

He nodded, confusion passing over his face. "My band was playing your fundraiser for the animal shelter. Why?"

"That night was Friday the Thirteenth. I was using Gremlin to gather luck, it's what cats do on that day. There was a woman in our coven who knew I was gathering luck to help Ashley pass the bar. She threatened to tell the Council, to bring them down on me.

"I was so scared of them then. That was just a year ago. And now? Now I'm working with one and have him in my back pocket. So that kind of threat now would be nothing. I could call O'Shay and have him bury it. I was just thinking I could start using that power for more good than just keeping me and mine out of trouble."

He smiled, kissing my knuckles again.

"The point of the story actually isn't this epiphany I've had. It's you. I was so scared then, keeping my eye on that woman who threatened to turn me in, but then I saw you. And for a second, or two, I was distracted. And Maggie got the drop on me."

"Sooooo, you're saying I almost got you arrested?"

"No, I'm saying you've been worth the risk since the day we met."

That made him smile.

"You, Evie Jones, are one smooth talking witch."

I leaned over and kissed him.

"What's in Wendover?" came from the front and we pulled apart.

"Wendover?" I asked.

O'Shay was twisted in his seat to look behind at us, his face just as contorted as his body. "I've got them dead ahead in about ten miles and the sign we just passed says around there is Wendover. Anything there?"

"Casinos," Corey and Ashley said together.

"It's basically Vegas's poor cousin," Ashley said. "It's on the border of Utah, and it has a cluster of casinos. Good place to go with girlfriends for a binge weekend."

"The only reason to go there is to gamble and hit the warehouse liquor store," Corey said. "Maybe see a band coming through, but yeah, gambling and drinking pretty much covers it."

"Evie, you know how you were joking it could be some sort of heist?" Chet asked. "What if you were right?"

I looked at him.

"Think about it," he said. "Only reason for anybody to be in Wendover? Vegas is big and has some serious security, but the casinos out here? Not nearly as big a fish, means less security."

I nodded along and pulled out my phone, pulling up Wolf's number and calling him.

"Evie? Have you found him?" Wolf said on answering before I could say hi.

"No, but we've got them narrowed down to Wendover," I said. *Here's hoping he doesn't ask how.* "Is there anything Sean was working on or knows that'd make him useful in a heist?"

"Haven't you been over this?"

"We're revisiting considering where they are."

"Not unless they are attempting to predict an earthquake so they know when to rob the casinos. Considering how unlikely one is… the math does not make sense."

I paused, covering the mouthpiece. "It's a casino and we're pretty sure it's witches behind this, right? What if they aren't trying to rob? What if they're trying to win?"

I looked over at Chet and he nodded, mouthing, "Gambling?"

I nodded, putting the phone back up. "Wolf, is there anything a geologist would know that'd make him useful in helping someone rig a win out of a casino? Like… use a machine to make the craps table shake at just the right time to bump the dice or something?"

"Not for craps, no," Wolf said so slowly my heart jumped. "But for roulette wheels? They just might. And roulette is a big enough payout compared to your bet to make it worth it."

"Explain."

"Roulette wheels have variations. A geologist who studies vibration could study a roulette wheel and predict with some amount of accuracy approximately where it will land next based on the microscopic variations, as long as he knows the previous sequence of numbers."

"How accurate?"

"Not down to one number, that's for sure."

"But down to an area?"

"Yes."

"Thanks Wolf, you don't know how helpful that was."

"Just get my TA back."

"Working on it." I ended the call. "Oy vey, I know what they're planning."

"What?" Chet asked.

"C-" My bag wiggled and I squinted at it. "What the?" It wiggled again.

"Meow!"

Chet burst out laughing and unzipped it.

Gremlin jumped out, scolding me with meows for leaving him in there so long as he jumped on my lap and spun a circle before laying down.

"At least now we know why your bag was so heavy?" Chet chuckled.

"You didn't check for stowaways?" I asked, petting my baby. He purred, sounding way too pleased with himself.

"Didn't occur to me."

"WOLF SAID A ROULETTE WHEEL has variations in it," I said after we were inside our hotel room.

We'd got one so we'd have a base of operations, and a place to stash our furry stowaway, but we'd grab more if it looked like we were staying the night. Dad was downstairs, scanning the casino with the spell O'Shay had whipped up to pinpoint Sean.

"Someone who studies motion could study an individual roulette wheel, what numbers it lands on, and estimate where the ball is likely to land," I said.

"So they're going to what?" Ashley asked. "Place bets on all the slots in that area?"

"No. They're witches. They're going to figure out the general area, place bets on one or two of them, and as the ball gets close, nudge it over into the slot. It falls approximately where it should, so the casino doesn't get suspicious, and since it'd only have to be nudged a bit since they'd already be in the area, they could do it with the minimum of magic."

"Why here though?" Chet asked. "Wouldn't Vegas be better? Much bigger payout."

"Practice," Corey said. "They want to make sure he can estimate it close enough tonight before they pull it in Vegas tomorrow. It's the dress rehearsal."

"It's brilliant," O'Shay said, sitting down on the edge of one bed. "Don't use magic tonight, just study it, maybe place some small bets, and watch to test the geologist. Bring him to Vegas tomorrow, and let the power of the equinox and those using it cover up very minor magic. We'd never have detected it if they didn't use magic to maim that body."

"That was stupid of them," I said. "Considering how careful they're being, why take such an unnecessary risk?"

"It's a group, right?" Chet asked.

O'Shay nodded, head jerking like it physically pained him to answer Chet's question.

"One of them is the leader, he's the one who planned it carefully. The one who was responsible for dumping the body is stupid, sloppy, probably young and cocky. He maimed the body, fast and dirty, and set off a magical imbalance he probably didn't expect."

"Group dynamics like that?" Corey said, rubbing his chin. "I'm guessing a family. Pros wouldn't bring in someone young and green then leave him alone, even a group of people with similar ideas wouldn't do that. Probably family business, maybe with the older ones' close friends, but it was probably someone's kid."

I nodded. "The experienced witches take Sean and make sure there's no trail or evidence while they leave the younger one to do the simplest task, cut off identifying marks. It was probably harder than he thought it'd be, and he took a shortcut."

"They wouldn't trust him alone after that," Corey said. "But they wouldn't all want to be seen together either. We need to look for people around the roulette wheels; not playing, or betting very low, with one young enough to be someone's son."

"Why are we assuming males?" Ashley asked. "Woman can be thieves too, ya know."

"Profiling," Corey said. "Most likely, these are middle aged males with something in life that tipped them over the edge. They might have a wife or girlfriend along, especially the one with the kid, but probably mostly guys."

"Go down to the casino, fan out around the roulette wheels," I said. "If you see anything, call me or my dad."

"If you see anything, call *me*," O'Shay said. "I'm the one who can track their energies and compare them to the reading from my tracking spell."

"Dad's the one who *has* the tracking spell right now," I said, grinding my teeth.

"For a preliminary scouting mission." O'Shay stood, leaning like he was trying to tower over me. Ha, he had maybe two inches on me.

"And yet," I said, "we still have it."

"And yet, I can take it back."

"We have three main casinos to hit," Corey said, pushing between us, knocking O'Shay back on the bed.

No clue if it was on purpose, but it was funny.

"Three casinos, with a nice spread of roulette wheels to cover," Corey continued. "We're going to have to split up to hit them all while the kidnappers are possibly still on the floor. It's already late, and I'm guessing they'll rise early to make it to Vegas. We'll need one witch at each casino. Evie, you take Chet, Ashley can go with your dad and I'll take the Council cop. We'll probably get along better than he will with the other two."

Chet smirked and whispered, "He's not doing anything for you right now with this taking charge thing, is he?"

I shrugged. "A little."

"I'm going to have to give you another lesson, aren't I?" He wrapped an arm around my shoulders, squeezing me into his side.

"Yep, but not tonight. We've got kidnappers to fry."

"You meant bigger fish to fry, right?"

"Yeah, sure."

O'SHAY REPLICATED THE SPELL HE'D made for Dad, and we each took one, a green ball the size of a bead that was supposed to grow warm as we neared our target.

Ours was stone cold.

Chet and I took the casino of the hotel we were staying in, The Pepper or Rainbow something, Dad and Ashley took the next one over, and Corey and O'Shay took the biggest one, about half a mile down the road.

We walked around the floor for a few minutes to get the lay of the land, the endless maze of slot machines and thick blanket of smoke making me dizzy.

"Is it wrong I kind of want to gamble right now?" Chet asked as we stood next to one of the roulette wheels.

It spun too many times to count and landed on numbers seemingly at random. If Wolf said it could be studied and predicted to some semblance of accuracy, I believed him, I just didn't see how it was possible.

"I'm a little worried," I said. "I don't think I'd deal well with a boyfriend with a gambling problem."

"I don't have a problem, it's fun, long as you go in knowing what you're willing to spend and don't go one cent over."

"I like to keep my money. Losing it on chance where the odds are definitely stacked against you has never appealed to me."

We walked between the craps tables to get to the next roulette wheel. My bead hadn't so much as glowed in the time we'd been on the floor, let alone heated.

"I don't think they're here," I said after we'd wandered between all the tables and watched each wheel for a few minutes each.

I called Corey and he said the same. They were still circling theirs since it was the biggest, but the stone was dead stone cold.

He thought that was hilarious. I chuckled to humor him.

I called my dad and his phone went right to voicemail.

"Dad," I huffed, rolling my eyes.

"What?" Chet asked.

"For someone who runs his own business, he's a freaking Luddite. Can't remember to charge his phone half the time, and can't work it the other half."

I left a message for my dad and called Ashley.

She didn't answer.

My heart sank and I hung up, hitting her number again.

"Evie?" Chet asked.

"Ashley's not answering either."

"And?"

"And that girl is glued to her phone. Having to part with it during the bar exam for a whole twelve hours nearly killed her. It was like she lost a hand."

"She's had a long day, and none of us packed anything besides you and your dad grabbing a few things. She probably doesn't have her charger with her."

"Then her phone would go directly to voicemail, not ring before."

I called again.

The phone clicked on.

"Ashley! Oy vey, give me a heart attack," I said, grinning.

"Oh, is that her name?" a male voice asked.

My stomach hit the floor and my hands shook. I met Chet's eyes, and he paled as I switched the phone to speaker.

"Who is this and where is my friend?" I said in a low voice.

"We're borrowing her," the man said. "When she showed up, our new friend grew quite excited. Figured we could use her for a little extra leverage. Can I assume her escort is also a friend of yours?"

Heat buzzed through my muscles and I tasted copper on the back of my tongue as my stomach lurched.

Dad!

"If you hurt them, I will gut you and feed you your intestines fried on a stick."

He chuckled.

"And then I'll turn you over to the Council."

The laughter shut off.

"You're one of us." It wasn't a question.

"You're caught. We're closing in on you. Surrender, and we may consider mercy."

"The girl isn't a witch. The man is?"

Honestly, I was surprised Dad hadn't fried them already.

"How'd you knock him out in the middle of a crowded casino?" I took a wild guess, after all, this town was about gambling.

"Chloroformed him in the bathroom, hauled him out saying our buddy drank too much."

"No magic. You're smart. Not smart enough not to kill a man and take off his face with enough magic to set off an earthquake. But then again, that was the young one, wasn't it?"

"You…" He paused and I smiled. I had him spooked at least. "If you were that smart, you'd already be on us."

"What makes you think I'm not?" I whispered.

He hung up.

"WE CAN'T RUN OFF HALF-COCKED," O'Shay said. "We need a plan of attack."

"They've got my dad and my friend!" I yelled, clenching my fists to keep from decking O'Shay myself.

"And that's why we need to be calm," Chet said. "We have to think this through and come up with a plan so they don't have the chance to hurt anyone."

"They won't have the chance to hurt anyone if I cook them alive," I said.

"We'll call that Plan B," Corey said. "We know where they were. Is there any way to track them from there?"

"Same spell we used before," O'Shay said. "But there's only so much it can do. It tells us the general area, but then it's up to us to get close enough for the smaller, more delicate sensors to work."

"There aren't that many hotels here," I said. "I say we walk down hallways with the trackers until they warm up."

"That's not efficient."

"Do I look like I give a flying rat's *fuck* about efficiency right now?"

O'Shay got in my face. "You look like you're ready to burn the entire town to the ground to find your dad, which is why we're not listening to you right now."

"Get away from me." I pushed him hard enough to knock him back on the bed, and he smiled, tight and nasty.

"Keep it up, Evie."

"Is that supposed to be a threat? Because yours need some work."

"You could teach me. Your threats are downright terrifying."

"Stop flirting," Chet said.

"As I said," O'Shay said slowly, straightening and wiggling his shoulders like he was getting his brain right side up too. "We need a plan."

"Fine," I snapped. "What do you suggest?"

"We need to find them. Since they were in that casino, they probably weren't staying at the adjoining hotel, too much risk of exposure if the casino decided to come looking for them. They're probably at the one next to it, where I was. We go there, and yes, walk up and down the halls looking for them with the beads. If they aren't there, we'll check the others."

"Then why did you just say it wasn't efficient!"

"Because it's not, but I can't think of anything better right now."

I tossed my hands up.

"These places aren't like Vegas, we should be able to do that fairly quickly," Corey said. "Four floors? Maybe six in the bigger ones? Yeah, we go in teams again and walk down the halls. We'll find them."

"WELL?" I ASKED AS WE met back in the lobby. It was obvious none of us had found anything, because if we had, we would've called.

O'Shay shifted on his feet. "Since we're here, they may have run. If they really have been trying this as a practice arena, they're probably going to Vegas tomorrow. Maybe they already left."

"Do the spell again then."

He met my eyes, a smile inching onto his face. "I was just about to suggest that."

Chet growled next to me and I rubbed his arm.

"I know," I said. "It's not ideal, but they've got my dad. If this is the only way to do this, I can live with dealing with his slimy water powers again."

"His powers aren't what I'm worried about sliming you," Chet said, stomping away.

I took a deep breath and nodded at O'Shay. "We'll go back to the hotel and do this again. Don't pull anything."

"Same to you, Ms. Jones."

I made a face. "If I didn't know better, I'd think someone from the Council actually cracked a joke."

"Heaven forfend."

O'SHAY BEHAVED HIMSELF DURING the spell. It wasn't nearly as disturbing the second time. The intimacy had already been reached. It was like having sex. The second time was always better because it was easier to get to the necessary intimacy with the person since you'd already been there and you knew the person's rhythms and desires better.

This time when the waves hit my shores, I ignored them and held onto the slimy little sucker just hard enough not to lose him.

If my friends and dad weren't kidnapped, I'd be tempted to.

"They're on the move," O'Shay said when we came out of the spell. "Going south."

"Towards Vegas," Corey said.

"That's the most reasonable assumption."

"I guess we won't be needing this room," I said. "I'll check us out.

Corey, call Chet, get him back here. O'Shay, can you drive a stick?"

He looked at me. "No. Can anyone under forty?"

I scowled. "I can. And so can Chet and Corey. We'll take shifts, get some sleep. The chairs in the first two rows lean back, and one of us can lay in the backseat."

"Chet and I can split it," Corey said. "It's not that long of a drive, you can sleep."

"It's six hours. No-"

"Evie, you and O'Shay are the witches. We come up against these guys, we can shoot, but that's all we got. You need your strength because you have magic. We're going to need you then. Let us do this now."

"Oy vey, good point."

"I'VE NEVER BEEN TO VEGAS," Corey said with wide eyes as we walked into our hotel suite and dropped our bags. The lobby had him staring like a tourist, and he hadn't even seen the stream running through the place with gondolas taking people on rides, let alone the shops. The casino we could see as we checked in almost knocked him over.

"The city of sin," I said, reaching for the bag cuddled in Chet's arms as it started to wiggle. Grem could sleep for hours in a bag or box, but the second you made him get in one?

Yikes.

I unzipped the bag and Gremlin exploded out of it, scolding loudly as he jumped on the first bed, flopping down at the bottom and licking his paw.

"I came here on my twenty-first birthday and decided sin and good little Jewish girls don't get along."

"When have you ever been a good little Jewish girl?" Chet asked.

He'd calmed down over the night, but only three hours of sleep, if he did sleep when his turn driving was over, wasn't doing great things to his anger.

The sun was barely rising over the buildings, and Vegas was already up and going. The casinos were near deserted but the restaurants were doing roaring business with overpriced breakfast buffets.

"Hey, I was good once," I said. "Well, I was better at pretending to be."

Chet nodded and flopped on the bed. "I've got to ask, how are we going to find these guys in Vegas? Have you seen the size of the hotels and casinos here? And there are dozens of them."

"We have it narrowed down to the Strip, but that's not saying much." O'Shay and I had done the spell again in the car when we were about half an hour out of town. "If you were going to go on a gambling spree, with a surefire winner, what would you do?"

"I'd spread it out," Corey said. "Too much in one place, and they'll toss your ass out, but someone who wins big once and is like, 'I won, I'm done,' and leaves? Yeah, I'd buy that. So until someone connects the dots and realizes these guys were in five to ten casinos and won big at every one of them, they'll get away scot-free."

"Do casinos do that? Compare winners' photos and stuff?" I asked.

"No idea. I could try calling up some cops here and see what they're willing to tell a fellow cop."

"Do it."

"No," O'Shay said. "We can't call attention to ourselves. If you call the cops and tip them off, they may find these men before us."

"Good," Chet said. "They're kidnappers. They need to go to jail."

"And we'll take care of it," O'Shay said. "A human jail wouldn't do much to them anyway. They'd escape and risk exposing us all."

"I don't get this obsession with hiding witches," Corey said. "And I don't care. I'll call and say it's professional curtesy." He paused. "Actually, that would make them suspicious, even after checking my credentials."

"Let's assume they wouldn't be matching winners on a regular basis between different casinos," I said. "Unless something gave them reason to look into it. These guys might get put on some security system for the casinos to be on the lookout for, but people win big in Vegas all the time. If they spread it out, they'll look like guys who got lucky and not much else."

"How much time do we have, do you think?" Chet asked.

"They're going to have to study the roulette wheels for a while for Sean to calculate stuff, based on what Wolf said. I think they'll gamble at one until Sean makes the calculations and then win big and leave. It'll look less suspicious because they'll be there for an hour or however long it takes, losing most of the time, maybe winning, betting bigger and bigger, probably getting drinks so it all looks real, and then have Sean tell them when they're ready."

"Video and earbuds?" O'Shay asked.

"No," Corey and Chet said.

"The security would definitely pick that up," Corey said. "You don't realize how much casinos spend on security. Everything in a casino is meant to prevent theft and cheating. Everything from the chips and cards being specially marked to the design of the casinos. They're meant to be mazes to keep people in."

"I think that's more for marketing," I said. "People can't get out, so they keep gambling. It's pop psychology, so take it with a grain of salt, but that's the point of them. Or one of the points."

"Means they'll have to have him on the floor," O'Shay said. "We can find him."

"That's a lot of casinos to hit," I said. "Wendover was easy. Three main casinos with only so much square footage. You could fit all of those and their hotels into this one hotel and casino. And we've got like twenty to look through."

"Actually," Chet said, holding up his smart phone, "there's thirty-one on the Strip and another dozen in the immediate vicinity, but not technically on the Strip."

"Forty-three," I said, licking my lips. "That's... not good. Can you find out what ones have high roller roulette wheels?"

"On it." Chet went back to his phone, fingers flying with a ferocity usually reserved for crazy writers.

"So they got Sean, and he wasn't exactly cooperating," I said. "Then Ashley shows up, probably runs up to him or something dramatic, because *Ashley*, and they realize they have some leverage. She lets it slip she's with someone or something, and they ambush him in the bathroom?"

I shook my head. "This all seems a little too staged."

"They didn't happen to grab her while he was in the bathroom," Corey said. "She shows up and they stay back, let her talk to Sean, maybe let him think he's getting away, wait to see who she meets up with and grabs him then."

"But they said they got Dad in a bathroom?"

"And you believed them?"

"Why would they lie... Huh, I shouldn't assume murders and kidnappers are going to tell the truth as their first option, should I?"

"No, but they probably did have a reason for lying. They didn't want you to know how they really got your dad. Means they have a trick up their sleeve."

"Fantastic."

"I can't find a master list of high stakes roulette," Chet said, holding the phone out for me to see. "But there is a list of the single zero wheels, which are better odds, so this website says there's only a few and all of them are high stakes. Gives us someplace to start at least."

"Sixteen on the list," I said after counting. "And half of those have hundred-dollar minimum bets going on all the time."

"Instead of?" Corey asked.

"Seven on the list say there's twenty-five-dollar ones with hundreds available on demand. I don't think they'll want to have to ask for one."

"Nine." O'Shay nodded slowly. "That gives us a place to start. I'll make a fresh batch of the beads."

"Why can't we use the last ones?" Chet asked.

"Because they were calibrated for that specific area. We're in a new one, we need new beads."

I nodded. "You do that, but first, we need to get breakfast."

"THIS IS THE BEST BREAKFAST place on the Strip," I said, leading the guys into the bustling buffet.

"How do you know?" Chet asked. "I thought you just came here for your twenty-first birthday?"

"No, I came here to party for my twenty-first birthday and decided not wanting to lose money, a sensitivity to smoke, and only ever drinking in moderation really are not what Vegas is about. I do come here every year with Dad for SHOT Show though."

"I'm sorry, a sensitivity to smoke?" O'Shay asked. "Since when?"

"Tobacco smoke, obviously not the other kind."

"Yeah. What's SHOT Show?"

"Biggest weapons convention in the country. It's where Dad picks up new clients."

Corey looked between us. "What does your dad *do*?"

I grinned. "Dad's an engineer, he's been inventing parts for guns since he was a kid. He started getting patents on the stuff he invented, got investors, started making them in bulk and selling them."

"Wait, wait, wait… the Jones Bolt? That was your dad?"

"Yeah! That's one of his."

"Awesome!"

"So you know the area?" Chet asked.

"Not really," I said. "I'll walk through casinos to get to the show and back, but I don't do anything in them. Even just walking through, it was hard to keep track of the path to get you to the other side. Hitting the casino floors and walking around isn't going to work," I said. "The casinos are too big. They are more of a maze than the casinos at Wendover could ever hope to be."

"But we know they'll be around the roulette wheels, why don't we just stick to those?" Corey asked.

"We can, we *will*, but we'll look suspicious real fast." I glanced at O'Shay, he wouldn't like this. "I could do a perception spell on all of us, let us hang around places, waiting for these guys to hit. We don't need to find them, not if we can guarantee they'll come to us."

Corey snapped his fingers. "We narrow their options. Call up casinos, send them a picture of Sean and say he's part of a gambling scam and to kick him out if he shows up. It'll push them to go to one of the ones we'll be waiting at."

"What if it tips them off and they abort?" I asked.

"Then good?" Chet said, wrinkling his forehead at me. "That's what we want."

"No," I said, "we want our people back. If they're no longer useful, they're disposable. Sean and Ashley at the very least have seen their faces. And my dad could turn them in to the Council if he wakes up while they have him. How do we do this without tipping them off? Without making anyone else suspicious and deciding it'd be a good idea to hold them for the cops too?"

We looked at each other.

I tossed my hands up. "Oy vey, there has to be *something*."

"Are there any kind of attraction spells or ones to repel witches?" Chet asked. "Something subtle."

O'Shay and I looked at each other.

"He's brilliant," O'Shay said, apparently forgetting he didn't like Chet.

"I always thought so." I grinned. "Charles Jonathan Lampart, *you* are an amazing man."

He smiled too. "I agree, but why?"

"A protection potion," I said. "Witches use protection potions to line the front doors of their businesses and homes to discourage thieves. It's so subtle, humans don't notice it, people looking to steal just happen to go elsewhere. But witches keep an eye out for it. If we put that on the front of all but a few of the big, likely casinos, they'll sense it and know witches work there and it'll be too big of a risk. They'll go to the other casinos, where we'll be waiting."

"WE STILL NEED TO FIGURE out how to capture them without alerting humans," O'Shay said as he finished the last of the marbles.

The protection potion was taking me longer because we didn't bring all the ingredients for it and I'd had to hit a grocery store for the last of the herbs.

Turns out finding a good grocery store in the middle of Vegas was harder than finding a good liquor store in Utah.

"I know," I said, giving the pot a vigorous stir. The suite was great because it came with a few rooms and a full kitchen. Not something you saw a lot of in Vegas either.

We'd already decided we'd put the potion in front of all the high limit roulette places but Caesar's and the Bellagio, and stake them out.

Why those two? Because we rolled on which ones so we'd stop arguing about floor layouts and escape routes and just get things moving, and those were the two we settled on that didn't already have the protection spell over them and were next door to each other.

Apparently there were a lot of witches working in Vegas.

"Knockout spell or a potion, basically make them seem really drunk and haul them out? Like we're taking drunk friends back to the room," I said. "Like what they said they did to Dad."

"It's risky," O'Shay said.

"Anything we do is going to be risky, but it's Vegas. Odds are the gamblers will be focused on gambling."

"The onlookers won't be, and security sure as hell won't either," Chet said.

"And you can't pull a perception spell on a camera," I said. "Cameras don't perceive, they just record."

Corey jerked, head whipping up so fast it made me flinch in sympathy. "What if we didn't have to take them down in the middle of the casino?"

"What were you thinking?"

He grinned.

"I HATE WAITING," I WHISPERED, shifting on my feet, trying to keep a smile and interested look on my face.

"I know," Chet said, sipping his drink and putting a small bet on the table.

We split up, me and Chet at Caesar's, Corey with O'Shay at the Bellagio. We hovered at the craps table just outside the partitioned high stakes area, Chet betting tiny amounts and not doing too bad. Soon as those guys got near us with Sean, our beads would warm.

Everything in me hoped they'd show up here first.

I wanted to take them down. They had my dad.

If he was still alive.

My heart seized. Of course he was! They wouldn't kill him.

The woman next to Chet ended her turn and he took the dice, grinning big as he had during paintball. The man liked his competitive games.

I sipped my glass of wine, willing the warmth to calm the cold pit in my stomach. My dad *couldn't* be dead.

I'd know it.

They didn't have a problem with killing someone just to be a decoy for Sean, an evil voice whispered inside. *What makes you think they wouldn't kill a witch while he was down?*

I took a longer gulp. If they killed my dad, I wouldn't let O'Shay arrest them. They'd answer to me first.

Chet rolled for a few minutes, apparently doing well based on the people shouting around the table, and I hoped the fake smile was still plastered on my face. I couldn't feel it anymore.

"Not having fun?" someone asked next to my elbow. I turned and the guy smiled at me. He didn't look old enough to gamble but hey, they wouldn't let him on the floor if he wasn't. I'd already been carded three times.

"I don't approve of gambling," I said quietly. "My boyfriend's having fun and I'm over here trying to be supportive. It's not like he's gambling a lot so I'm trying not to worry. But I don't get why people like it. Odds are you'll lose."

"I'm here with my dad. He's having a blast. I'm just taking some of his free drinks." He held up his highball glass filed with a dark liquid, probably a Jack and Coke.

I snorted, lifting my glass and we clinked. "You even old enough to drink?"

He grinned. "I'm twenty-one. I know, my sister calls me a walking tree with a baby face."

I chuckled. "I like that. Walking tree with a baby face. I'll have to remember that."

Cheers rocked the table and I flinched at the noise. Chet hadn't even turned.

Huh, maybe people gambling really were that caught up in it. If we did have a magical smack down, we probably would just have to worry about cameras, the security and pit bosses, and the random people there watching instead of playing.

I held out my hand. "I'm Evie."

"Jorge." He shook my hand a little tentatively, like he wasn't used to shaking hands with people. Not exactly hip with the young people these days.

"I don't get this game," I said.

"My dad taught me. He normally... hey, what's that?"

I looked down where he was pointing.

A green glow showed through my woven purse like a laser, and I yelped.

"Oh, it's a reminder on my phone," I said, smacking Chet's arm.

"Ow, what?" Chet turned and I jabbed a finger at the pocket he had the bead in. He glanced down and his eyes grew huge. "Stay cool, girl," he whispered, turning back to the table and placing his next bet.

Right. Had to play it cool. Had to pretend all was well here.

But they were here!

I pulled out my phone, swaying like I'd had a bit too much to keep me steady on my feet, and text Corey and O'Shay they were here.

"Got it," came back from Corey a moment later.

It'd take them at least ten minutes to get here from what I could tell by the size of the places. They may have been next door to each other, but in Vegas, that was akin to saying two city blocks were next to each other.

"Hey sweetie," I said loud enough to be heard over the music and cheers of gamblers, "if the cocktail waiter comes back, ask him for another red wine for me?"

"Got it," he said, shooting me a confused look.

"Recon," I mouthed, nodding to the high rollers area.

He nodded and I went by, switching the glowing bead to my pocket.

I peeked into the high stakes room and saw a variety of slots and tables just like out on the main floor, just fewer of them, and scurried my tuchus by fast enough that hopefully it just looked like I was curious.

I hit the bathroom just in case and circled back out, peeking into the high stakes room again.

"You want to go in?" came from behind me, making me jump.

I turned and the kid Jorge stared down at me.

"I couldn't," I said. "I think they'd take one look at me and toss me out."

"If you're worried, my dad was talking about going in there. You could come with us to watch. I'm always tagging along with him and watching and they don't mind."

I grinned and nodded. I told Chet I was heading in with my new friends and he asked if he could come along because that would be awesome to see. Jorge's dad introduced himself as Gabriel, and we exchanged pleasantries before heading in.

He went straight for the craps table again, obviously he had a favorite game, but it was close enough to the roulette wheel to see it.

I glanced around, letting the tourist in me come out, making my eyes wide with wonder at the glitz and the thousands of dollars being tossed around like so much change.

It took a few passes, but I finally saw Sean. He hung near the roulette wheel. The wheel hit a number and he nodded, eyes ticking back and forth like he was doing the calculations in his head.

Maybe he was.

Was that even possible?

Hey, never underestimate a nerd at their craft.

Sean texted something then looked up and around as the wheel went again.

I knew the second he spotted us because he jerked, eyes flying huge. He gave a subtle shake of his head and I grinned, turning back to the craps table.

I pulled out my phone, typing we were here to rescue him.

We're coming, Sean. Hang in there.

We had them!

Just had to wait for our reinforcements. Wasn't like these guys were going anywhere.

A text came in, Sean typing so much the bad guys probably didn't notice the extra messages.

Not too bright of them.

"No!" it said. "They've got magic. Not kidding."

"So do I," I typed. "Not kidding. Which ones are they?"

A moment later. "It's the guy with the Utes cap, the one on his left with the ghetto braid, and the woman in the blue dress on the other side of the table with a tall glass and umbrella."

I checked out the people. Utes cap could've been anywhere in his thirties or forties, but the other guy and woman were definitely at least fifty, probably the couple Corey was predicting.

Meaning they'd left two or three with their hostages, one of which was going to be the sloppy kid who'd set off the quake. They had Dad drugged, might have Ashley the same way, and they had the drugs still on them. And didn't want us to know. Probably meant they could pull out the needles and use them at some point.

I looked up, playing spot the camera. If anything went wrong on film, we'd have security all over us. As though they weren't already. There were at least three guys combing the high stakes area and those were just the obvious ones. Something told me they wouldn't appreciate any shenanigans.

"I'm not sure we're going to pull this off," I whispered to Chet and he smiled slowly.

"I'm sure you'll think of something. You always do." He kissed my cheek, turning to shout for our new friend as he got the dice.

O'Shay and Corey got there while Gabriel was still rolling, and hung outside the high stakes area so they didn't attract attention. He apparently was on a quite literal roll and everyone was screaming.

It took everything in me not to roll my eyes and to keep on smiling. These guys realized this was a great, big scam, right? That no matter what, the odds were in the house's favor, and if you won now, unless it was your first time, you'd probably already lost more to them than you'd ever get back?

Then again, some might call me cynical when it came to games of chance.

Jews don't play with money; we just earn it.

I wandered around a bit after the guys got there, checking out the different games with a glass in my hand and a slight wobble. People always cut you more slack when you'd been drinking. Something about alcohol excusing bad behavior.

"You okay?" Jorge asked as I came back, smiling and tilting my head to the side so Corey would know where to look as he poked his head in.

"I'm fine," I slurred slightly, waving my hand. "I have the tolerance of a guinea pig, that's all."

"Yeah."

"Thanks for getting us in here," I said, making sure that indoor voice thing was out the windows. "This is so cool." I giggled and shushed myself. "Oy vey, I'm loud when I drink."

I grinned as I stumbled away, catching myself on Chet's arm. We watched the game at the roulette table for a bit before he went back to watch the craps game, keeping us from catching the eye of the bad guys probably.

Sean kept looking at the wheel and pounding on his phone. Putting the numbers in maybe?

I knew when he had it down because Utes hat upped his bet. Not too much, just threw down two hundred instead of one. The ball landed close to his and he did the two hundred bet again and again, then jumped it up to five hundred.

Utes hat looked at Sean and he typed something into his phone, then downed his drink.

Poor Sean was the one with the tolerance of a guinea pig. Probably trying to drown himself, get a little emotional insulation from the situation.

We'll get them, Sean. I swear.

Utes hat bet a thousand dollars, and I nodded at the front, hoping the guys were keeping an eye out. This wasn't the best plan, but hopefully good enough to keep them from winning anything from their cheating, and get them out of here.

We could just let them win; they'll probably leave after that.

I shrugged to myself, but letting them win didn't sit well. Sure the casinos were sucking money out of people every day, but they were upfront that they were cheating people. Hell, they even broke down the odds for the mathematically challenged.

Nah, letting them get away with this, even for a few minutes, wasn't happening.

The wheel spun and I focused on the number the man put his money on. He'd have to make the ball jump at the very end to get it in there and make it look natural.

The wheel spun. I kept my body loose as I finished my drink and put the glass down on the table, watching the ball as intently as any of the players.

It slowed, and as it started skipping through the notches slower and slower, I squinted, focusing my senses. The magic came out so light and subtle, even waiting for it I almost missed it. The ball skipped into the slot and I nudged it.

It skipped down three more, landing and going around again before the dealer scooped up the chips.

The angry growls weren't audible from where I was but I could see from the corner of my eye the guy was pissed.

He obviously thought he was pushing too hard because he tried landing it in the slot before his chosen number the next time. I let it sit and he lost another thousand.

He tried again and again, missing by one or two each time.

With a little help from me.

Corey had suggested we mess them up just enough until they got sick of it and left to try another.

Only problem was, after doing this another half a dozen times, he still wasn't leaving.

He upped his bet to two thousand instead.

The ball went round and round again and I squinted at the wheel, halfway through another glass of wine.

If this kept up, I really would be drunk.

Maybe it was time to let the bastards win. We could always take the cash off them and donate it, and it wasn't like the casinos didn't expect to lose here and there.

Still, letting them get away with it churned my stomach. It wouldn't be right.

The ball slowed and I focused on the wheel.

Something bumped into me and I went stumbling on my heels and to my knees, scraping them on the hard carpet.

Whoops and cheers echoed through the casino so loud I flinched against the noise.

"I am so, so sorry," a woman said loud enough for me to hear over the hollering, helping me to my feet. "I was watching the craps game and didn't even see you."

Everything about her screamed motherly, from her rounded body to her middle aged, pleasant face, to her slacks and sweater set. She could be Faye in ten years.

I looked from her to the roulette table. The men were cheering and screaming how they finally won and were going to keep going, let it ride.

Yeah, like that was a coincidence.

They were onto me. And this woman was in on it. That put four of them on the floor, and somehow Sean didn't know this one was in on it, meaning she had probably kept her distance during the travel.

I blinked at the woman, twisting my face so I hoped it looked confused. "You ran into me? I just thought I was drunk." I giggled and she smiled with me.

"Dear, I am so sorry. You're bleeding. I'll grab you a first aid kit and get you cleaned up in the bathroom."

"No," I said, "It's okay. I-"

"Please. It's the least I can do."

Oy vey. I smiled and nodded. "Well, I can clean myself up, but I wouldn't say no to the kit. Bring it to the bathroom?"

She nodded, looking so relieved I almost bought it. "Back in a jiff, dear." And she ran off.

I hobbled to the bathroom, laying it on thick for anyone watching.

When I got out, I tapped O'Shay's arm and jerked my head to the bathroom. They were probably trying what I'd been thinking they'd done to my dad. Get me to the bathroom and jump me there.

"When the woman who ran that way gets back." I pointed towards where the exit was hiding in the maze of machines. "Follow her into the bathroom. We'll ambush her."

"How do you know she won't have someone go in there with her?"

"I don't. Why do you think I need you?"

He met my eyes, nodding once. "I've got your back."

I was trusting a Council rep.

How did I get here?

"Goddess help me," I said, making him frown.

I quickly texted Corey to keep an eye on Chet. They probably knew we were together if they were paying enough attention to figure out I was the one messing with them.

Corey nodded at his phone, casually walking to the high rollers area, and I went to the bathroom.

I cleaned up my knees with warm water and paper towels, looking around like I was expecting... what? For her to burst in, magic whipping?

Kind of.

The woman walked in and I nearly jumped out of my skin. She just smiled, putting the kit on the counter. "There should be antibiotics and Band-Aids in here. I'm so sorry, again. I'm usually not that clumsy. I feel just awful."

"It's fine, ma'am," I said as she came over, waving a hand. "I've done worse, trust me."

She smiled again, still so sweet and motherly as I took the little pack of antibiotics from her.

I kneeled to dab it on my knee but keep her in sight.

She jerked, producing a cloth from nowhere and advancing in one motion. I fell on my butt, lifting my hands as she swooped down.

I sprayed flames and they slid off a shield like Vaseline, barely pausing her long enough for me to kick off my heels and scramble up. I pulled my gun from my hip, shooting as I scurried backwards.

I tapped the wall and the bullets fell from her shield, clattering on the ground loud enough to echo.

"Suppression spell on the gun, dear? she asked, walking forward. "Impressive."

I flung up a shield and she bumped into it, giving me a condescending smile.

"You're not going to be able to keep that up long. I can taste your magic. It's far better at fighting than defending."

"The best defense is a good offense." I focused on her, imagined the blood in her body boiling, the body's natural energy cooking it, and let the spell out with a whoosh of breath, sagging under the effort of spelling while I held up the shield.

She raised her eyebrows at me. "That may impress the teenagers, but I'm afraid that spell is a lot of flash with no substance to a witch who knows what she's doing. How long can you keep that shield up now? A minute? Less?"

I pointed my gun at her. "How long can you keep yours up? All I need is one shot. And you can't touch me with whatever's on that cloth without dropping that shield."

She whirled just in time for me to see O'Shay blast her with water. It splashed against her shield, sloshing to the floor harmlessly. I ran around her as he blasted her again, and let my shield fall with a sigh. Had to save some magic. And she was obviously occupied.

O'Shay dropped his arms and she crossed hers, staring him down through the bubble. "How many of you are there?"

"Funny. I was going to ask you the same thing," I said.

"You do realize I told my friends what I was doing? If I don't go back, they'll kill the hostages."

Hostages! My heart jumped. Meant they were both alive.

"They'll have to get to them first," O'Shay said.

"We have people watching the hostages," she said.

He shrugged. "Thanks for confirming. Ma'am, I am Representative O'Shay of the Council."

She paled and he nodded.

"You're under arrest," he continued. "You can come easily, tell us where the hostages are, and save us some trouble, buy yourself a deal with the Council, or we can take you in."

He smiled and I mimicked it, making mine nasty.

"Either way," I said, "we're not going to kill you. We are under very strict orders to bring you in alive."

I let the threat hang and she visibly gulped, nodding quickly.

Ha! She was so scared she didn't even notice I'd changed my story from I'll shoot you to we have to take you alive.

"I'll take you to them," she said.

O'Shay opened the door, keeping his eyes on her as she walked through and back to the casino.

"In case this is a trap, one of us should stay here," I whispered as we walked past the high roller's room.

O'Shay nodded. "I'll go to the room."

"No. They have my dad."

"You can't go in alone."

"I can't risk these guys taking off with Sean either. Two humans won't be able to stop them."

"That's why you should stay."

"What if they have more people in there than the one or two we were thinking and they kill my dad?"

"Which is why I should go, since you're low on magic." O'Shay stayed by my side as we followed the woman through the maze of ringing dinging casino games.

"Oy gevalt," I said, pulling out my phone. I texted the guys to watch the men there, make sure they didn't wander off with Sean. And to follow them very carefully if they did.

When Chet asked where we were going and I told him, I swear the phone melted in my hand with his anger.

"NO!" he texted back. "It's probably a trap."

"Yeah, that's why we're both going. Watch your backs, please!"

I put the phone away so I couldn't see his response.

"I don't like this," I whispered.

"I don't either," O'Shay said as we hit outside and followed the woman into the next casino. "It's the perfect opportunity to take off with Sean, maybe your friends too."

"Except she hasn't had a chance to tell those guys what's going on. Hopefully they'll keep playing."

"They'll expect her back."

I nodded, half-shouting, "Hey!" at the woman.

She turned.

"Toss me your phone," I said.

She did without question.

"Keep going," I said loudly before saying to O'Shay, "I can see why you guys cling so tightly to your power. This is going to go to my head."

He didn't say anything. Probably smart.

I read through her texts to see if I could tell who had Sean on the floor, and get a handle on her writing style. I texted one of the guys who obviously had Sean based on the texts that I was taking the woman I drugged back to the room to put with the others.

"Need help?" came back.

"No," I text, figuring the less said the better.

We walked through another casino and in the next she took us to the elevators.

"I don't need to tell you what will happen to you if this is a trap, do I?" O'Shay asked as we entered the elevator, voice sharp, somehow threatening even with that accent.

"No," she said, staring at the ground. "I know what happens to witches who cross the Council."

"We get the hostages, take you all in, and I promise you'll be treated fairly," I said.

"This from the woman threatening to shoot me?"

So she did notice the discrepancy. "It was you or me in that moment. I would've been in trouble with my superiors if I had, but they would have understood. We can still make this okay, though. Still give you a chance."

The elevator doors slid open and we followed her down the hall. I kept my hand on the grip of my second gun under my jacket, ready to pull it out the moment we got inside.

The woman opened the door and we followed her in, calm as anything. Soon as we were in, I closed the door behind us and now that I was pretty sure there were no cameras to capture me, I pulled my gun.

I shot the woman, the paintball splatting against her shield.

She'd had it up this entire time? No way.

She turned on us, throwing her arm up. I flew backwards, hitting the door hard enough to bruise.

I hit the ground on my knees, flinching as they got scraped again. Kept ahold of my gun though.

Two guys jumped off the beds they'd been lounging on, watching some action movie. The younger one really did look young enough to be the woman's son, maybe eighteen.

He should've been playing beer pong at frat parties and flashing fake IDs to campus cops, not playing gangster with his murderous parents and fighting witches playing cop.

I shot him with the paintball and his eyes rolled up into his head as he crashed down.

We'd infused the paintballs with a sleeping potion so strong it could drop an elephant, that way, even if the person only got a little through their clothes, it'd still knock them out.

O'Shay and the woman went at it, magic flying so fast and thick I couldn't even tell what spells they were trying, only that both had shields strong enough to keep them from landing.

The other guy looked about my age and I shot at him, hitting a shield. I switched the paintball gun to my left hand and pulled out my real gun, shooting the shield with another few bullets. Couldn't get through, but hopefully they would put enough stress on the shield to make him drop it.

He pulled out his phone, fingers flying over it, and I screamed like a banshee, running at him full tilt, only now realizing I'd been walking barefoot through Vegas since the bathroom.

What a funny thing to notice. I smacked into his shield. The thing bounced me back like a jelly bubble and I huffed, backhanding it with the butt of my gun.

My hand bounced off, but only slightly.

I met his eyes, grinning as I shot the shield with my last bullet.

It fell. I dropped the gun and grabbed the paintball gun with two hands.

He swung at me and I ducked, bringing my paintball gun up and dancing out of his way. I shot and he dodged to the side, smacking into the table in the little hotel room with his legs and yelping in pain.

I shot again, hitting him dead center, and he went down.

"Whoop!" I yelled, turning to the dueling witches.

O'Shay popped in and out of the bathroom, shooting spells at the woman as she poured magic out in bursts like a machine gun, keeping him pinned.

I shot her in the back and she dropped.

"Couldn't keep the shield up through that, could ya?" I taunted her unconscious body as I grabbed the guy's phone.

"Your dad and Ashley are unconscious in the bathroom," O'Shay said.

I ran, and he got out of the way so I could poke my head in and see. Dad and Ashley sat in the tub, propped up against the back wall and leaning into each other.

I breathed a sigh of relief as I pulled up the phone.

The breath snagged in my throat. The phone showed the text saying they'd been caught had already gone.

O'Shay joined me as I straightened and showed him the phone. "Shit!" he said. "After that, I'm drained."

"We can't leave these guys alone in case any of them come to or anyone comes looking for them," I said. "Do you think you could see what's in that potion and come up with a potion to counter it? And make sure these guys don't wake up until we can get you repowered to take them in?"

He licked his lips. "I don't know if I can take them down if they wake up."

I handed him the paintball gun. "You know how to use this?" He nodded. "Tie them up with something if you can. If they wake up, put them back out. There's about twenty more in there. Anyone comes through that door, drop them."

I grabbed my gun, pulling extra bullets out of my pocket and reloading the revolver before tucking it away.

"Evie," he said, voice heavy, "I-"

"I know," I said, opening the door and running out, swinging it shut behind me before he could say anything else.

I ran down the hall, hitting the stairs instead of waiting for the elevator. I'd never been fast, but now I practically had wings on my feet.

I took the shortcut through the casinos we'd taken, definitely faster than going around the monstrosities outside, even if I couldn't run flat out in here.

I hit the casino floor at Caesar's and hustled back to the high rollers room. I poked my head in.

The trio along with Sean were gone, Chet and Corey nowhere in sight. I tried calling Chet. No answer. Called Corey. No answer. I texted them both just in case they hadn't heard their phones or couldn't talk.

Nothing. I huffed, looking around.

I did see one familiar face. "Jorge!" I half jogged up to him. He smiled but it slipped off as I got closer. Maybe I looked as disheveled as I felt.

"Where are your shoes?" he asked.

"Oh, right. They were hurting my feet. Did you see where my boyfriend went?"

"Left with a buddy of his, maybe five minutes ago."

"Do you know where?"

"Said they were going to meet you at the next place, to tell you if you showed up here looking for them."

"Thanks," I said, quick walking back out. I kept my phone in my hand as I hustled through the casino to the side it shared with the Bellagio.

Why would they be going to the next casino if they knew they were blown?

They wouldn't! They left, and Chet must've assumed they were going to the next place.

They could be anywhere, and if the kidnappers caught them following them…

My phone buzzed with a text from Chet. It just said, "Our room. We're stalling. Hurry!"

I hurried.

THIS TIME I DID PULL OUT my gun in the hallway, cameras be damned. The door was open a crack and I slammed it open, gun up and out Cagney and Lacey style.

Two guys rushed me in a flash of clothes, and I barely had time to pull the trigger before one was on me. The bullet got him pointblank in the chest, and he barreled into me, taking me to the ground.

I slammed to my back, barely keeping my chin tucked, and the wind burst out of me in a painful huff.

The man coughed, blood hitting the ground next to me. I pushed out from under him, scrambling to my feet. A fist came out of nowhere, clocking me across the jaw so hard I dropped again, birdies flying around my head.

The world went blurry as the arm came down again.

Then it wasn't.

I blinked, trying to clear my vision as nausea took me. Chet had the guy in an arm lock and slammed his fist into my attacker's face. Blood exploded and Chet hit him again and again, letting the captured arm go just long enough to pull his hand back and pound the man across the face with a hook, then shot him with the paintball.

The man dropped.

It was the guy who'd been playing roulette. Maybe his magic was better for delicate work like that than fighting. It'd explain why he didn't have any shields up or use magic for the smack down.

Chet ran to me and helped me to my feet. My stomach heaved and I bent, breathing heavy through my mouth to keep my stomach down.

Chet turned, paintball gun up, and shot.

Oh yeah, there were more of them.

I grabbed my gun from the ground, willing my stomach to settle, and pointed it at the room too.

The woman in the blue dress held Sean in front of her like a human shield, and the guy with the thin ghetto braid coming out of the base of his otherwise shaved skull traded swings of magic with Corey's fists as Corey tried to get the paintball gun up to shoot him.

"Evie?" Chet asked, moving his arms like he was trying to get a clear shot of the woman. She grinned out from behind Sean's back, way too small a target to hit.

"Trade," I said to Chet. He handed over the paintball and I gave him my gun without having to explain.

I shot Sean in the chest.

He dropped out of the woman's arms, way too much dead weight for her to hold.

I shot her and she waved an arm, barely deflecting the ball in time.

I shot at the guys, three in a row, figuring one would get one of them. It smacked the arm of the guy, but the splat must've gotten Corey, because he dropped too.

The woman put a shield up and I blew out a huff. "I'm getting really sick of you guys pulling those. You know we took down the rest of your team, right?"

She didn't say anything. Apparently witty banter was for TV shows.

The world shook under us and I slammed to my knees, jaw dropping as she grinned.

Oy gevalt, an earth witch.

Chet hit the ground behind me, heavy enough to give the room another shake.

"Really wish we weren't on the ground floor now." I grinned, meeting her eyes with a look I knew wasn't friendly by the way she paled. I focused on the bed next to her. Lots of cloth in here.

And subtle really never had been my strong suit.

I set the bed on fire, the power push leaving me shaking. She jumped away and I shot another paintball as I pulled flames in front of her face. She screamed, scrambling back.

The fire alarm screeched and I fried it.

I pulled the flaming covers off the bed, wrapping them around her shield, my brain pounding to get out as I pushed my powers and squeezed.

I dropped to a knee as I squeezed harder, and felt it when the shield fell.

The flames snuffed out and she glared at me, murder in her eyes.

The floor rolled up under me, bucking me back into Chet, and we both went down. I grabbed my gun from where he dropped it and shot off a few rounds at her to keep her occupied. She tossed up a shield just in time, but I could see the effort in the sweat on her hairline.

"They really can cause fucking earthquakes?" Chet asked as we unmixed our limbs.

"Not usually." I shot again, and the bullet broke her shield with just enough momentum left to tap her chest.

She rubbed the spot on her chest and pulled a knife, rushing me. The ground picked up under me and pitched me forward.

Straight towards the blade.

A black ball of furred fury flew out from under the other bed.

Gremlin latched onto her back with his seriously sharp claws, and she howled, half turning with the knife so I stumbled into the bed.

"Gremlin!" I screamed as I bounced back up. She had a knife!

Grem had already pushed away before the knife could even catch his fluff. He ran under the bed and slingshot around, pouncing her face before she could pull up the knife, or do much more than scream.

He clawed up her face before bouncing off, and I shot her in the belly with the paintball once he was out of the way.

She collapsed, smacking her head on the nightstand as she went down.

"Oy vey." I lay back on the bed.

Gremlin's furry face appeared above mine and he meowed. He climbed on my belly and turned in a circle before settling down.

"Evie," Chet said, sitting next to me. "Where are the others?"

"In their hotel room, O'Shay's watching my dad and Ashley. They're knocked out."

"I'll call O'Shay, tell him this is over."

I grinned.

"What?" he asked.

"I told you there were too prisoners in paintball."

I drifted off to the sound of him cracking up like it was the funnies fucking thing he'd ever heard.

"My colleagues have them safely tucked away on a truck and are taking them to Oz," O'Shay said, putting the phone down and resting the icepack on his head again.

"The guy I shot?" I asked, closing my eyes again as I pet my purring baby. The room spun every time I opened my eyes, moved, or so much as breathed too heavy.

"Stomach shot. They stopped the bleeding in time and are pretty sure he'll live. The woman is swearing revenge against you and"—he hitched his voice up—"your little cat, too."

I burst out laughing, my stomach cutting it off with a gag as it fought to get out.

"Shhhhh," my dad said from somewhere to my right. "Here's your soup."

The door opened and closed and I groaned. "That better be Corey, I can't deal with any more attacks today."

"It's me," Corey said. "How about some good news? The guy they got to play Sean? It was a body from the morgue. He died of natural causes three days ago."

"Nobody died?" Ashley asked. "Oh thank god."

"Well, technically he did die," I said.

Grumbling came from my left and I grinned.

We'd decided to stick around until we got enough of our energy back to fix the damage we did to the room. Trying to explain the ripped-up carpets, ashes of the comforter, and the destroyed fire alarm would take way too much, and it'd be easier just to mend a few things magically and buy the rest.

Also, O'Shay and I were in no condition to be moved until we recovered from the severe magic drain.

O'Shay had called the Council reps in Vegas and told them what happened, making it sound like he stumbled onto the scheme when he was in Vegas on an impromptu trip, and asked them to get the perps since he was drained after fighting and capturing them.

We were fine with him taking the credit and leaving us the hell out of it.

Once O'Shay woke everyone, Dad used his powers to patch the guy I'd shot, then to magically cover Corey and Sean as they hauled the unconscious bodies out of our room, and to the kidnappers' hotel room.

"Thanks, Daddy," I said, cracking my eyes enough to see him sit next to me and hand me the half-filled bowl. It was thick chicken stew from the restaurant downstairs, sitting on a plate next to a bunch of little packets of crackers.

Ashley sat curled up next to Sean on the stiff hotel couch like a cat. He watched her eat with an intensity that made me think no matter what she was saying about them being casual, and that's why they hadn't told their friends, there were definitely feelings there.

I smiled as Chet put an arm around me and Dad passed out the rest of the food they'd hauled up.

Chet handed me a Body Armor sports drink. "Keep hydrated."

"Goddess bless you," I said, opening it and downing a few sips to test my stomach. It was cool with it.

"And to you," Chet said, bowing his head and making me giggle.

"I still can't believe you shot him," Ashley said, making me jerk.

"What?" I asked. "He was rushing me."

"No, not that guy. I mean Sean."

"Oh, it was just a sleeping potion. It was the only way to get him out of the way so I could get to the woman."

"I still object to the friendly fire," Sean said, not sounding terribly upset. "I could have been more use in the fight."

"I'm sure you could've, but it was the only thing I could think of at the time."

"What happened to the money they won?" Sean asked.

"I'm glad you asked," I said. "They made out with nearly a hundred grand after I stopped messing with them, according to O'Shay's count. I think that'd go a long way towards helping out some of the animal shelters in Utah and Nevada."

"I was thinking the Science Center in Salt Lake," Sean said. "They've got an after-school program that could use a little help."

"Okay, animals and kids. Sounds like a good way to spend it. Does anyone know where to go get the money? I mean, all we got is their ticket saying they had that many chips, right?"

Chet chuckled. "Nope. They took the chips up to the cashier and got their money. Weren't planning on going back."

"That's convenient." I sipped my soup and my dad stroked my hair. "Yes?"

"I'm just glad you're okay," Dad said, sitting next to me judging by how the bed shifted. "You were incredible today. I am so proud of you."

I grinned, cracking my eyes open. "What do you expect? I am a Jones."

"That was pretty fast thinking, Evie," O'Shay said from the other bed. "You'd make a damn good Representative."

That made me open my eyes and look over at him. "I'm sorry. What!"

"I'm serious," he said.

"You think I'd make a good witch cop? What happened to me being an anarchist?"

He shrugged. "You think we're so corrupt? Our tactics are wrong and one size fits all? Leaves no room for exceptions? Right?"

I nodded.

"Then change us. Show us a new way. Join us."

"You're serious? You think I should apply? They'd laugh me out of their offices, and then they'd be keeping a sharper eye on me than they already do."

"I'm not saying you should apply." O'Shay met my eyes. "I'm a high-ranking rep. It's why I was sent to check out how Covens were doing in different cities. I'm saying the job is yours if you want it."

O'Shay stared me down. "So the question is, do you want it?"

Become part of the Council? It had never even occurred to me. Could I stomach it? Could I really change things from the inside?

I licked my lips and turned to my dad. He looked as dumbstruck as me.

I stared down at my soup like it could give me the answer. "Ummmmmm."

Thanks for reading!

- If you would like to know when my next story is out, you can sign up for my mailing list at https://mailchi.mp/afc38083307c/amie-gibbons, *and get a free story not available anywhere else.*
  Check out my blog https://authoramiegibbons.wordpress.com/.
  Like my Facebook page https://www.facebook.com/AuthorAmieGibbons/, and friend my author profile on Facebook https://www.facebook.com/authoramie.gibbons.10

- Reviews help readers find books. I appreciate all reviews: good, bad and ugly. You can leave a review for this book on its Amazon page.

- My other shorts and novels are available on Amazon from my page at http://www.amazon.com/-/e/B01651YIZU.

ABOUT THE AUTHOR

Amie Gibbons was born and raised in the Salt Lake Valley. She started making up stories before she could read and would act them out with her dolls and stuffed animals. She started actually writing them down in college, just decided to do it one day and couldn't stop.

She took an unplanned hiatus from writing when she went to Vanderbilt Law School and all of her brain power got consumed by cases, statutes, exams, and partying like only grad students in Nashville can. She graduated and picked her writing back up as soon as her brain limped back in after the bar exam.

She loves urban fantasy and is obsessed with the theory of alternate realities. Whether or not she travels to them in the flesh or just in her mind is up for debate.

She spends her days living the law life and her nights writing when she's not hitting downtown Nashville to check out live music or inflict her singing on the crowds at karaoke bars. She lives with her familiar and baby, a beautiful black cat named Merlin, who keeps her in this reality… most of the time.

To hear about new releases, sign up for her mailing list: https://mailchi.mp/afc38083307c/amie-gibbons, and get a free story not available anywhere else.

The Evie Jones Shorts Series
EVIE JONES AND THE CRAZY EXES
EVIE JONES AND THE GOOD LUCK FUNDRAISER
EVIE JONES AND THE MAGIC MELTDOWN
EVIE JONES AND THE SPIRIT STALKER
EVIE JONES AND THE SHADOW OF CHAOS
EVIE JONES AND THE ROCKY ROULETTE

The Laws of Magic Series
THE TREETOPS EXPERIMENTATION (A MILLIE LEHMAN SHORT STORY)
SHIFTING ICE (A TYLER CARMICHAEL NOVELLA)
THE GODS DEFENSE
THE GODS' APPEAL (Future Release)
THE GODS' COURT (Future Release)
PATENTING MAGIC (Future Release)

The Order of the Sphinx Series
SPHINX ORIGINS (A SPHINX SHORT)
PARATA'S SHADOWS (BOOK 1 Future Release)

ONE IN INFINITY (A REALITY CROSSING NOVELLA)
CHAOS CANDY (A REALITY CROSSING NOVELLA)

The SDF Series
WE INVESTIGATE ZEBRAS (AN ARIANA RYDER SHORT)
PSYCHIC SEEKS (AN ARIANA RYDER NOVELLA)
PSYCHIC OVERBOARD (AN ARIANA RYDER NOVELLA)
PSYCHIC UNDERCOVER (WITH THE UNDEAD)
PSYCHO (AND PSYCHIC) GAMES
PSYCHIC FOR SALE (RENT TO OWN)
PSYCHIC WANTED (UN)DEAD OR ALIVE
PSYCHIC SPIRAL (OF DEATH)
PSYCHIC ECLIPSE (OF THE HEART)
PSYCHIC (WILD WILD) WEST (COMING 2021)

The Elemental Demons Series
SCORPIONS OF THE DEEP
SCORPIONS OF THE AIR

Printed in Great Britain
by Amazon

78541871R00108